THE
HOTEL

BOOKS BY EMILY SHINER

The Wife in the Photo

EMILY SHINER

THE
HOTEL

bookouture

Published by Bookouture in 2023

An imprint of Storyfire Ltd.
Carmelite House
50 Victoria Embankment
London EC4Y 0DZ

www.bookouture.com

ISBN: 978-1-83790-625-3
eBook ISBN: 978-1-83790-624-6

For Natalie, Kelsey, & Lauren
Y'all are 10/10 in all the best ways.

PROLOGUE

The air is so cold against my nose that it seems to burn. Snow has soaked through my pants, making the wet fabric cling to my skin. I take another step, then another, the tops of my boots filling with slush.

Wind whips around me, howling as it cuts through the pass between the barn and the house. Each time it blows hard like this, it carries small frozen particles with it, the tiny bits of ice stinging me as they're flung against my face. I pause, close my eyes for a moment, wait for the wind to die down.

When it doesn't, I exhale hard, adjust my grip. Behind me, the B&B towers overhead, four full stories, the windows dark, like blank, unseeing eyes. I cast an eerie shadow ahead of me as I lurch and stumble through the drifts.

At first, I'm grateful for the light so I can see where I'm going without having to rely on my dancing flashlight. But then I realize where the light is coming from. Halfway between the barn and the B&B I freeze, then turn slowly, my heart pounding.

My breathing comes in short little gasps, and I rub an icy hand across my face as I stare at the house. It was loud a moment ago but now has fallen silent. I can feel someone watching.

Their flashlight is pointed right at me.

Fear spurs me to turn back to the barn. I have to get there, have to make sure this all worked out the way it was supposed to. If it didn't, and I'm the reason, I don't know if I'll ever be able to forgive myself.

One step, then another. I find it difficult to catch my breath in air this cold. It fills my lungs, sucking all the warmth it can from my body. Right now, I'm running on nothing more than adrenaline and anger.

The heavy bundle I'm carrying is slowing me down and I push forward, leaning into the wind as it howls around me, gritting my teeth as I force myself to keep moving.

If I don't get there, if I trip and fall...

I will my body to move faster. It feels like I might freeze to death out here, but that would be preferable to what's waiting behind me in the house.

I just have to keep moving.

It's not only my life that depends on it.

ONE

ABBY

Monday 19 Nov

No matter how many times I go over the books, something just isn't right. My eyes ache and all the numbers start to run together the more I stare at the pages.

Sighing, I lean against the kitchen counter, the computer printouts still warm in my hands. Mark will be back from some handyman job soon, and even though I know he hates talking about the gritty details of the B&B with me before he's had something to drink in the evening, this is something I need him to focus on.

Just one glass of whiskey in his hand and he'll resort to telling me over and over that *everything is fine* and *all businesses go through lean years*.

But I don't think that's what this is, and I don't want to listen to him lie to us both.

Lean years aren't supposed to happen when you've been in business for almost a decade and suddenly it seems like all the guests you used to have pouring in through the door every month have dried up. Maybe they're all on a beach in Mexico, where they can work on their tans instead of worrying about frostbite. Maybe they're all saving for college or paying off a new convertible. Whatever it is they're doing, they're doing it somewhere else, not here, in the B&B I dreamed about having since I was a little girl.

The front door slams and I stiffen, mentally preparing myself for what I'm going to say to Mark. With him—like with most men, I'd wager—it's best to keep it short and simple, to state the facts without getting all bogged down in emotion. The only problem is that this *is* emotional for me.

"Hello, wife!" Mark sweeps into the kitchen in his usual fashion. While some people walk into a room, that's not how Mark operates. He swaggers, drawing attention from everyone, no matter what they're doing. My husband is larger than life, towering over me at 6'4", and his personality is just as big. Even though I'm worried how this conversation will go, I can't help but rush to him.

He wraps his arms around me, and I snuggle into his chest, breathing him in. "Hello, husband," I say, pulling back after a moment. I still have the printouts clutched in my hand, but he hasn't seemed to notice them. "Good afternoon of work?"

"You know it. I was down in town at the Fitzsimmons house. They hired someone last summer to come in and run some wire for a new outlet in the kitchen. Let me tell you, whoever they brought in didn't know his ass from his elbow."

I grin in spite of myself. This is why I felt like Mark and I would be fine here in Oyster, Maine, well away from any friends and family we've ever had. He's a force to be reckoned with, and his confidence is why I knew we could make it here.

"Where's Henry?" Mark makes a show of looking around the kitchen for our son. It's early afternoon and outside the sky is still light, but dark comes early this time of year, sneaking up to the house to wrap it in a blanket of night. The light won't last long.

"Taking a nap. He didn't feel good after lunch, and it took me over an hour to rock him and get him to settle. I'm not sure if he ate something or if it's just a little bug he caught when we were in town." He motions for me to move so he can grab a glass from the cupboard behind me, but I don't. Next will come the whiskey, then any concerns I have about our future here will be washed away with the rest of his worries.

Nope. Not tonight.

"Hey, while he's sleeping and before I make some dinner, there's something I want to talk to you about." I take his hand and lead him over to the kitchen table. It's huge, made from a few thick slabs of oak, with a live edge. Henry loves to pick off bits of bark during meals, and even though it makes Mark mad, I let him.

It's hard for me to say no to Henry about much of anything. We fought for that little boy, and I know I spoil him, but I can't stop.

"You look worried." Mark takes his usual seat at the head of the table, and I sit to his right. Next to me is the highchair where Henry sits. "Did something happen while I was gone?"

"No. Yes." I exhale hard, blowing a stray strand of hair out of my face. Mark's eyes flick to follow the movement then land back on me. "I was checking the books, and this hasn't been a good year."

He raises an eyebrow, and I can see the argument in his eyes, so I keep talking, almost tripping over the words in an effort to explain what I mean. "In fact, it's our worst year, second only to our first one in business."

He exhales. Sighs. Waits for me to continue.

"It's not sustainable, not if we continue on this trajectory. I think—"

"I think we're in a slump." He drums his fingers on the table but won't look at me. "It's not unusual for places to have to tighten their belts for a while."

I'm prepared for this, and I nod, letting him finish before launching back into what I've been planning to say.

"Yes, that's true, Mark, but we've been at this for a decade. We're not bringing in as many guests as usual, and we need to do something about that. Even when it's nice out, we don't have the traffic we did. And now, going into winter, I'm a little worried that things will only get worse. But I have an idea."

"It's really that bad?" His voice is tight, his eyes locked on me.

"It's not good."

He nods, then reaches out and takes my hand. "You've always been a planner, Abby. I wouldn't be surprised if you not only have a plan but also a backup plan."

"I want to run a special to celebrate ten years in business. At least, that's what we'll tell people on social media. Really though, you and I will know we're doing this to bring in a bit more money so we can make it through the winter."

"What kind of special?"

I know I need to hurry before Henry gets up from his nap and needs us, so I talk faster, spreading the printouts in front of us on the table so he can see what I've already planned. "New guests will get ten percent off when they book with us, regardless of how many days they stay. We can take that little bit of a cut and still turn a profit, especially if it means people will book for longer than a night or two. Everyone loves a deal. And as for returning customers, I want to offer them the opportunity to book three nights and get the fourth free." Finished, I exhale hard and sit back.

"How long will this special run?" Mark's invested now and he leans forward, his eyes locked on me. He may not have believed me at first that there's a problem, but I think I got through to him. "I think it's a great idea, Abby, but do you have an end date in mind?"

"Just through the end of the year. I'll release this information as soon as we agree on it. I can even spin it as a way to treat yourself or your loved one for Christmas. Imagine how great it would be if we filled this place up and had a huge Christmas dinner with all of our guests."

Across the kitchen from us, the baby monitor on the counter squawks. The row of small bulbs across the top lights up then goes dark before illuminating again. Henry's up, and from the sound of it, he's hungry.

"You are amazing," Mark tells me, already pushing back from the table. He takes my hand in his and lightly kisses my fingertips. "I'll get Henry; you sit here with that big brain of yours and let me know when I get back if there are any other details we need to iron out."

"You like it?" I stand as Mark walks through the kitchen towards the stairs. "You think it's a good idea?"

"I think," Mark says, pausing to look back over his shoulder at me, "that if we're in a pickle, you're the person I want on my team to make sure we get out of it. I trust you implicitly, Abby. You're the brains, I'm the brawn. Whatever you want to do, I support."

Then he's gone, and just like he brings a crackle of excitement into a room when he enters, it feels like the space falls silent. I watch the empty door where he left for a moment, then turn and grab my printouts from the table. At the bottom of the stack are some statements. Some from the bank.

Some from another company.

My cheeks burn and I snatch them up, glancing at the door to make sure Mark hasn't come back. It was silly to look at them, but I had to double-check.

Him finding those would put an end to it all, wouldn't it?

Right now, I need to get Henry something to eat, but soon

I'll get everything posted online. Mark's right—I'd do anything for my family.

What he doesn't know is just how far I'm willing to go. Or who I'm willing to drag into this.

Who knew good revenge takes years to orchestrate?

TWO

ABBY

Henry's hiccupping cry rips through the silence of the kitchen, startling me from my daydream. There's an open crossword book on the table in front of me and I leave it there, rushing to the stairs to get him.

For over a week he's been sick. A fever. Throwing up. Lethargic. Glassy eyes.

For over a week we've been stuck in the house, the wind shrieking against the walls, making the windows rattle, all while Mark goes off to work and I'm left at home with a sick kid.

And now it finally feels like it's coming to an end.

"I'm coming, Henry!" I call to him as soon as I reach the second floor.

He's just been so sick. So quiet. So quiet, like he was going to—

Nope, not going to think that. He's fine.

I hit his door at a run then force myself to take a few deep breaths before walking over to his crib.

"My sweet boy," I coo, carefully picking him up. "You don't

feel hot, did you know that? You're so cool and you sound hungry. Do you want something to eat?"

Something falls from his hand as I lift him. His Spider-Man flashlight, the one he loves to use when we play hide-and-seek. I snuggle him against my body and kiss him on the forehead.

He nods, leaning his cheek against my shoulder. "Hungry." Henry yawns and repeats the word. "Hungry, Mommy."

"Yes, I bet you are. And I'm so glad you are! Daddy's outside getting ready to go to a job, but we'll see if we can catch him before he goes. And then we'll get you something to eat." *And then,* I think, *I can finally post on social media about the sale.* The kitchen still smells like bacon from breakfast, and Henry shimmies against me, slipping out of my grasp and walking to the table. He puts his hands up on his highchair and grunts like he's going to be able to pull himself up.

"Let me help you, darling boy," I say, scooping him up into the seat and buckling him in. "Now, how hungry are you? Could you eat a mouse or an elephant?"

"Elephant." He has dark circles under his eyes, and he yawns, rubbing his fists into them before slumping back into his chair and staring at me.

"Elephant it is," I say, my voice a singsong. It's relief making me sound like this, I'm sure of it. Relief that my baby boy is okay, that Mark has had steady handyman jobs for a while.

That things are finally going to change.

Along with the bacon this morning, Mark and I had pancakes, and I heat up a leftover one in the pan before cutting it into bites and pouring syrup in a little cup to go on the side of the plate. It only takes a moment to quarter grapes and pour Henry a cup of juice. After snapping his tray in place, I put his food in front of him, then drop a kiss on the top of his head.

"Listen, kiddo, I'm going to lean out the front door and yell to your dad that you're up and see if he can pop in to say hi. He has a few jobs this morning. And one is an emergency call-out, which let me tell you..."

Henry barely glances at me as I rub my fingers together in the air to mimic how much it's going to cost for Mark to show up at someone's house without a prior appointment.

Henry stuffs a piece of pancake in his mouth. Syrup drips down his chin and I wipe it with a napkin before rushing to the front door. We need new weatherstripping around it. Cold air seeps in around the door, insidious, always flowing in to chill the house. It's not so bad when the weather is temperate, but right now it feels like the foyer is ten degrees cooler than the rest of the house.

Welcome to Oyster, Maine, where even the good weather is bad.

I stuff my feet into my boots and grab a heavy coat from the closet before stepping outside. The air is bracing, and I suck in a lungful, surprised, then exhale hard, watching my breath cloud in front of me. It's the kind of morning that makes me want to curl up with a cup of tea and a good book.

"Mark!" Cupping my hands around my mouth, I yell as loud as I can. He's been letting his truck run to warm up and now he's already halfway down the driveway, backing his old red Ram up slowly.

"Mark!" Now I wave, both arms over my head, the excitement of how much better Henry is finally feeling fueling me on. Still, even though I don't think he's going to turn around, I hope until the last minute, when he jerks the wheel hard to the side, slipping out backwards onto the main road.

And he's gone. Saltside Inn is at the top of a curvy hill, the barn and the B&B itself the only buildings up here. In the snow, we don't get our mail until after everything has melted and the roads are clear again, but the view is worth it. Scrubby pines form a thick forest around one side and the back of the pink house, but the view from the porch is incredible.

From here I can see across the road and straight down into the ocean. We're on a cliff, so I can't see the huge rocks that break up the shoreline, but I can hear the waves battering against them night and day. I love how the spray shoots straight up into the sky, how the droplets of water seem to hang suspended, then how they fall back down into the ocean to do it all again.

Guests always comment on how amazing the views are, especially the sunrises. Fingers of light stretch over the land, glittering on the water like an explosion of jewels. In the soft morning light, our home looks even more pink than it is, with the white shutters I painted and installed myself taking on a rosy glow.

It's gorgeous up here but lonely, and I hurry back into the house. "He's already left, Henry," I call from the foyer as I strip out of my coat and boots. "But he'll be home for lunch! Isn't that great?"

There's no answer.

THREE

ABBY

"Henry?" I'm moving too quickly, and I trip as I try to kick out of my right boot. When I fall, I catch myself on the wall. The impact makes my palms sting. "Henry! Are you okay?"

He's quiet. The entire house is quiet. There hasn't been anyone but the three of us in here for weeks and now the silence feels oppressive, like it's pressing in on my eardrums.

"Henry, answer me!"

Something happened to him.

The knowledge comes to me, hard, like a punch to the gut.

He was fine, just fine, and I turned my back long enough to let something terrible happen to him. I shouldn't have gone to say goodbye to Mark, shouldn't have stood there for as long as I did. Guilt rips through me as I grab the doorframe to the kitchen and spin into it, my eyes searching the table for my son.

And he's there.

He's there.

"Henry, why didn't you answer me?" I hurry to him, my heart still pounding in my chest. When I reach him, he tilts his head back, lifting his sticky face to mine. His mouth is stuffed with pancake and grapes, his cheeks distended. I have a sudden, terrible vision of him choking, of me not being able to save him, his eyes bulging out, his skin mottled red, but then he swallows, the gulping sound loud enough to break the vision in my mind.

He's fine. I don't have to watch him every second of the day.

"Daddy?"

"Daddy's gone," I say, lifting him from his highchair. I ignore how sticky he is and pull him close to me. "He's gone, but what do you say we go upstairs and have a nice warm bath? You can play with your duckies."

"Duckies."

He's still exhausted and must have used up most of his energy eating his breakfast. Once again, he's dead weight in my arms, but he's not hot like he has been for the past week so I'm no longer really worried.

On my way out of the kitchen, we swing by my office and grab my laptop. "I have some work to do while you get all clean, my darling." As soon as I get him settled in the water, I'll log on, post all the information about the sale.

Henry is fine.

The B&B will be fine.

Henry is fine.

I run the bath and get him settled in the warm water, handing him the bottle of bubble bath. He flips it over and squeezes the bottle hard, his tongue poking out of the corner of his mouth as he concentrates. The smell of fake raspberries is so thick in the small bathroom I feel like I can taste it. But it's better than the sweaty smell he's had all week.

Perching on the toilet, I open my laptop and start typing. Every few seconds, I look up, my eyes landing on Henry.

He's fine.

But what if he slipped and hit his head? If he got too tired to hold his head up and slid under the water? What if, after all we went through to have our baby boy, I lost him?

I fought for him. It can't end like this.

I'd hear him if he had trouble in the bath, I know I would. But I keep watching. He keeps splashing.

In under ten minutes I have everything posted on social media.

"Okay, that's all sent," I tell Henry, closing my laptop and setting it outside on the floor in the hall. I have a text to send, easily the most important part of all of this, and I do that, tapping the screen with triumph before putting my phone to the side as well.

"You ready to hop on out?"

He shakes his head and holds up a rubber duck, laughing as water drips down on his head.

"Twenty minutes," I say, grinning at him. It's nice to see him feeling better, to know that he's turned a corner.

I grab my phone and doom scroll for a bit longer than I meant to, then finally shake my head a little to focus.

"Okay, Henry," I tell him, yawning and putting my phone down. "I vote we get out and go downstairs to snuggle."

I grab a fluffy white towel and pull the plug on the water. Just as I'm about to yank him from the tub and dry him off, my phone beeps.

Again.

Three times.

I pause, staring at Henry. He's trying desperately to plug the drain so the tub will remain full. His little chubby hands splay flat on the bottom of the tub, water still gurgling down the drain.

I stare at him. Look at my phone.

Henry's laughing, still trying to keep the water in the tub, and I turn away, to my phone. My fingers tremble as I tap the screen to see what caused so many notifications.

"We have a booking," I say, hating that I sound so surprised.

That was fast. Faster than I thought it would be.

The only person here with me is Henry and still I cringe,

not wanting anyone else to know how shocked I am about how quickly this happened.

"It's a big booking." I flick the screen to scroll up.

I stare at the contact info. How many times have I cursed this woman's name? She has no idea the mistake she just made.

FOUR

LOTTIE

My heart hammers in my chest as I stare at the computer screen. Like the mouse burned me, I jerk my hand back, press my fingers to my lips.

It's done.

Tim mentioned wanting to go on a family vacation, and I know why.

Things between the two of us have changed so much. Taking your vows means believing that everything will work out the way you want it to, but we've been married so, so long. We need help.

Things have to change. I've seen the open tabs on our computer's browser, clear signs of the place he wanted to book.

And then he sent me the post about their promotion.

The Saltside Inn.

It's romantic. Secluded. He won't have any distractions— not from his friends coming by, no trivia night at the bar—and I'll be able to rest a little, not work around the house so much.

Going there will be different enough from our day-to-day around the house that it might work.

I exhale, then a laugh escapes from my lips. Clapping both

hands down over my mouth, I try to hold back any future giggles.

I'm obviously over-tired.

That has to be what this is. I'm tired. I'm beyond tired, if I'm being honest. Exhausted. Money doesn't stretch as far as we all want it to. Things are tight, even with Tim managing to bring in cash the way he does. I know there are a lot of people who would think my plan is insane, but they don't know what I do.

They don't see the way out.

I have a way out, a plan, a way to fix all of this.

But it's only because I've been pushed so close to the edge.

A lot of it is because of Chelsea. I can blame a lot of things in my life on our teenage daughter, if I'm being honest with myself. Nobody ever said having a kid would be easy, but what they don't tell you is that it only gets worse as the kid gets older. I'd do anything to go back to changing diapers if it meant I didn't have to deal with the teenage angst that radiates from Chelsea 24/7.

That and the eyeliner. The jeans with *strategic* holes placed all over them, the way she pops her gum at me and rolls her eyes and...

I'm getting a headache. Moaning, I lean forward and press my fingers hard into my temples. Tim will be home anytime now and I'm going to have to tell him we're going on a trip. Just our little family, just the three of us, off on a trip that will change our lives.

He'll be thrilled.

Sighing heavily, I close my laptop and stand. My knees feel a little weak and I close my eyes, count to ten.

As soon as I open them again, I smile. It feels strange on my face, like my skin is stretching, and I pull a small mirror out from my desk drawer. No, I look fine. Not like I'm about to come out of my skin.

Not like a woman pushed to the edge.

Not like a woman with one last plan, one last Hail Mary to try to fix everything. I've done what I can to set this into motion. I've planned, I've thought it out. And if this doesn't work?

Well, there is no plan B.

I'm about to head downstairs to wait for Tim to get home when my phone rings.

FIVE

ABBY

My fingers trembled as I dialed the phone number on the booking request. I'd double-checked it to make sure I didn't type it in incorrectly, then I'd tapped the green call button and pressed the phone up to my ear. I'm standing in the kitchen, probably one of my favorite places in the house. Under my feet are wide wood planks, and the huge cottage sink is deep enough for me to soak all of my pots and pans.

Thick exposed rafters span the entire kitchen, the rough wood stained dark. In front of one window, I have a row of succulents, houseplants I hoped would grow without a lot of care. They're leggy and stretched out, their fleshy leaves pressed up against the glass, desperate for more sun. I ignore them and turn around, run my finger along the edge of the granite counter.

None of it is custom, but I love it so much it might as well have been.

"Hello?" a woman answers, her voice soft.

So that's what she sounds like.

"Lottie Rowe?" My throat sounds thick, and I clear it. I'm terrified she's going to tell me there was some mistake, that she doesn't really want to rent the entire B&B for three weeks. There's no way she really wants to do that; she had to have typed something in incorrectly.

"This is Lottie."

I exhale and wipe one sweaty palm on my jeans. From where I'm standing, I can see straight into the main living area where Henry's watching a cartoon. I don't love plopping him in front of the TV, but he's felt so bad recently that I want to make it up to him. If he wants to watch TV while I make this phone call, then that's fine.

"Lottie, hi. This is Abby Hardy from the Saltside Inn. I received your reservation request and I wanted to reach out to make sure you didn't accidentally make a mistake." *Dear God, don't let her have made a mistake.* "I saw you want to stay with us for three weeks, which is great, but you want to rent out the entire B&B?"

"Yes, that's right."

She sounds calm, perfectly in control. While her voice had been quiet when she first answered the phone, there's a bit more power to it now.

"Is that a problem? I thought I saw online the rooms were all available, and since we're return guests, I was hoping we'd get the discount. My husband really wants to come stay with you."

"Oh, that's not a problem at all." I clear my throat again. "It's just that we believe in providing personal service to each of our guests, and I always like to touch base after booking. It gives me the chance to verify dates and make sure we have any important information like allergies or special accommodations you might need."

"No, we want to rent the entire building, if that's not a problem."

"It's not."

"Great."

She laughs, the sound light and airy. She sounds like she doesn't have a care in the world, not at all like she's struggling to figure out how she's going to keep the lights on at home. I feel a stab of jealousy.

"I really wanted to take my family away for a vacation. We stayed with you years ago, and my husband and I loved it. I thought it would be a good surprise for him to come back."

"Oh, that's wonderful. What a gift for him. Well, if you and your husband are happy with the price, then we can't wait to see you both."

"And our daughter, Chelsea."

There's a bite to her voice and I mentally kick myself. Most guests don't care if you mention their children or not because they're confident they'll be included.

Obviously, Lottie is not that woman.

"Yes, I see her information listed. Sorry."

My mind races as I try to think about how to smooth this over with her. Lottie sounds like the kind of woman who knows what she wants, knows how to get it, and isn't ever interested in people standing in her way.

"Let me ask you this, Lottie. You three will be the only guests for most of December. Is there anything special you want me to have on hand for meals?"

There's a pause and I wonder if I made a mistake. With my luck, she's now going to launch into this convoluted story about food allergies and how picky an eater Chelsea is and I'm going to spend the remaining time before they get here worrying about what I'm going to feed them, but she laughs again.

"Oh, no, Abby, you don't need to worry about us. We're not coming to get waited on, so you don't have to worry about that. We want to get away, spend some time together as a family. Nothing's more important than that, wouldn't you agree?"

"I do agree." I swallow hard, trying to push away any doubts I have of how amazing this is.

Good things can happen to me. I'm allowed to have nice things in my life. When something good happens, it doesn't mean that something terrible is going to happen later.

Manifesting your dream life. Sounds like a crock, doesn't it?

"Well, if you think of anything you need or any questions you want to ask, give me a call." I'm grinning now and I do a little dance in place. "Otherwise, I'll get your contract signed and emailed back for you to send your deposit and we'll see you in two days."

"We can't wait. Thanks so much for checking in, Abby. I appreciate that you wanted to make sure we're on the same page, but we are. We're going to love it."

"See you then." I hang up, making sure the call is completely disconnected.

"Yes!" I cry, thrusting my fist into the air. "Yes, yes, yes!" Through the door I see Henry turn from the TV to look at me, but he doesn't get up. "We booked the entire place for three weeks!" I call to him.

He turns back to the TV.

No matter. I don't expect my two-year-old to have any idea why I'm so excited, but I know who will. My hands shake as I swipe my phone back on and send a text to Mark.

We rented the entire B&B for three weeks.

I barely have time to take a breath after sending the text before my phone buzzes in my hands.

You're kidding! It's time to celebrate!

Time to celebrate, indeed.

Are they new or repeats?

Of course Mark wants to know all the details. I would too. But I ignore his question.

Tim and Lottie Rowe. And their daughter, Chelsea.

I'm grinning as I type out their names. I'm never going to forget to mention Chelsea again, that much is for sure.

Mark doesn't immediately respond, and I turn my screen off and plug my phone in to charge. Even though I have two days to get ready for our guests, who knows what will happen? Maybe someone else will call and book a room before their arrival.

I have a lot to do.

I'm humming to myself, so happy I feel like I'm going to explode. A lot of it is nervous energy, I know that, but I might as well put it to good use and get some things done around the place.

As I get out my rags and bucket to start the baseboards, I remember I need to e-sign and send the contract.

It's easy to get distracted when you're so excited about something.

Hurrying back to my computer, I pull up the software I use to send invoices. Lottie wants the discount for being a repeat guest, and I can't say I blame her.

A vacation like this isn't going to be cheap. Even though we just talked and she assured me they want to come, part of me's afraid she's going to see the final price on the contract and change her mind.

I'll have to sweeten the deal for her.

Whatever we might lose out on by giving her the biggest discount will be more than made up for thanks to them renting out the whole place. Everything's going to change thanks to them coming to stay with us.

"Just send the invoice with a coupon code. Who cares about the rate being a little bit lower, really? They're making it easier than you thought, booking the whole place. You won't even have to worry about other guests bumping around while they're here," I mutter to myself, my fingers flying across the keyboard.

There. Hopefully she won't balk at the final price on the contract. Just in case, I apply another coupon code to make it as low as possible to ensure she doesn't. I click send.

In the other room I hear the cartoon end and I sigh, pushing myself up from the kitchen table to check on Henry. My laptop closes with a soft click, and I run my fingers across it before turning to grab my phone. The message light blinks, and I tap the screen, swiping it on.

It's from Mark. My heart beats harder, which it always does when I get a text from my husband. We've been married for twenty years now but he still makes me feel like I'm the most special woman in the world. After trying for so long to have a child and finally getting blessed with Henry, I'm grateful we still feel like this.

Abby, did you already send them a contract?

I swell with pride. Mark has no reason to worry. I'm on top of it, like I always am.

My thumbs fly across the screen as I tap out my answer.

Already done. No worries, honey, I'm on it.

My phone beeps and I grin when I see it's an email confirmation that Lottie has already paid the deposit.

And they've paid. I've got everything handled.

He can't argue with that. He has nothing to worry about, not when I've got things under control.

My plan is going perfectly.

SIX

MARK

I have to force myself to put my phone down and not immediately call Abby. My fingers twitch to text her, but I leave my phone in the cupholder of my truck, slamming the door hard as I walk away from it.

Working will help. Working always helps.

My toolbox bangs against my knee as I walk up to the Moran house. Tucked back in the woods, it looks like something from a storybook, with huge patches of moss on the roof, a cute little fence around the garden, and a curl of smoke coming from the chimney.

She'll need to keep the fire burning during the upcoming storm.

I knock twice then step back so Maggie Moran will be able to see it's me and won't worry about who's knocking on her door this time of morning.

"Mark!" Maggie opens the door a crack, grinning out at me for a moment, then throws it the rest of the way open, gesturing for me to come in from the cold. There's a bit of frost on the ground, and I scuff my shoes on the welcome mat before following her inside.

It's like walking into the Sahara Desert.

"Warm enough in here for you, Maggie?" I ask, putting my toolbox down by my feet and stripping out of my jacket. She laughs and takes it from me, hanging it on a hook next to the door.

"When you're as old as I am, you need heat to keep your bones moving." She gestures for me to follow her, her finger twisted and thin as she crooks it at me.

I do, grabbing my toolbox from the floor and walking through her living room to her kitchen. Maggie Moran told me over the phone that her garbage disposal was possessed and that it was going to be the death of her if I couldn't fix it. She's gotten a bit dramatic since we first met, when Abby and I moved to Oyster, but as soon as I walk into her kitchen, I see what she means.

"This," she says, pointing at the sink as she pulls out a chair at the table to sit down, "this is a living nightmare. Can you fix it?"

Her disposal isn't just broken, it looks like it's on strike. Her sink is full of water and bits of food, like whatever she tried to put down the disposal fought its way right back up.

"Oh, I can fix it, but I'm going to need one thing." I try to keep a smile on my face. Maggie's told me before how much she loves me coming to her house because I'm always in a good mood. I'm not in a good mood right now, but if that's the reputation I have, then I need to try to keep it up.

"Anything." Her eyes are bright. Even though she has to be pushing eighty, you'd never know it thanks to how spry she is. Maggie was my first handyman client here in Oyster and I have a soft spot for her.

"Coffee," I say. "Stat. So dark and thick it might be able to get out of the cup on its own and walk across the kitchen."

She laughs, waggling her finger at me, then slowly rises from her chair. "I figured you'd want that. Is it too early for a little something special to go in the mug with it?" She pauses, her eyes locked on me, obviously trying to guess what I'm going to say before I answer.

"It's a little early," I tell her. Even if it weren't, I don't think I could drink any alcohol right now. My stomach feels like it's flipping over and over, and every time I let my mind wander back to Abby and the B&B, I want to throw up.

Maggie walks to the coffee pot and I settle myself in front of the sink. At least this is an easy job, one I'm pretty sure I could do with my eyes closed. While there are plenty of calls I go on where I really need to focus on what I'm doing, repairing a garbage disposal isn't one of them.

My hands seem to move on their own, but my mind won't slow down. I'm honestly grateful to be out of the house right now. It's one thing to lie to your wife; it's another to try to do it on the spur of the moment. I know what would happen if Abby knew the truth.

She'd leave me.

She'd divorce me and take the B&B.

Worse than that, I have a very good feeling she'd make it so I never saw Henry again. Abby isn't the type of woman who easily forgives. When we first met it was because she was throwing my roommate's things out of our apartment for cheating on her best friend.

Never mind that her best friend didn't seem too upset about moving on to someone new. Never mind the fact that Abby broke into our apartment through a window to pitch his clothing, books, and toiletries out the window onto the lawn. I can't help but grin at the memory of the expression on Danny's face when he got home from work and everything he owned was outside.

By that time, I'd calmed Abby down enough to sit and talk to me. We were in the kitchen while I cooked pancakes for dinner, completely oblivious to Danny's rage. From that moment on, it's been like the two of us are alone in our world and we can easily handle anything.

"Coffee." Maggie thrusts a mug into my face, and I put down my tools to take it from her. The mug is warm, and I breathe in the steam, taking a small sip before groaning.

"That is good. I don't know how you make coffee that amazing, but I appreciate that I'm on the receiving end of it."

She beams and totters back to the table to work on the crossword. "Do you think you'll be much longer? Is it bad?"

"It's not bad." Standing, I turn on the sink to flush out the disposal. "In fact, my dear, I'd say I'm done."

"Oh, you're a hero." The crossword forgotten, she claps her hands together and gestures to me. "Sit with me a moment, Mark, unless you have somewhere else you need to hurry off to."

I think about the next jobs on my list and shake my head. I have no problem taking my time.

I sit down, perched on the needlepoint cushion resting in the seat, and take another sip of my coffee.

"Tell me, how is Abby? And Henry?" Maggie's eyes are bright with excitement.

"Oh, they're great," I say, leaning back a little bit in the chair. There's a loud pop from the leg and I stiffen then stand, walking to my toolbox to get some wood glue. While I search for the loose joint, I continue. "We're coming up on our ten-year anniversary at the Saltside Inn, so that's exciting. And Henry is all-out all the time. He's one hundred percent boy and keeps Abby on her toes."

There it is. Some glue will tighten it right up.

"I love it." She claps her hands together. "And you'll have to forgive me for asking, but I feel like you and I have known each other long enough that I can be a little forward."

She pauses and I wait, already guessing what she's going to say.

It's the one question everyone asks, isn't it? As soon as you walk down the aisle, people want to know when there will be a baby.

And then, when you have one, they want to know when you'll have another.

Even if we hadn't had trouble getting pregnant with Henry, I hate these questions. Everyone asks them.

But little old ladies? They're the worst.

"Do you think there will be any more children?" Her face is bright, her expression so hopeful, so happy, that I almost feel bad for what I'm going to tell her.

"Oh, Maggie," I say, putting the glue back in my toolbox and walking over to her. She's staring at me, holding her breath, looking for all the world like what I'm about to say is the most important thing. "You know we'd both love that. And Henry is the best thing to ever happen to our little family. But having him and making sure he was safe? That was almost too much for the two of us."

Even thinking about how hard Abby and I tried to get pregnant and the stress she went through, going to the doctor all the time only to find out that we'd need help to get pregnant in the first place, makes me feel ill.

It almost destroyed us. How is it fair that some people get pregnant so quickly and easily and we didn't?

She nods. "I shouldn't have asked. Just know how much I love you and your sweet family." She reaches for me, and I take her hands, letting her squeeze mine. "Please give Abby and Henry my love, okay? And I'll call you if I need you for anything else."

She looks past me to the clock on the oven. "And look at the time! I know you didn't come all the way down the mountain just to help me out. You better get going, or you're going to have a long line of desperate clients." Moving quickly, she grabs a twenty-dollar bill from the table and presses it into my hand.

Twenty dollars is a lot less than I'd charge anyone else to come to their home, but Maggie's word of mouth is better advertising than anything I could pay for. I grin at her and pull her into a hug.

"I'll make sure Abby sends cookies down the mountain for you for Christmas," I tell her, then break away to head outside. She calls to me from the front porch and I turn and wave, but already I'm lost in my thoughts.

This was a nice distraction.

But now it's back to the real world.

SEVEN

ABBY

Even from across the living room I can smell the whiskey on Mark's breath. He came home and went right for the bottle like he was on a mission. He's gotten better about that, about not diving head-first into the bottle as soon as he walks in the door, but today he doesn't even speak to me before he pours a glass and takes a sip.

"Was it a long day?" I'm perched on the sofa across from him. We have a blazing fire in the fireplace and it's doing a pretty good job of chasing away the chill of the evening. My entire body aches from cleaning baseboards for an hour this afternoon before launching right into dusting all of the guest rooms.

It's one thing to prepare for a single guest to come stay with us, another entirely to have to clean the entire B&B from top to bottom. And Henry is feeling a lot better, which is amazing, but he's been full of energy. After his bath and cartoon time, he took a short nap and woke up acting like he felt better than he had in weeks.

Kids somehow bottle all their unused energy when they're sick, then let it all out as soon as they start feeling better.

And now? Henry feels great.

But I'm exhausted.

In between cleaning and dusting and making snacks, I've been building forts with him and nervously checking my email. Just in case. Just in case Lottie changed her mind.

She hasn't, by the way. The endorphin high I was on all morning is still here; it's just tempered a little bit by how drained I am now.

"The day was fine." Mark swirls his glass, the amber liquid catching the light from the fireplace, then drains it. Leaning forward, he puts it on the coffee table between us and sighs as he settles back in his chair. "Tell me again how it all went with these guests."

So I do. I'm animated as I launch into an explanation of how I posted the information on social media and Lottie jumped on it right away. I leave out the coupon codes, how I was careful to lower the final price as much as possible so they wouldn't cancel.

But those are the only things I don't tell him. Other than that, I don't leave out a single detail when telling him how nervous I was and how that nervousness gave way to exhilaration when I realized she was serious about renting out the entire place.

"So, it's not perfect," I say, exhaling hard and wrapping a blanket tighter around my shoulders, "but things are looking up."

"Don't you think renting the entire place to one family is a bad idea?" Mark scrubs his hand down his face and then locks his eyes on me.

"Not a good idea? Why do you think that? I think it's a great idea."

"Sure, but what about anyone else who might want to stay with us? Don't you think they'll be disappointed when they realize the place is booked and they can't get in?"

I'm shaking my head before he can even finish his thought. "I know what you're saying, Mark, but no. Nobody else has reached out today to book. If we had people falling all over themselves to stay with us, then maybe, but we don't. Why in the world would we push the Rowes out of the way to make room for guests who might not ever materialize?"

"It's strange, that's all." Mark stands. He seems unsure of what to do with his hands and finally shoves them in his pockets. It's impossible for me to tell what he's thinking, not when his face keeps changing. One moment he looks calm, the next he looks like he's going to blurt something out.

"Do you know them?"

Mark stares at me and I hurry to cover the question. "They're not from Oyster though, so you might not. They're from a few towns over, but I don't remember which one."

"I don't know them." He crosses his arms over his chest. "I can't get over how weird it is that they'd want to rent out the entire place."

"Well, get over it." Shrugging the blanket from my shoulders, I cross the room and hug him. When Mark gets inside his head like this, there's only one thing to do to bring him back down to earth. "Seriously, you're going to have to let this one go. They're coming to stay with us in two days and it's going to be great. Now, Henry is sleeping, after demanding one game of hide-and-seek before bed, I'm sore from working all day, and I think I know a way I can help you blow off some steam."

He's still, then he relaxes and hugs me, his strong arms wrapping around me. I exhale hard, in relief. It's one thing for Mark to be unhappy about something, but he never takes it out on me. He's never once, in our decades of marriage, made me feel like I'm the problem.

"You said Henry's sleeping?"

I nod against his chest.

"And we have guests coming for three whole weeks soon?"

Another nod. "Yep. It's going to get a little crazy around here. It'll be nice to have people around, but if we're going to enjoy ourselves—"

He scoops me up, one arm under my knee, the other behind my back. I laugh, then clap my hand over my mouth to stifle the noise. I have to be quiet so we can avoid waking up our son.

"Let's enjoy ourselves," he tells me, carrying me to the stairs. "And then tomorrow we can talk about this again, see if we really want to rent out the entire place to one family. It seems like we're shooting ourselves in the foot and preventing other people who also might want to come stay with us from getting that opportunity."

I don't respond. He may not like it, but there's no way I'm going to cancel this reservation. The Rowes are coming and staying with us for three weeks.

Let Mark worry. This is the right thing for us.

EIGHT

MARK

Thursday 29 Nov

I told you I'd pay you. Don't do this.

The nine words blink back at me from my cell phone before I tap send. The screen clicks off and I slip my phone into my pocket.

My phone sits heavy there, and I try to ignore the way it feels like it's weighing me down. Any secret can do this, I've learned. Any secret you keep long enough, especially from someone you love, can be enough to make you feel like you wronged the mob, were put in cement shoes, and thrown into the bay.

That's exactly how I feel right now. It's like what I just did can't ever be taken back, and when it all comes to light, I'm going to have to answer for it.

"Hey, Mark." Abby walks up behind me and loops her arms around my waist, snuggling her face into my back. "Are you getting excited to have some more people in the house?"

My heart sinks.

"It's going to be great," I lie, carefully unwrapping her arms from around me so I can turn and hug her. "And I think Henry will like having someone else in the house too."

"Oh, definitely." From the other room we can both hear Henry playing with his cars. Normally I'd want to go join him, to get on the floor with him, to spend some time with my son.

"Well, you'll be pleased to know that everything's ready." Abby speaks with pride, and I can't help but smile at her. "I've done all the grocery shopping, and even with the storm coming in, I think we'll be fine. Our medical kit was looking a little empty, so I replenished what we were missing." She begins counting things off on her fingers. "I also topped up the extra gas can for your truck, and even remembered to pick up extra batteries for our flashlights. Just in case."

"Just in case." I reach out and brush her cheek where she has a bit of dirt from playing with Henry. "You're so on top of it, Abs. What would I do without you?"

She laughs. "Let's hope you never have to find out, mister." Her laugh has always been addictive to me. I'm about to compliment her again when my phone beeps.

I don't move to get it. Abby tilts her head as she looks at me.

"You need to grab that? It might be a handyman job. Oooh, or maybe someone is canceling thanks to all the upcoming snow. That storm is supposed to move in tonight, you know." She mock shivers and rubs her hands up and down her arms.

"Oh, I'll get it. I'm just enjoying talking to you."

There's another beep.

And another.

Abby frowns. "Seriously, Mark, don't let me keep you from work stuff. I know how hard you've worked to build up a good reputation, and I don't want to be the reason that you don't get back to someone right away."

If I didn't know my wife as well as I do, I'd think for sure she was trying to trick me.

But that's not who Abby is. She's kind and generous and always thinks of other people before herself.

"Yeah, you're right." I fish my phone from my pocket as it beeps again. "Man, someone's toilet better have exploded or something for them to keep texting me like this."

She laughs and slaps my arm. "I'm going to check on Henry. If you do go, please make sure you keep an eye on the weather and let me know before you leave." She turns around and chews on her lower lip. "I'm serious, Mark, I know you love your truck and think nothing bad will ever happen to you when you're driving it, but you know how slick the roads here can get. And I don't want you to get stuck down the mountain away from us. I need you here, especially with guests coming."

"I won't do anything dangerous," I tell her. My thumb is on the side button on my phone, ready to click it on, but I want to make sure Abby really walks away from me. Not that she ever tries to read my texts. She wouldn't.

She's so sweet. So trusting.

But what if she did today? The thought is irrational, but once it's taken root in my mind, I can't stop thinking about it. Abby is trusting. That's what got us into this mess in the first place.

The texts fill my screen.

Obviously not fast enough.

You knew this was a possibility.

Is there going to be a problem?

I sigh and hesitate before answering. This is a can of worms I never should have opened, but, now that I have, I'm not sure I'll be able to close it back up.

No, of course not.

That's it. That's all I want to say, and I hope there's no response.

Just as I'm about to tap the little trashcan button to delete the entire thread, Henry runs into the kitchen and slams into my legs, practically scaling me for a hug. He laughs as I stumble forward and catch myself on the counter.

"Hey, Henry!" My phone goes back in my pocket, and I bend down, scooping him up. "What in the world has got into you, my little monkey?"

"I want to play outside!" He wraps his arms around my neck and snuggles close before pulling away to get a better look at me. "With you, Daddy."

"Oh, buddy," I say, carrying him to the kitchen window so we can look outside. "Look at how cold it is out there. There's snow coming later and it's freezing. Why don't we stay inside and play a game?"

He shakes his head hard, his baby-soft blond hair flying out around his head like a halo.

"I want to go out. With you." He pouts, then snuggles his little face into my neck. Over his head I watch as Abby walks into the kitchen, laughter all over her face.

"You did this," I say, freeing one hand from my son to point at him. "You're sacrificing me to go outside even though it's freezing."

"Hey," she says, holding up her hands. "I thought it would be good for you."

"Good for me?"

She's laughing harder now.

"What if I told you that was a job and I'm headed into town right now and that you were on duty to go play outside in this freezing weather?"

That sobers her up. She stops laughing and stares at me. "No, seriously? I don't want to become a popsicle today."

I laugh, making her roll her eyes. "No, not seriously. I'll take him out, but why don't you come with us? You've been working so hard getting ready for our guests, and once they get here, you'll be working even harder. Why not take a little break and go on a short walk with us?"

"Because it's cold enough to freeze spit?" she offers, but she's already leading the way to the kitchen door. We go through this song and dance from time to time and I know what's going to happen. She'll tug on her old boots, the ones that look like she lifted them from a dumpster, then spend at least five minutes fussing over Henry and making sure he's warm enough to go outside.

We'll all bundle up and head out. By the time we get back, our noses will be bright red, and Abby will declare it's time for hot chocolate. I'll have forgotten all about the texts, and so will she.

That thought is the only thing that drives me outside. We'll go to the front yard, have a good time as a family.

I shouldn't have ever texted back, but that's done. There's no coming back from that right now.

But Abby never has to know. I'm going to see to it that she doesn't.

NINE

ABBY

Henry sleeps on me, his little face turned so he's breathing hot breath right into my face. His entire body is warm, but not the scary hot that it was when he was so sick. He's exhausted from our long walk earlier and then from playing outside after we got back. It's been a busy day and now it's time for bed, his body already full of that heavy feeling kids get when they're on the cusp of sleep.

Normally I wouldn't dare dream of letting him skip his nap, especially not on purpose. He's like any other little kid in that regard. He gets cranky and then refuses to eat because he's so tired. It was a risk to let him stay up through his nap, but a calculated one.

And now I have to make sure he wakes up and stays up.

I know he'll be exhausted, but I have good reason.

"Hey," I say to Mark, who's sitting next to us on the sofa. He looks almost as tired as Henry does after our excursion outside. There are dark circles under his eyes and he's leaning his head back on the sofa like he could fall asleep anytime. The shadow of stubble on his jaw is going to turn into a beard if he doesn't shave it soon.

It takes him a moment to answer. "Hey." Turning his head, he looks at me, blinking a few times like he was almost asleep. "What's up?"

"Can you take him to bed?" I whisper so Henry won't wake up. He should have had a bath this evening after so much playing today, but I wasn't about to deal with him throwing a tantrum as soon as we put him in the water. I needed him tired but that doesn't mean I have the energy for a full-on fit.

Mark's eyes widen. "You want me to carry him to bed?"

I nod. "Can you? I think my arms are numb from how he's sleeping on me. There's no way I'd be able to carry him up the stairs."

"Okay, sure." Mark exhales hard. I know he doesn't want to take Henry to bed. Our son is a ticking bomb right now, ready to wake up and start crying at any moment.

I'm counting on it.

Henry's head rolls to the side a little bit when Mark takes him from my arms. Immediately I'm chilled, and I wrap my arms around myself and start rubbing them to wake them back up. I wasn't lying to my husband about my arms going slightly numb, but I've had worse when holding Henry.

Mark moves slowly, scooping Henry to his chest. For a moment, the sight of them takes my breath away. Henry looks so much like his dad. He has Mark's nose and broad smile, and I have no doubt in my mind that he'll be a heartbreaker when he grows up.

"Okay, you've got him," I say, slowly standing up and leaning up to Mark's cheek to give him a kiss. "I'm going to clean up the kitchen really quickly and be right up. Need me to bring anything?"

"My—" Mark begins, but then he stops himself and shakes his head. "No, I think I'm good, thanks. I'll see you upstairs as soon as I get this little monster tucked in."

"You're the best."

Even though I'm dying to get into the kitchen where Mark charges his phone, I wait until they're halfway up the stairs before walking that way. Henry hasn't started crying yet, and maybe I was wrong. Maybe he's not going to wake up and give Mark a hard time, which would keep my husband occupied for a little while.

As soon as I have that thought though, I hear a hiccup from the second-floor landing. Mark's footsteps stop and I hold my breath, already fully aware of what's going to happen.

And there it is, right on time. Exactly why I didn't want Henry to take a nap earlier today. He's crying now—not the terrible screaming little kids do when they're overly tired, but he's working up to it. It's my cue to get moving, and I hurry from the living room, down the hall, and into the kitchen.

There's not a single thing I need to clean up in here. I did it all right after dinner, all while keeping an eye on Mark's phone to make sure he didn't disappear with it. When we first got married, I told myself I wouldn't be a paranoid wife who wanted to check her husband's phone all the time.

And I wasn't, for a while.

Until a little voice in the back of my head told me to keep tabs on Mark. He's devastatingly good-looking. Even when I'm right next to him at the park and he's holding Henry, I see the way other women turn to check him out. He doesn't see it though.

At least I didn't think he did.

Keeping one ear out for any footsteps on the stairs, I rush to our little kitchen command center. This is a point of pride for me. A few years ago, when I was struggling to stay on top of everything for the B&B, I set it up with our calendar, cell-phone chargers, a cup of pens, and sticky notes. There's a pad of paper for us to make grocery lists and even some business cards for both Mark and the B&B for us to hand out.

In short, I'm prepared.

Also, I know exactly where Mark's phone is when he's not using it.

I grab it, my fingers trembling as I type in his password. There's a pause, then the screen shakes, kicking me right back to the keypad.

"What in the world?" I mutter and type the numbers in again. Three. Seven. One. Nine.

The screen shakes.

Heat blooms in my cheeks.

He changed his passcode.

A cold mixture of anger and fear washes over me and I stand completely still, my ears on high alert for any sound of Mark coming down the stairs, my mind racing as I try to figure out why he changed his passcode.

And, more importantly, what it might be now.

"Okay, Abby, think." I know I only have one more shot at guessing his passcode and then it will lock me out. The last thing I need is for Mark to see that I tried to get into his phone and wonder what in the world I was doing. He has no idea that I like to check his messages from time to time.

So why would he suddenly change the passcode?

It started a few years into our marriage, and I haven't stopped yet. Once a week, at least, like clockwork. I wait until he leaves his phone unattended and turn it on, check his messages, his social media, and his internet search history.

We were having so much trouble getting pregnant, and I was worried he'd find someone else.

Is it wrong? Maybe. Maybe it is. Maybe I should feel bad about checking up on him when I'm almost certain he doesn't do it to me, but what wife in my position wouldn't make sure? It's insurance, that's all it is, just insurance that things are going okay.

Or that they're not.

I turn his phone over and over in my hand as I think.

Henry's crying from upstairs has decreased a little but I can still hear him whimpering. In a moment of brilliance, I reach over and snap on the baby monitor.

Now it sounds like he's in the room with me. Wincing, I turn it down, making sure I'll be able to hear what's going on upstairs without blowing out my eardrums.

"Hey, Henry, you're okay." It's Mark, his voice so calm even in the face of a meltdown that I feel my heart soften. "You're going to be okay, bud. You're exhausted, and I get it. I'm tired too. I don't know why you're so tired, but it will be okay."

His voice keeps getting louder and then softer again. He must be carrying Henry as he walks around our son's bedroom, trying to calm him.

"But tomorrow's a big day, okay?" His voice grows quiet again and I turn up the monitor, trying to hear what he's saying. For the moment, the phone is almost completely forgotten, although I do want to see what those texts were earlier.

"... need to be on your best behavior. You want to impress them, don't you?"

Mark has never worried about impressing our guests before.

I'm frozen, my fingers on the volume, listening to every word Mark's saying. Some of them though, I can't hear. When he walks away from the monitor, his voice gets so soft, it's difficult for me to make out the words.

"... just be yourself. We'll get through this okay. Now, are you ready for bed, little man? I think you are. I think—"

I don't listen to what else Mark thinks because I turn off the monitor. Checking his phone tonight was supposed to give me some answers about what he's been up to. It was supposed to allow me to check his browser history and make sure he wasn't doing anything we'd both regret.

But now I have more questions than answers. And even though I wish I had a clue about what passcode to use to get into his phone, I don't.

And I need to hurry.

He'll head downstairs in a moment if he's already putting Henry in bed.

Moving as quickly as possible now, I click off the kitchen light and grab my phone from the charger next to his. Holding both our phones so he can see I have them and so he'll think I wasn't doing anything with his, I plaster a smile on my face and walk to the stairs.

Just as I thought, he's halfway down the staircase when I reach the bottom. He stops, grins. Runs his hand through his hair.

"He's sleeping. You going to bed?"

"Yes." I wait for him to join me at the bottom of the stairs then offer him his phone. "I thought you might want this."

"Yeah, thanks." He takes it and gives me a kiss on the cheek. "I think I'm going to stay up a bit longer. Maybe have some whiskey, try to relax a bit before our guests come tomorrow. I'll be up in a bit."

"Sounds good."

He walks away from me, and I turn so I can watch him go. As he walks, he looks at his phone, types on the screen to unlock it, then gives a little sigh.

Of relief? Of happiness?

I have no idea, but I'm determined to find out.

TEN

LOTTIE

Friday 30 Nov

The road in front of us keeps turning. It's a steeper incline than I would have thought, and our Jeep groans a little bit as Tim presses down on the gas, inching us forward, carefully navigating around slick spots of ice that have already begun covering the road.

"Just be careful," I say, my teeth clenched. I have to squeeze my hands together in my lap to keep myself from reaching over and grabbing his arm. We hit a patch of ice and I close my eyes, my fingers cramping as I grip them together.

"You need to relax," he tells me.

When I glance over at him, I'm not surprised to see his wrist resting lightly on the steering wheel, his other hand on his travel mug of coffee.

"You think I can't handle icy roads like this? This is nothing. Just wait, we're going to be snowed in for three weeks."

His words make me glance in the backseat. Chelsea has earbuds in, and even though I've already fussed at her twice to turn down the music, I can still hear the low thrum of the bass.

Her face is turned away from me and she's staring out the window. I'd give just about anything to know what she's thinking, but as my daughter has grown older, she's done her best to keep her thoughts hidden from me.

She was passive when I told her that we were coming here to Saltside Inn for a few weeks. Most teenagers would throw a fit, I'd think, and refuse to get snowed in with their parents somewhere they don't know. But not Chelsea. She got really quiet, even more than usual, and simply nodded.

And now we're here.

There's one final turn in the road. We hit another patch of ice, but Tim keeps the wheel straight. The feeling of the back wheels slipping out behind us a bit makes my stomach turn, but then he's straightened us out and the Saltside Inn is there—*right there*—and it takes my breath away.

I knew it was big, but the pictures online didn't do it any justice. It's four stories, a soft pink with white molding, trim, and shutters, the entire thing perched on the top of the hill like a sentry. It's on our right as we pull up, the ocean on our left. Even without entering the building I can tell there are going to be incredible views of the waves crashing against rocks from the upper floors.

There's a rugged forest, the trees closer to the cliff clinging to the rock, the forest growing thicker and darker deeper inland. From here, it's almost impossible to grasp the sheer scale of the cliff, the ocean, the forest. No neighbors, as far as I can see, just the ever-encroaching wilderness.

I shiver at the isolation.

A barn is set back a bit from the B&B. I glimpsed it in a few pictures of the property and thought for sure there would be horses, but according to Google reviews, it's used for garden equipment and to house a tractor that can be used to winch people out of the ditch in bad weather.

I hope we won't need that.

Tim taps the brakes and slowly pulls into the driveway. I keep craning my head up, my neck back, trying to take in the entire house. It's hard when it's so overwhelming.

The front porch wraps all the way around the building, with huge white columns to support the roof. Most of the other floors have small balconies off their rooms. They're surrounded by twisted iron railings to keep people safe outside. It never crossed my mind to warn Chelsea to stay inside and not venture out, but now I'm wishing I'd done just that.

A person could fall from up there.

The thought is unbidden, and I do my best to push it away. It circles like a vulture, and I already know it's going to be one I struggle to keep at bay the entire three weeks we're here.

But that's something I'll have to deal with later. Surely, she won't go onto her balcony, not in this terrible weather.

Tim parks the Jeep, and I reach out to touch the window, surprised at how cold it is. It was chilly when we left the house an hour ago, but the temperature keeps dropping. The gray clouds hang low, like I could reach up and touch them, and I shiver, unbuckling before zipping up my coat.

"Are you ready?" My voice is high and tight as I turn back to look at Chelsea.

She sighs, takes her earbuds out. Nods.

"And you?" I ask, turning to Tim.

"I'm ready." Tim squeezes my hand, unfolds himself from the front seat and steps out of the Jeep. Our Jeep is big enough that I feel safe on the road, but there are few vehicles designed for someone built like Tim. He's tall and thin, his dark-brown hair longer than he normally wears it, so it curls a little around his ears.

When I don't get out, he leans back in. "Now, Lottie, don't you want to meet the innkeepers?"

My stomach twists but I nod, finally getting out.

Chelsea does the same, stamping her feet as she swings her backpack over her shoulder. "Coming, Mom?"

"Yes, of course." I swallow anything I might want to say. There's no turning back from this now, no matter what happens. Tim waits for me to join him in front of the Jeep then takes my hand, pulling me slowly towards the house.

It looms over us. I thought it was big when we pulled up but now that we're standing at the base of the porch, I can't believe how giant this place is. Every picture I saw made it look like something from a fairytale, but up close I see the cracks. Some of the pink paint is peeling, probably from the salt blown in from the ocean all day long. The porch is a little warped. One of the white columns has a patch of lichen growing on it, close to the ground.

As gorgeous as the building looks in pictures, I'm a little surprised to see how many flaws it really has. There's no way anyone besides a professional photographer could capture the full feeling of this place.

"Come on, Mom." Chelsea's halfway up the stairs. "I want to get in and warm up."

What she's saying is that she wants to wait inside while Tim and I get the rest of the bags from the Jeep, but I'm not going to argue with her. Getting her inside and getting our vacation started is the smartest thing we can do right now.

"Yes, I'm coming."

I glance around one more time. Our Jeep is right behind us, the blue paint slowly getting covered with snow. No other vehicles are visible, but I guess the owners could have parked around the back of the building. Still, it feels a little strange that there aren't any other signs of life.

Tim bangs on the door then steps back, mashing his finger into the doorbell. My heart beats in my throat as I watch him. Chelsea's next to him, her long red hair tucked behind her ears.

She bounces on the balls of her feet, unable to contain her excitement about the trip.

I never thought she'd be this excited to come here.

I take a deep breath, almost ready to tell my family there must have been a misunderstanding, that nobody is here, that if we leave now, we can still make it back down the mountain safely, but there's footsteps and a loud *thunk* as someone turns the bolt in the door, and then it swings open.

Tim and Chelsea both step back and to the side, and I'm finally face-to-face with Abby Hardy. She has a toddler on her hip, a huge smile on her face, and she beckons us in.

"I'm so glad you're here! You must be the Rowes. Why don't you come on in and we can all warm up, get to know each other? You have your pick of the rooms, and I'm sure you're going to have a wonderful time here."

A long thick braid hangs down her back, strands of gray peeking out from her brunette locks. There are laugh lines on her face—*crow's feet*—but she's not wearing any makeup to try to cover them up. Her cheeks are ruddy, probably from facing the blowing cold up here all the time, and her eyes dart around the three of us to drink us all in.

Tim says something and even Chelsea speaks to her, but I can't seem to find my voice as I walk past her into the foyer. A wave of heat washes over me, and I can smell coffee. Anyone else would be instantly at peace here. Anyone else would accept this place as the haven it is.

Anyone except me.

I can barely look Abby in the eye. I keep thinking this is all going to fall apart, that she's going to figure it out, but so far, I think she's clueless.

I can't believe it.

Does she really not know who I am?

ELEVEN

MARK

For the longest time after getting home, I sit in the driveway next to a blue Jeep, my hands tight on the steering wheel, my eyes locked on the windows of the house. Snow lands on my windshield, slowly obscuring the pink building, but even when all I can see through the layer of snow are soft lights from the house's windows, I still don't move.

My phone beeps in my cupholder and I glance down at it, not surprised to see Abby's name on the screen. She worries about me when the roads are bad which, in Oyster, means she worries about me for months at a time. I'm careful though. I haven't gotten in an accident yet and I have no intention to start now.

"Just pulled up," I mutter, typing out the words and clicking send. By now the cab of my truck is cold, I've sat here so long.

Shivering, I throw the door open and step out, sinking into about a foot of snow. According to the weather reports, the storm cell we're in right now is set to hover directly over Oyster, dumping another foot of snow tonight. Even the most seasoned weathermen were excited on the news today, saying that this winter is set to be one of the coldest and wettest we've had in decades.

I can't wait.

I slam my truck door behind me, well aware that I might not be going anywhere for days.

Or a week.

It takes the city a while to get the roads scraped this far away from downtown. Even though I put down ice melt, I have a feeling it's not going to help much against this storm.

Being secluded like this was part of the charm when Abby and I bought the B&B. We both loved the idea of being snowed in together up here, of how romantic it would be. And it was romantic. Especially before Henry came along.

Even then, we made it work. Being snowed in with your family is one thing, but being snowed in with three other people at the same time?

I know we need the money; I just wish there had been another way.

Abby greets me at the front door, flinging it open and throwing herself into my arms. She has on thick wool socks, and I pick her up to keep her from stepping in the snow that's blown up on the porch.

"I wondered when you'd be home!" She snuggles into me, wrapping her legs around my waist as I carry her into the house. "You're going to love our new guests. They're delightful."

"Delightful, huh?" I put her down, slowly unwrapping her arms from around me before giving her a kiss. "Where are these delightful guests?"

She shrugs. "Not sure, but I'm also not worried. They rented the entire place out, remember? But everyone's coming down for dinner in an hour, so you'll get to meet them then."

Everyone. "That's great," I tell her. "So they really came?"

Like I didn't just park next to their Jeep.

She looks at me nervously then starts to laugh. "Why, did

you already spend some of the money from the deposit? Of course they came, Mark. Why wouldn't they?"

"No reason."

She's eyeballing me like she thinks something is wrong, so I scoop her to me again and kiss her. "Where's the little man?"

"Playing in the kitchen. I was making dinner and he was banging on the pots and pans."

We're silent for a moment, both of us listening.

There isn't any sound coming from down the hall. Outside, I hear the wind whipping around the house, crying as it slams into the shutters, its cold fingers searching for a way in, but I don't hear Henry.

"You're sure he stayed where you left him? We both know that when he's excited about guests, he tends to be on the move."

"I'm sure," Abby says, but her voice is tight. "Come on—I'll show you."

She leads me down the hall, our fingers linked together. Normally I would stop and take off my boots, but I don't. I'm leaving big wet footprints behind me on the wood floor, but I'll get them later. Now I just want to see my son.

"Henry?" Abby turns into the kitchen, me right behind her. I barely notice how good the stew on the stove smells. It's simmering away, the scent of it thick and rich in the air.

But our son is gone.

"Where is he?" I let go of Abby's hand, turn in a slow circle. The kitchen is huge, with a big island and a dining table, but I still should be able to see my son without too much effort. While I drop to my knees to look under the table and between the tangle of chair legs, Abby hurries around the counter.

"The pots and pans are here," she says. "He can't have gone too far, Mark. He wouldn't wander off. Besides, he's two, so what's there to worry about? The house is baby-proofed, and there's no way he could get in trouble."

I ignore her. Maybe Abby isn't too worried about our son, but I want to hold him, want to make sure he's okay, don't want to pretend like everything is fine when there are strangers in the house.

Only they're not strangers, are they? Not really.

I shake my head. Clear the thought. "I'll look in the living room," I snap. "Don't let dinner burn."

She blinks at me in surprise, but I'm already turning away from her.

My shoes thunk loudly on the floor as I walk through to the living room. A blazing fire greets me, the heat drawing me in, making me want to sit in my chair with a whiskey, to enjoy a quiet night.

"Daddy!"

Henry's voice yanks my gaze from the fire. I turn, fully expecting my son to come toddling to me, his arms outstretched, his face wide and smiling, but there's no movement, no Henry running at me.

"Henry?" I look to the sofa. Nothing.

My favorite chair is sitting with its back to me. I can see a head in it, see there's someone sitting there. Not Henry—his head wouldn't reach the top of the chair like that. He wouldn't be able to sit there and have his head so high over the back.

"Did you find Henry?" Abby sounds worried.

"Sure did!" I take a step towards the chair, then another. The head doesn't move but then Henry's face pops out around the side, his familiar smile making my heart ache.

"Daddy!"

"Henry, come here." I'm moving faster now, but as I go to scoop him from the lap of whoever's holding him, I freeze.

A pointed chin.

Thick red hair.

A smile that barely turns up the corners of her mouth.

Bright eyes that are locked on me as tightly as her arms are locked around Henry's middle.

"Chelsea, hi." I remember her name. Of course I remember her name—Abby's drilled it into me—but it's still strange to put a face to it. "Thanks for hanging out with Henry, but you don't have to do that. I'll take him."

She shifts, Henry snuggling up to her chest. "Don't worry about it," she tells me. "The two of us are having a lot of fun together."

I hesitate, unsure how to handle this. Years of running the Saltside Inn have taught me to be as polite as possible to our guests. If she wants to hold Henry, I should let her. He's obviously not in danger. If anything, he's enjoying the attention and being able to play with his truck by the fire.

"Are you su—"

"I'm sure," she cuts me off, still grinning. "I always wanted a sibling, so this is kinda fun."

I nod. My mouth dry. "Just let me know if he gets to be a bother."

"Oh, he won't." Her attention is fully on my son now and she kisses the top of his head. "He's so perfect and sweet, right? What a good boy you are, Henry."

Henry laughs and holds his truck up in the air before slamming it down on the chair's arm. Neither of them pay any attention to me.

I've been dismissed. In my own house.

TWELVE

ABBY

I'm nervous as I wait for everyone to join us in the dining room for dinner. While there are a lot of B&Bs that don't offer full meal service, I like to not only offer something big to eat on the first night guests are with us but also join them so they don't feel so alone. Maybe it's overkill, but I've read a lot of reviews where past guests have stated how much they loved it, that it made them feel like they were at home.

So, a full family-style dinner it is, like usual, even though I'm worried the guests will be able to tell that something feels off with Mark. He's been distant since getting home today, which isn't like him. He's the type of man who always pours on the PDA in front of other people, and so for him to hold himself away from me, to not even scoop Henry up and carry him around on his back like a horse... that's strange.

"You ready to ring the dinner bell, Henry?" I ask my son. He's perched on the counter, a Lego car in one hand, the other resting on the giant bell we use to call guests down to the kitchen. I pat the bell, waiting for him to respond. He hadn't wanted to leave our guests alone, but I finally pried him away so they could have some space to unwind.

Henry grunts and picks up the bell. It's heavier than it looks, and I move to help him, cupping my hands around it so I won't dampen the sound but so I can easily grab it if it gets to be too much for him and he thinks he's going to drop it.

The sound rings out as he shakes it, the clapper smacking into the side of the bell, and he giggles as I take it from him, give it one more solid ring, then put it back on the little piece of green velvet it sits on before pushing it farther back from the edge of the counter.

"Alright," I say, scooping Henry up and putting him down on the floor, "why don't you go find Dad and then everyone will be here in a moment for dinner?"

"Okay, Mommy!" He darts out of the kitchen, his chubby little legs flying as he runs for Mark.

Sighing, I lean against the kitchen counter and watch him go for a minute. That should put my husband in a better mood and help get him out of whatever funk he's in.

You can't be mad at the world when a toddler comes running full speed at you, especially if that toddler thinks you hung the moon.

When Henry's out of sight, I work on finishing setting the table. In addition to the stew I've had simmering on the stove all afternoon, I also baked some bread. Living this far from town, I figured out pretty quickly that it's best to know how to do stuff like that. When a bad storm comes through, like the one right now, it's easy to get cut off from town for days, if not a week or two.

After our first winter here, when we survived a week on canned soup and saltines, I vowed to never let that happen again. It was fine when it was just Mark and me, but I can only imagine the terrible reviews guests would leave if that happened when we had someone in to stay with us.

"Hello?"

The woman's voice surprises me, and I put down the last

spoon in a hurry before turning and wiping my hands on my apron.

"Lottie, hi. I was so lost in my own world that I didn't hear you come into the kitchen." I give her what I hope is a winning smile so she doesn't think I've completely lost the plot.

"I heard the dinner bell, right? You mentioned that was a thing, and I'm pretty sure I heard it, but I didn't want to interrupt if I was wrong."

She doesn't move from the doorway. Her hands twist in front of her body as she speaks. I notice the way her shoulders round forward, like she's used to being told that she's wrong and is waiting for me to do that.

"You heard it," I say brightly. "You're the first one here, but come on in. I just sent Henry off to get Mark. and I have no doubt your family will be here any minute."

I grab the pot of stew from the stove, set it in the middle of the table, and start ladling it into bowls. "Did you all get settled in okay?"

"Sure did." Lottie steps into the kitchen but still hovers a few feet away from me. "This place is amazing, exactly like I remembered." A slight pause while I keep working. "Is there anything I can do to help?"

I eyeball her. *She's a nervous thing, isn't she?*

"Actually yes," I say. "If you don't mind. You are a guest, but if you could slice that loaf of bread back there and pop it in the basket next to it, then we can get that on the table. I don't know about you, but when it's so cold out like this, I just want warm food in my stomach."

"I'm the same way."

Now that I've given her a task, she seems much more comfortable, and she walks right over to the counter, grabs the bread knife, and starts sawing away. "Days like this make me want to curl up and hibernate."

"We're just mammals, when you think about it." I place the

soup ladle back in the stew and step back to look at the table. The food smells amazing and is piping hot. There's cheese for the stew and butter for the bread, and I baked an apple pie this afternoon for dessert.

"I never thought about it that way." Lottie appears at my side with the bread, and I take it to put it on the table. "It makes sense."

"Sure does."

We work in silence for a moment.

"Hey," I say, clearing my throat. Footsteps on the staircase tell me I'm almost out of time to talk to her, but I still push through, the words tipping from my lips. "When did you say you stayed with us last time? I can't find any record of it. Not that it's a big deal; I just was curious."

There's a flash of something on her face—there and gone—before I can put my finger on what emotion it might be. Her eyes narrowed a little, didn't they? Or her mouth set in a firm line before she forced herself to relax? I can't tell, can't figure it out, but it disappears like a dandelion seed blown in the wind.

"Oh, it's been years," she says, flapping her hand. "And Chelsea didn't come with us, so that's probably why you don't remember us being here. Everyone remembers her, but Tim and I tend to blend in with the background." She laughs.

I force myself to smile.

"I don't know about that," I say, lightly touching her arm before gesturing to where she can sit at the table. "I think you're probably a lot more memorable than you're giving yourself credit for."

It sounds like lip service, I'm sure of it. I can tell Lottie thinks so by the way she gives a little smirk as she turns her head to sit down in her chair, but I mean it. She carries herself with grace, although I don't like the way she acts like something terrible might happen to her at any moment.

No, she's definitely memorable. It's that dark hair that falls around her shoulders and her big brown eyes, the type that every movie starlet wants to have. There's no way anyone could look at Lottie and not remember seeing her.

I'm betting on it.

THIRTEEN

LOTTIE

I knew telling Abby that we'd stayed here before was a mistake. My hand shakes as I pick up my spoon and take my first bite of stew, but as soon as it hits my lips, I convince myself that I'll forget all about the problem with my lie coming back to haunt me.

This is delicious. The stew is warm, with huge chunks of beef and vegetables. I notice how Tim is dipping his bread into his bowl and I do the same, closing my eyes with pleasure as I chew it.

Okay, I'll give Abby this: The woman can cook. She might not be the sharpest tool in the shed, but she knows her way around the kitchen.

Conversation around the table snaps me out of my thoughts and I look up only to see Abby staring at me, a friendly smile on her face. She has her spoon held halfway to her mouth, like she was about to take a bite but is waiting on my response.

"I'm so sorry," I say, hoping for grace, "I was thinking about how delicious this stew is. What did you ask?"

"Not a problem. I was just asking if you and Tim work." She takes the bite of stew but never looks away from me.

"I don't work," I admit, feeling terrible telling that to someone who obviously never stops working from the time she gets up to when she probably passes out at night. "I stayed home with Chelsea when I got pregnant and never went back. And Tim—"

"I'm in sales," Tim interrupts, which is usually something I hate about him but, for once, I'm grateful for it. I don't like feeling like I'm in the hot seat, and that's exactly how I feel when Abby pins me in place with those blue eyes of hers.

"Well, you know what I do." Abby chuckles. "And Mark is a handyman. If you ever need anything done around the house that you don't think you can take care of on your own, he's your guy."

Silence falls around the table.

Abby clears her throat. "So, Chelsea, what are you into?" As she speaks, she leans forward, resting her chin on her fist as she looks at my daughter. "Any sports or anything?"

"I was in gymnastics," my daughter answers before I have a chance to speak for her, "but I was asked to leave."

"Oh." Abby blinks and looks down at her stew. The tips of her ears go red like she's embarrassed.

"Because I had a knife at practice," Chelsea says, volunteering the information. She pauses, rips a hunk of bread in two. "I wasn't going to do anything with it. It was my favorite knife."

I clear my throat, desperate to turn attention away from her. "How long have you two been married?" The question is out of my mouth before I even realize what I'm asking. Next to me, Chelsea shifts in her seat, but she doesn't say anything.

Abby looks surprised at the change in subject but smiles when she answers. "Twenty years." She reaches over and lightly touches Mark's shoulder before continuing. "High school sweethearts, you know. Nobody thought it was going to work, but it has so far."

"I love that." There are a thousand questions in my mind,

all of them begging to be asked, and even though I know it's probably not appropriate, I can't help myself. "You've been together a long time, but Henry is so young..." I trail off, hoping she's not going to be able to avoid answering the unasked question.

"Mom." Chelsea elbows me.

I ignore her.

"Well, I don't know how much you want to know, and I certainly don't want to bore you with the details, but getting pregnant wasn't easy for us. We tried and tried, and it took a little medical intervention, but we finally have Henry. He was worth it all."

Abby leans over and musses her son's hair. I watch her, see the expression of pure love on her face, then look over at Tim. He's studiously taking bite after bite of his stew.

"I'm glad you have him," I say. Swallowing hard, I continue. "Kids are such a blessing."

Abby grins at me. "Lottie, you're right. That's one thing I think people lose sight of when they're tired or overwhelmed or just need a break, but I wouldn't give up being a mom for anything. Yes, I'm exhausted, but it's worth it. And it gets better, right? How old is Chelsea?"

Chelsea looks up and answers before I can speak for her. "I'm sixteen."

"Sixteen. Wow. And where in the world did you get that gorgeous red hair from?"

Now it's my turn to speak over Chelsea. "It runs in the family but it's recessive, I guess. Somehow she got it but neither of us have it."

"Genes are so bizarre, aren't they?" Abby laughs, glancing over at Mark, who pastes a tight smile on his face. "Anyway, now that you're here and so is the storm of the century, I want to remind you that all you have to do is reach out if you need anything. Mark will hopefully be going to town from time to time, not only to go to the store, but also if he gets called in for an emergency. Fingers crossed he'll be able to get out. So, if you need anything, just touch base with me and I'll either take care of it or ask Mark to. He can handle anything."

She gestures at Mark with her spoon, and I look at him.

"That's so nice to have someone around who can take care of things." I scrape my spoon against my bowl, making sure to keep my eyes down so I don't glance up at Tim. "Honestly though, as long as there's something to eat and books to read, I think the three of us will be fine. Really, we're happy to be out of the house and to have the chance to get away for a little bit. You know how things can add up, and you never really feel like you're on vacation in your own home."

"Boy, do I." Abby rests her elbows on the table and leans forward, looking at me like the two of us are close friends hanging out.

She's good at this, making me feel comfortable. Now I see why so many people left glowing reviews about their time here. Her face, which certainly wouldn't grace a magazine, looks kind, welcoming.

Abby wrinkles her nose a little as she smiles but then looks more serious. "But I want you to feel totally comfortable while you're here, Lottie. Oh, one thing to note—our bedrooms are all on the second floor and we ask guests to stay off that floor. There are locks on the bedroom doors—both the inside and out —from when this place was built. I'm sure that won't be a problem, but it is something to be aware of. Besides that though, this place is yours to enjoy. There are bedrooms on both the third and fourth floor for you to choose from, but we find guests tend to stick to the third in winter because it's easier to get down-stairs to the warm fireplace. Either way, what's ours is yours, especially if you can't get out of the B&B and you start to feel a little stir-crazy."

"That's so kind of you." Tim speaks up for the first time.

He's wiped his stew bowl clean with a hunk of bread and now he grins at Abby. "Seriously, I don't know many people who are that willing to share everything they have. You're one of a kind, Abby."

The woman blushes. She dips her head down, then looks up at Mark. Her husband is staring at her, and when they make eye contact, he reaches out and brushes some hair back from her face.

"Well, we can't wait to get to know you all," I say, dragging my eyes from Mark and Abby over to Tim, who nods. "You both seem like some of the kindest people we've ever met, and I think this trip is going to be incredible."

Incredible for me, maybe. For Abby, probably not.

And for Mark? Well, that all depends on what he agrees to do.

FOURTEEN

ABBY

Sunday 2 Dec

The Rowes have been here for two days, and while we're not officially snowed in yet, it's coming. The deep gray clouds in the sky promise nothing but more snow, and the cold wind blowing in off the ocean carries with it a chill that I can't seem to shake.

Even with the fire going all the time, it's still chilly in here, one of the problems with such an old building. Frost covers the windows in all the rooms but the kitchen and living room, thanks to the heat from the fireplace and oven. Even so, when the oven and stove are off, little fingers of frost creep across the kitchen windows.

The howling wind has been so constant that it's more like background noise now... at least until it slams against the house, little whispers of cold seeping in through unpatched cracks.

I hope a customer doesn't call Mark. I don't think there's a chance he could make it down the mountain, not even with four-wheel drive.

I sigh as I sit down on the floor and look under our bed, taking a moment to hug my cardigan tighter around my body.

Mark wanted a king-size bed when we got married and I fought it tooth and nail for the longest time. I told him I wanted to be able to roll over and feel him in the middle of the night. The last thing I wanted was to feel like I wasn't in bed with my husband, like he could come and go as he pleased without me knowing.

He got the giant bed even though I didn't want one. They say compromise is imperative if you want to stay married.

But the one great thing about a huge bed? Plenty of storage underneath.

I'm looking for an extra box of blankets. The storm that's supposed to be headed our way is looking like it's going to be worse than we originally thought. Of course, I keep plenty of blankets on hand for cold nights, but the boxes get shifted around under the bed.

That means I have to crawl halfway under it to pull the box back out.

"Lord, give me strength." Taking a deep inhale to avoid breathing in any dust bunnies that may have been multiplying in the dark under the bed since spring, I slide under, on my stomach, a small flashlight in one hand.

I click it on, blinking at how bright it is, then look for the blanket box. It should be labeled, my careful print on the side. Every moment with Henry is a learning opportunity and I remember writing B L A N K E T S and telling him the name of each letter as I worked.

But it's not in this first section. I put the light down on the ground then reach out, shoving the first box, S W E A T E R S, to the side, only to reveal S H E E T S.

"Come on," I groan. This hurts my back. My arms. My pride, if I'm being honest. I thought I'd be the type of person to keep the house spotless, to know exactly where everything is at the same time. But life gets overwhelming, and even though that sounds like an excuse, it's not. It's the truth.

Between running around after Henry, doing everything to

keep the B&B afloat, and doing most of it by myself while Mark is out working random jobs to help keep our bank account padded, I feel like I'm losing my mind.

And now I can't find the damn blankets.

My shoulders feel like they're about to pop out of their sockets as I lunge forward, digging the tips of my toes into the floor to help propel me farther under the bed. Grunting, I stretch my arm as far as I can, my fingers barely pressing into the side of a box. It shifts to the right a little, then a bit more.

And behind it, B L A N K E T S.

Thank God.

Exhaling hard, I crawl a bit further under the bed then stop. I swear I heard footsteps behind me. I freeze, twisting my head to the side to try to see out behind me, but I can't from this angle.

"Hello?" My voice has to be muffled from the way my head is turned but surely whoever is out there heard me.

No answer.

"Mark? Henry?"

Nothing. Maybe I imagined it? But there's a prickle of fear at the base of my spine that's telling me to get a move on.

Clicking off the flashlight, I twist around to shove it into my pocket, then I grind my hips forward and grab the sides of the box, slowly crawling backwards. My butt keeps bumping up into the mattress.

It's slow going.

Sweat trickles down my back.

During a pause, where I try to readjust my hands so I don't lose the box completely, I hear something.

A soft *click*. The door being closed.

My right shoulder slams up into the bed as I twist farther, trying again to look behind me at who's in the bedroom with me. I can see the bedroom rug from here, the soothing blue color still as gorgeous as the day we bought it, but I can't see past it.

But who would come in here and not answer me when I called out?

I must be imagining it.

Fighting down my impulse to call out again, I shimmy faster now, pure adrenaline the only reason I'm able to move so quickly. I have the box, have pulled it with me, and when my head is finally free from under the bed, I yank it out, then press my hands down on top of it to stand.

A wave of dizziness washes over me and I bend over, grabbing the edge of the bed for support while my head clears. There's nobody here. Nobody in the room with me.

Still, I know someone was here. I'm sure of it.

When I look at the bedroom door, it's closed.

"What?" The blankets forgotten, I stumble to it. Mark's clothes from the day before didn't make it to the hamper. They're in a pile by the door, waiting for me to take them down to the laundry room. Maybe he leaned in to toss something onto the pile. Surely, if it had been him at the door, he would have said something.

I grab the handle and twist it hard, first to the right, then to the left. It doesn't turn and I step back, trying to catch my breath. I feel like I'm breathing through a straw, like each inhale only gives me half the oxygen I need. Exhaling, I grab the handle again, feeling the way it slips from my grasp.

My palms are sweaty. I wipe them on my jeans.

Again.

Panic bubbles in my stomach and I slam my open palm against the door. It rattles in the frame but doesn't open.

This? This is a sick joke.

No, not a joke. An *accident*. I told Mark when we moved in that he needed to change the knobs. That having it possible for them to lock from the outside of the rooms was an accident waiting to happen.

I told him.

"Mark!" I call, and even though I feel panic starting to work its way through my veins like a cold chill, I'm pleased to hear that I don't sound terrified.

Angry, maybe. Frustrated and put out, sure. But not scared.

Whatever just happened, this had to have been an accident.

"Mark!" I'm louder now and I rattle the door again, enjoying the sound it makes in its frame. Someone has to hear this. Yes, the building is big, but it's old, and sound travels.

He'll hear me.

Even if he's downstairs. Even if he has music on. He has to hear me eventually.

Or he'll wonder where I am. *Eventually*.

"Mark! Let me out!" I pound my fist into the door. The wood is solid, the doors all original to the house. It was part of the charm when we looked at the place and I fell in love with it. No foam-core doors for me, no thank you. I wanted solid wood ones, with carvings along the doorframe, with heavy old knobs that feel good in the hand.

Until you're locked in the bedroom, that is.

"Anyone! Help me!" There's a prickle of sweat at the back of my neck and I reach up. Wipe it away. Lean against the wood. When I press my ear against it, I hope I'll be able to hear something, but my heartbeat is the only sound.

It's erratic. Fast.

It's silly, this feeling that I'm running out of oxygen and soon won't be able to breathe. There's plenty of oxygen in here, and even if there wasn't, I could open the window. I'd be cold, sure, but I'd be able to breathe. The air would rush into the room, into my lungs, it would fill me up, it would—

A floorboard creaks.

Someone's on the other side of the door.

I swear I heard someone.

Dropping to my knees, I look through the crack under the door. It's too narrow to see much of anything, but I can see shadows, and I see the way they move across my field of vision.

"Who's there?" This time my voice fails me. I'm trying to be loud, to sound brave and strong, but it comes out in nothing more than a whisper. "Who's out there?"

Nothing. No response. No sound.

Just shadows moving away from the door, whoever was out there walking away, leaving me.

I stare, my cheek pressed against the cold floor. It's crazy, what's happening. It's insane I left my cell downstairs, thinking I'd just pop right up. It's beyond imagination that someone in the house would want to lock me in my bedroom.

Maybe I'm not nearly as in control as I thought I was.

FIFTEEN

CHELSEA

I think I hear something as I hurry down the stairs from my room on the third floor, but I don't pause. Everyone's occupied right now, which means it's the perfect opportunity for me to do a little exploring.

Poke around. See what neat things I can find.

Snoop.

I'm practically skipping as I hurry down the stairs to the foyer, then stop and listen for a moment. Mom and Dad are in the kitchen, their voices low as they discuss... something. They do that a lot. Hiss at each other quietly, thinking I don't hear them.

So, to another room then.

I don't know where either Mark or Abby are, but I can guess. With Henry, no doubt. That kid spends a lot of time playing by himself, but there's always a parent nearby, always willing and ready to leap into action if they think something might be wrong.

They hover, that's what they do.

Turning away from the kitchen, I wander down the hall to the living room. My fingers trail along the wall and I slow my pace, knowing I finally have time to look around on my own. There are family pictures all along the wall and I pause at a few of them, taking in Abby's smile, Henry's laugh.

But mostly I'm looking at Mark.

I examine his eyes, the way he holds his mouth when he's happy.

Finally, I turn into the living room and he's there, right in front of the fire, his feet propped up on a leather ottoman. It's older, the leather so old it's cracking, but its appearance adds to the shabby-chic thing they've got going on here.

I guess some people find it charming. I think it looks dirty.

Henry's on the floor, as always, his little toy truck clutched in his fist. Next to him is a plate with a stack of crackers and some grape quarters. He looks up when I walk into the room and waves but doesn't say anything.

Not that I'd have the energy to respond. There's only one other person in here, and that's Mark. Just like Henry, he must feel my presence as I walk into the room, or maybe the floor-boards squeak under my weight. Whatever it is, he looks up, a smile on his face—probably for Abby—then his smile changes, fades, settles into a frown.

I frown back before I catch myself. Fix a smile back on my face. Throw my shoulders back, say hi.

"Hello, Chelsea." He moves to get up, going so far as to put his hands on the chair arms and press up, but I'm right there before he can stand. If he stands up, he'll step into me.

He sits back down. The leather sighs as he settles in, the cushion forming to his body.

"What are you doing?" I perch on the edge of the ottoman. It's not nearly as soft as it looks and I frown, wiggling around a bit to get comfortable.

Mark watches me for a moment before he answers. "Just spending time with Henry."

While I watch, he reaches down and chucks Henry on the cheek.

"He's cute. You and Abby had to try a long time to get him, huh?"

He doesn't respond.

"I'm just saying, Mom said she got pregnant with me really quickly. I didn't know it could take a long time."

Mark lets out a soft sigh. "Sometimes it does, sometimes it doesn't." A shrug. "Was there something you needed help with?"

"I just wanted to get to know you. I figured I'd try to get to know all three of you since we're going to be here for so long. And I don't know where Abby is. My parents are talking. I got bored." I shrug to get my point across.

I'm bored. It's snowing. There's literally nothing to do here. It's horrible.

To get my point across, I grin at him, and he stares at me, tilting his head to the side a little bit like I'm some strange insect he's never seen before. He's taking in my face, the way I'm sitting, how my one foot is propped out a bit from my body, ready to—what? What does he think?

"Okay then. Tell me about you. I know you were in gymnastics, but what else is there to know about Chelsea?"

Oh, good. We're all here, together, all of us snowed in, and time will pass faster if I'm not trying to entertain myself.

"Well, I loved gymnastics. And I play the flute. I was in the marching band, but I got kicked out."

"Knife?" He raises an eyebrow while he asks the question, and I nod to confirm.

"Yep, knife." I sigh and spread my hands out on my knees then look back up at him. "But I wasn't going to do anything with it. I liked having it, you know?"

"Like a toy truck?" He nudges Henry's truck with his toe.

I laugh. "Yeah, kinda like that. Although if I'd been carrying around a toy truck, I doubt I would have gotten kicked out of gymnastics. Or marching band."

"You're probably lucky you didn't get kicked out of school." He moves to stand up and I let him, swinging my legs out of the way.

"That's what Mom said, and she's probably right. I got lucky and she told me I wouldn't get lucky again and that she didn't want to homeschool me."

He laughs and bends down, picking up Henry and propping him on his hip. "Homeschool sounds terrifying." He gives a mock shiver. "It was nice talking to you, Chelsea. I'm going to go see if this little man needs a nap. Then I need to find Abby. Have you seen her?"

"Nope." Now it's my turn to stand and I do, walking over to the bookshelf to see if there's anything here worth reading. "Hey, do you mind if I borrow a book? And maybe I can read to Henry later—what do you think?"

"Make yourself at home," he calls over his shoulder as he walks out of the living room. "You heard Abby. What's ours is yours."

Yes, I did hear what she said.

But I don't think she meant it literally.

SIXTEEN

MARK

I climb into bed, moving slowly, taking my time as I lay down and pull the covers up so I can do my best to keep from accidentally waking Abby. Not only was she on her feet all day getting ready for our guests and looking close to passing out shortly after dinner, but something had her on edge.

She'd somehow gotten locked in our room while looking for blankets and was furious with herself when I found her. I've told her time and time again to be careful with some of the doors, that the outside lock can drop into place if you're not lucky. Of course, she didn't want to talk about it.

Probably embarrassed. When I brought it up, she got angry at me, so I dropped it.

To try to keep her from falling asleep in the shower or falling apart, I told her to go to bed and I'd tuck Henry in.

She rolls over a bit, her breathing changing as I tug the blankets up under my chin. My body is exhausted, but my mind won't stop racing. Ever since the Rowes arrived for their vacation, I haven't been able to catch my breath.

And now they're sleeping in the same building as my family and there isn't a thing I can do about it.

The ceiling fan is on, and in the glowing light of the moon off the snow outside, I can see how lazily the blades turn. When we first bought the place, I offered to buy Abby a white noise machine to help her sleep, but she refused, saying it was too expensive when a ceiling fan spinning above her did the trick. No matter the weather, she has it on, the whirring sound helping her drift off to sleep while the cool air in my face can sometimes keep me up. It's going to be a cold night but at least the snow has stopped for a while. I don't have much hope of getting out of here tomorrow but maybe the next day.

Or the next.

"Hey." Abby breathes the word out and rolls over to me, reaching out and lightly resting her hand on my chest. "What time is it?"

"Just past ten." I feel a shock of guilt that I was up with Henry so late, but he didn't want to settle tonight, and I wasn't interested in heading to bed any earlier than I had to. I didn't want to accidentally wake Abby up, and yet here we are.

I hate that she's awake. She needs to sleep, but more than that, I need some time alone. It's impossible for me to relax right now, not even in bed next to my wife. I haven't been able to relax in days, and lying awake in the middle of the night isn't going to help.

"Why so late? Is Henry okay?" My wife's voice has the thick sound of someone barely hanging on to consciousness. She could probably pass back out if I didn't answer her, if I let the silence grow around us, but I clear my throat.

I already know I'm not going to get any sleep tonight.

"He was having trouble settling," I tell her, rolling over so I can try to see her in the moonlight. Her back is to the window and all I see is the lump of her body under the covers. "I think having three new people in the house like this wired him a little bit. But he's fine."

Abby's quiet for a few minutes and I think for sure that she's fallen asleep, but then she speaks again.

"New people are exciting. He'll calm back down." A pause. "Chelsea was enamored with him earlier today. Henry doesn't get a lot of chances to be with other kids, and she's so much older, but I think he still enjoyed hanging out with her. I caught the two of them in the living room and she was reading to him."

"That's great." My voice is perfectly flat and even. I'm proud of myself. "He'll go to kindergarten soon and then he'll have his fill of other kids, but it's nice he can spend time with someone other than family right now."

"I think so too." She sighs and falls silent again.

I wait. Count to ten. Finally, moving slowly again, I roll onto my side. From the soft breathing next to me, it's clear Abby has fallen asleep. I envy my wife and the ease with which she passed out.

Overhead, the fan whirs. There's a soft click with each revolution. I stare up at it and the shadows it casts while my mind races.

Groaning, I rub my hands across my eyes, trying to clear my thoughts so I can figure out exactly what's going on here. If I saved my messages and calls, then I'd be able to look back through them, see how things got this bad.

But I don't save those, and for good reason. Abby has never once asked to go through my phone to see who I've been talking to, but what if she suddenly started? It seems like one of those things that wasn't ever worth the risk.

Fear twists my stomach. I've never felt this way about any guests we've had at the B&B before.

I roll back over and sit up, letting the blanket I so carefully pulled up under my chin a moment ago fall down around my waist. My head pounds and I grip it, squeezing it hard as I try to think through what's going on.

It's one thing for us to open our home to random guests. That was the plan all along. The dream, in fact. Both Abby and I love meeting new people and getting to know them. We both enjoy sharing our lives with people for a short period of time before they leave us.

Some come back. Most don't. One trip to the coast of Maine is more than enough for a lot of people, so it doesn't surprise me when most of our guests are one-time.

But opening your home to strangers is totally different than opening it to people who know your deepest and darkest secrets. I'm not a man who wants to have a lot of secrets from my wife. I never wanted to keep anything from Abby, and, for a while, that was how it was. We kept each other in the loop about everything going on.

Until I didn't.

I'm sweating now and unable to shut off the part of my brain that's telling me I won't get any sleep the rest of the night. My skin feels tight, and I scrub my hand down my face before I finally stand up, my bare chest covered in goosebumps in the cool night air.

"Mark?" Abby's voice is quiet.

"I have to pee," I lie, then flip the covers back on my side of the bed. I'm antsy. Until I know what exactly is going on with the Rowes being here, I don't know if I'm going to be able to sleep.

I can't go for a walk, not in snow this deep and when it's this cold out, but I can go downstairs, maybe make a cup of tea. I have to do something to try to clear my head.

The door whines on its hinges and I wince, freezing in the doorway for a moment until I'm sure Abby isn't going to get up. We have a bathroom attached to our bedroom and I'm sure she'd question what I'm doing going out into the hall when I could just as easily use the bathroom here.

But it's not about having to pee, is it?

That's just another lie.

In the hall I feel myself relax a little bit.

Exhaling slowly to try to calm my pounding heart, I close the door, making sure to turn the doorknob before pushing the door closed so it won't click loudly into place. Still moving quietly, because now I have to walk past Henry's room, I start down the hall. By sticking to the middle of the floor and staying on the thick runners Abby bought at a garage sale, I should be able to move undetected through our wing to the stairs.

There's one final door separating our floor from the rest of the house, and I unlock it, pausing a moment before stepping through onto a landing on the stairs. This door was my doing. Abby had told me over and over that she didn't think we really needed a door to keep people from accidentally coming onto our floor, but I told her we needed it and then I put it in without asking permission.

It was better that way. The last thing I wanted was for any guest to think they had a right to come into our private rooms. In fact, that thought makes me feel sick. I'm especially grateful now that I put my foot down about that and installed the door. And the lock.

I can only imagine what would happen if a guest showed up in our bedroom while Abby and I were in bed. Just the thought makes my stomach twist, and I grip the handrail as tightly as possible as I walk quietly down the stairs.

At the bottom of the stairs I pause, listening for any sounds of someone else awake in the house. Then slowly, carefully, I pick my way to the kitchen. I'm quiet, but sounds tend to carry in old houses. Even though I highly doubt anyone else in the B&B will be able to hear me, I don't want to run the risk of waking someone up.

In the kitchen I turn on the light, finally relaxing as I fill the kettle and press the button to turn it on. Closing my eyes, I lean against the counter, listening for the familiar sound of boiling water.

It heats up quickly then a soft click lets me know the water is hot. Just as I'm about to open my eyes and grab the kettle to fill up my mug, I hear a sound.

Footsteps.

SEVENTEEN

LOTTIE

How I ever thought I'd be able to sleep a single night here at Saltside Inn, much less three weeks of nights, is beyond me.

I keep trying. It's one thing to sleep in a new bed, a new room, a new building. That's hard enough. It can be almost impossible to get used to unfamiliar sounds.

But staying here is different.

In the mornings I wake up, surprised I fell asleep at all.

Right now though, I'm wide wake.

I hear Tim snore.

The creak of the bed when he shifts position.

The wind battering the house.

And someone on the move.

I slip from bed, curious about who's awake and moving around. My money is on Mark. He's got broad shoulders and large feet, and there isn't any way the person making that much noise moving down the stairs could be his wife. I bet it's him.

As carefully as possible, I make my way down the staircase. It's so dark in here that I grip the handrail tightly. Only when I'm on the first floor do I feel like I can relax. I pause, my eyes still adjusting to the dark. There's a light on in the kitchen, and I walk in the direction of the soft glow.

"Hi, Mark," I say, pausing in the kitchen doorway. He's got low-slung pajama pants on, flannel plaid ones, and a hoodie.

At the sound of my voice, he freezes and slowly turns around to look at me. I give a small wave, then walk into the kitchen. "I thought I was the only one who couldn't sleep tonight."

He swallows hard. Puts his mug down on the counter.

"There's something about a storm that makes it hard to sleep sometimes." His voice is low, tight.

I nod, rubbing my hands up and down my arms. "It's always weird sleeping in a new place, but the wind battering against the walls has made it even worse than usual."

"I get it. That's my problem tonight, too The last thing I wanted was to keep Abby up with my tossing and turning."

A silence falls between the two of us, but I'm in no hurry to break it. It feels nice knowing I'm not the only one who couldn't sleep, that I'm not alone in being awake in the middle of the night.

But then it hits me that he might think I'm suggesting there's a problem with the beds, and that's not it at all.

"Not that this place isn't comfortable," I say, suddenly wanting to explain myself. "The problem is me. Not the beds."

He chuckles. "Yeah, I get it. Tell me what you think about this place." Casually, like he hasn't a care in the world, he waves one hand around, encompassing the entire B&B.

"It's exactly what we needed. You know, we wanted a vacation. When we saw the post Abby made on social media, it seemed like the perfect way to get out of the house, get Chelsea out of her own head. She thinks a lot; she sometimes needs a break."

"Teenagers." He leans back against the counter. "We have a few years until we hit that stage, but I've heard horror stories."

I nod eagerly, wanting the conversation to continue. This is nice, talking to him. Much nicer than staying in bed, staring at the ceiling.

"Well, Chelsea has been wild from day one. But she's a good kid. Being a mom isn't always easy, but it is rewarding. I'm sure Abby can attest to that."

He smiles. "I'm sure she can. She's an amazing woman. How she handles running this place and staying on top of Henry, I'll never know. But I'm so glad I have her."

His words make my heart hurt. Has Tim ever talked about me like that to another person? I'm not sure he has.

"This was her dream, you know," he says, and there's a faraway look in his eyes that tells me he's not talking to me, that he's talking more to himself. "The B&B. She's wanted it from day one. She's the one with the vision; she's the one who made it happen."

"You obviously had some role in it," I say. "I wouldn't sell myself short if I were you."

"Yeah, well, you don't know Abby as well as I do," he tells me, scrubbing his hand down his cheek. "She's tenacious. I love that about her, how there's literally nothing that can stop her from getting what she wants."

I want to be like that. I want to be so tenacious that people say the same about me—and say it with the same hint of wonder that Mark has in his voice.

"She sounds like an amazing woman."

"You have no idea." He gives his head a little shake. "Driven, focused, loving, but dogged, that's for sure." Now he's nodding to himself as he speaks. "And, on that note, I think I could also add *freezing cold* to the list. I better get back to bed before she realizes I'm gone and not keeping her warm any longer."

"You didn't want tea?" I'm grasping at straws, not wanting to be left alone by myself in this huge B&B. It's unnerving to be the only person awake someplace like this. "The water won't take long to heat back up."

"Oh, no, I better get back to bed. I'm sure I have a busy day tomorrow, but don't feel like you have to head back too. Feel free to have some tea or even get into the leftovers." He gives me a nod as he walks past me.

I turn, keeping an eye on him, not wanting him to leave me here.

He keeps walking, his pace steady, unbothered. I, on the other hand, am flustered. Adrenaline courses through my body, pushing me to chase after him so I'm not left alone.

But I don't move.

Mark doesn't want to stay with me to keep me company. It's perfectly reasonable for him to go back upstairs, to head to bed with his wife. My loneliness is not his problem, no matter how much I'd love for someone to keep me company.

So, no, I'm not going to make a scene by asking him to stay down here with me. Not now, not when Tim is asleep.

I can't wake up my husband.

That's the last thing any of us need.

EIGHTEEN

ABBY

Monday 3 Dec

I slept great last night and now the smell of coffee and bacon fills the air, making my stomach rumble. I love early mornings; love being the only person in the house awake as I putter around the kitchen, poking at the bacon, taking a sip of my coffee. There's something incredibly decadent about being the first person up when it's still dark out, about being able to move quietly through the house, flicking on lights to push the shadows back, maybe even turning on some soft music to help wake up.

The sun hasn't fully risen yet, but I've already been outside to see how bright the light is, bouncing off the thick layer of snow. It's like icing, glittering with diamonds, the white drifts up against the house probably close to three feet deep. I don't know what our guests are planning on doing today, but I highly doubt they'll be able to spend much time, if any, outside.

Of course, we do have some snowshoes in the barn, but I don't know if that's something they'd want to do. There are few things in this world that offer a workout like strapping those to your feet and heading out into the cold. Movies make it look so glamorous, like you'll get to float on top of the snow and explore at the same time, but that's not half of it.

Movies don't accurately show how exhausted you'll be after snowshoeing, how your thighs will burn and how you'll never want to do it again. That's why we have them in the barn and not in the house for easy access. I went snowshoeing with Mark one time when we first moved to Oyster and declared I'd never do it again.

And I haven't. It's a nightmare, but for some people, that nightmare is preferable to being locked up inside without anything to do.

Still, that's not my problem. They had to know what they were getting into when they booked the entire B&B for three weeks. I can't be their activities coordinator. Yes, we have puzzles and board games. And sure, I don't mind if they raid our bookshelves for something to read while they're here.

But I made the mistake of trying to keep guests happy all the time when we first opened Saltside Inn. I still get a bad taste in my mouth when I think about the Hendersons, how they'd sit around the dining table every time I went into the kitchen so they could watch me, how they always seemed to be *judging* me.

Nope, I'm not allowing that to happen any longer. If guests want advice on what to do, I'm happy to offer that, but I can't do it all for them.

That's why I have so many pamphlets from attractions around Oyster. Not *in* Oyster, because there's not that much to do once you're actually here, but there are plenty of places to visit within an hour's drive. Of course, the Rowes are from the area, so they might not want to go drive to the aquarium or to get the world's best lobster mac and cheese, but the options are there if they want them.

I'm incredibly nervous as I wait for everyone to make it

downstairs to start the day. Mark was in a bit of a mood yesterday, which isn't like him. And then when he finally came to bed, he felt... off. It's one thing for him to be stressed about work, another for him to bring that stress home.

I know he said he had to pee, but I heard him coming downstairs. What was that about?

I rearrange the pamphlets, wanting to make sure they look their best. It's not like I can fix how glossy or bright they are, but I can organize them. They're in a little basket on the coffee bar so guests can flip through them while they wait for their brew, and I pat them into place before stepping back.

The sound of feet on the stairs snaps me from my thoughts. Grabbing my mug and holding it in front of me like a shield, I plaster a smile on my face and turn to the kitchen door.

Who's it going to be?

What's behind door number one?

The thought makes me giggle, and I stop myself by taking a sip of coffee.

A flash of red hair in the doorway tells me it's Chelsea. She's dressed in leggings and an oversized hoodie that hangs halfway to her knees. One thing I've never understood—and probably never will—is teenage fashion. She seems like a nice girl and there is something rather familiar about her, but why teenagers dress the way they do, I'll never know.

The thought of sweet little Henry growing up and dressing like a typical teenager gives me pause, but I put a smile on my face and greet the girl.

"Good morning!" My voice is chipper and bright, thanks in part to the coffee I've already had, and she winces a little bit. "I'm sorry. Do you drink coffee?"

She nods and I'm glad I read the expression on her face correctly. "Hang on, I'll grab you a cup. Creamer and sugar are over there." I gesture at the coffee bar I set up our first year in business then pour her a mug of coffee, carefully handing it over.

"I take it black, thanks." She takes a small sip, then another.

"So does Mark," I say, topping mine off before stirring in some sugar and French vanilla creamer. "But I don't know how he does it. I like my coffee a little sweeter and milky."

She perks up. The caffeine works fast, I guess. "He does?"

I nod. "Yep. It's one of the things I don't get about him, but I guess I don't have to."

We fall silent and I search for a topic of conversation that won't be awkward or uncomfortable. As great as I am with Henry, two is a far cry from sixteen, and I don't really know what to say to Chelsea.

Luckily for me, she fills the silence.

"So, you've owned the B&B a long time, huh?"

"Sure have." I'm leaning against the counter now, watching her while she sips her brew. "This was always our dream, so when I found the building for sale ten years ago, we moved right up here and bought it. I was worried there was going to be a bidding war, but I guess not many people want to live right on the ocean like this."

She shivers. "It is cold. You run it, but he's a handyman too, right?"

"That's right." She was paying attention at dinner that first night. "He likes handyman stuff because he says it keeps him sharp and prevents him from forgetting simple things like plumbing and electrical work. That way he can take care of repairs here without having to call someone." I laugh at the thought.

"That means he's gone a lot?" She pulls out a stool at the island and perches on the edge of it. "I mean, during the day? Or does he ever spend the night away from home? I think I'd get lonely up here."

"No, he doesn't spend the night away," I say, tapping my

chin while I think. "And yes, sometimes he'll be gone all day and then get up and do it again the next day, but what do you do?" I shrug. "That's the nature of his job. And I do get lonely, but I have Henry. And trashy TV." I grin at her.

She turns her mug on the counter. It makes a grinding noise in the spilled sugar as she does. "My dad travels a lot for work. Or he did, before I was born and when I was little, but that stopped."

Ahh, I see. Chelsea's at the age where she's trying to see where she fits in the world and how normal her family is. I've read about this in child development books. "I bet it's nice to have him home. My dad traveled a lot for work too, and I remember it could be kinda hard not having him around."

The sound of someone else coming down the stairs draws my attention away from Chelsea. I can't see the base of the stairs from here, but I'll be able to see whoever it is as soon as they make it onto the first floor.

"That's probably my dad," Chelsea says, pushing back from the counter.

The stool legs scrape hard against the wood floor and I wince, but she doesn't seem to notice as she hops down and hurries to the door. "Oh, hi," she says, greeting whoever's out there before I get a chance to see who it is.

Her voice is different. Lower. Thicker.

There's a pause and I find myself walking across the kitchen to stand behind Chelsea. It's always a little strange opening the B&B to new guests, especially long-term ones like the Rowes. We'll all find our routine, I'm sure of it, but until then, I have to figure out how we all fit together.

"Hi."

It's Mark. I'd recognize his voice anywhere. There's something about the way it warms me that makes me feel safe. I know how it makes me feel and I also know the way I stare at him when I get to see him for the first time.

He still isn't in view, but Chelsea is. I turn to look at her and my stomach sinks. Her eyes are wide, her mouth dropped open a little bit. There's bright color in her cheeks and she nervously runs her hand through her hair, pushing it back from her face.

If I didn't know any better, I'd think she was in love with my husband.

NINETEEN

LOTTIE

Every time I walk into a room where Mark is, he gets up, yawns like he can hardly keep his eyes open, then slips out the door without saying a word. His movements are smooth, slow, like he's not in a hurry. But he always leaves, refusing to be caught on his own.

I just want to talk to him.

Moving slowly, like I'm a hunter on the Savannah and Mark is an unwitting antelope, I walk into the living room, a Lee Child book tucked under my arm, a cup of coffee in my hand. Mark's sitting by the fire, which is apparently where he lives half the time, and doesn't look up.

So far, so good.

Henry's playing on the floor with metal cars, slamming them into each other before picking them up and dropping them from as high up as he can reach. They clatter against the wood and Mark looks up sharply.

"Hey, Henry, let's not do that."

Even though the words themselves have an edge to them, his tone is soft. It's obvious how much Mark loves his son.

The thought makes my heart squeeze. It's silly, because you

can't go back and change the past, but I close my eyes for a moment, trying to imagine what life would have been like for me had things been different, if Chelsea had had a dad who loved her like that. Not that Tim isn't a good dad. But she could have had better.

We both could have.

Not that it matters. We all learn at a young age that you can't change the past any more than you can predict the future.

I take a step into the room, my eyes locked on him, and not on the little boy at his feet. There's a smile curling Mark's lips and I take a deep breath.

Another step. I'm close to him now, not close enough that I feel comfortable speaking and getting his attention, but maybe this time he won't leave the room.

Then he sees me. His eyes dart from his son to me and the smile that had been forming on the corners of his mouth disappears.

My heart sinks.

"Hi there, Mark," I say, but before I can say anything else, he's up, walking towards Henry, bending and scooping him into his arms before brushing past me.

"Mark," I say, turning to him, "I just want to get to know you and Abby," I tell him, but he's gone.

I sigh and drop down onto the sofa. This trip was supposed to be the best thing for my little family.

One way or another.

Right now though, I want nothing more than to be back at home. I'd love to be in my own kitchen, watching the snow fall, not looking at it from someone else's house.

Why Tim thought this was the best way to handle the problem, I don't know.

Full of resolve, I push off the sofa and head upstairs. Tim has mostly kept to himself since we got here, only coming down briefly to eat. I know he wants to talk to Mark, but I have a feeling he's probably having as much luck as I am.

Not that hiding upstairs is at all helpful.

Our bedroom is on the third floor. There's an incredible view from here and I'm not surprised Tim is sitting in front of the window, a book on his lap. Next to him, on a small table, is a steaming cup of coffee. Each of the rooms has a small coffee bar, which means he doesn't even have to go downstairs to get his morning fix.

The bed is ornate, a huge king-size thing with four carved posters. I like a firmer mattress and my back was sore this morning, but there's no reason we can't try out another room tonight. We did rent out the entire B&B, after all.

"Tim," I say, closing the door behind me and perching in front of him on the edge of the bed, "we need to talk."

He takes a sip of coffee before clearing his throat. "About what? Are you not enjoying your vacation?"

I have to fight down my annoyance. "Of course I am," I say, smiling sweetly. "But I thought we came here because you had a plan. I wanted to make sure we didn't forget the real reason we're here."

This makes him put his book down. He carefully dog-ears the corner, moving slowly, like what he's doing to the book is an act of love. How many times have I given him bookmarks? How many times have I asked him not to do that to the books he's reading?

Not that it matters. Tim is going to do whatever he wants, and I learned a long time ago there's not much I can do to stop him.

"I'm here to enjoy a vacation."

I stare at him. Take a deep breath. Do my best to choose words I know won't anger him.

"Right, a vacation," I say. "But you also wanted to talk to

Mark. You know that was the main reason we rented this place. I wanted to make sure that was still the plan."

Can he tell how nervous I am? My cheeks feel flushed, but I'm not going to reach up and press my fingers against my skin to check. He doesn't need any more proof of how uncomfortable this conversation makes me. This is my *husband*. It doesn't make any sense that talking to him would make me feel as uncomfortable as I do right now.

But my skin feels too tight. I feel the beginning of a headache coming on. More than anything, I want this to be over.

No, scratch that.

More than anything, I'd like to be at home. Tim and Chelsea could be there with me of course. I'm not a monster. I just don't want to be *here*.

"You don't need to worry, Lottie." Tim's voice is honey, smooth and rich, like he's going to be able to sweet-talk me into doing what he wants, or believing what he wants me to believe. Tim hasn't ever had a problem getting me to do the things he wanted.

Except for once.

And even that he was able to turn on its head so he was the one who came out on top.

"When are you going to talk to him?" I reach out, wrapping my fingers tight around his arm. I want him to look at me, dammit. He's too distracted, too comfortable here. It's like this conversation isn't even happening.

"When I'm ready. Listen, Lottie, I know you're on edge, but you don't need to be. This is how it's going to go. I will talk to Mark; you have to trust me on that. But first I want to enjoy myself."

There's nothing to say to that. As much as I'd love to argue with Tim and tell him that he's not right, that we can get this over with faster than he thinks, that we'd all be much happier back at the house instead of here, in a B&B perched on a windy hill, there's no arguing with my husband.

He hates it.

And I never win.

We're here, whether I like it or not. Until my husband talks to Mark and gets what he wants from him, we're not going anywhere. And I don't have a choice in the matter.

Unless I get what I want first.

TWENTY

ABBY

I curl up on the sofa next to Mark, my cold feet tucked under his thigh, an open book on my lap. Instead of reading though, I'm staring at the fireplace, watching the flames as they die. One of us needs to put more wood on the fire or it's going to die down, but I'm exhausted, and our guests are already in bed.

Surely Mark won't want to stay up much longer. Part of me wants to have a bit of alone time tonight before going to bed, but I do enjoy his company. It's just that guests are so exhausting, and it's nice to have some time alone to let my brain slowly shut down for the night.

Next to me is the baby monitor. I've been carrying it around with me everywhere. Mark commented on it once, but that's only because I never used to keep it with me all the time. And then Henry got so sick. Now, I'm attached to it.

As soon as I put my son in his room and leave him there, I carry it with me like a talisman. It's silly, I know, but having it with me makes me feel so much better about leaving him alone.

Henry was so sick in November, much sicker than he's ever been before. And Mark wasn't here for the worst of it. He was always out, working to bring in some extra cash while we waited for more guests to book with us, but when he did see our son, it was clear what bad shape he was in. I'm grateful he never had to go to the hospital.

But sometimes, in the middle of the night when I'd get up with him, I was surprised he didn't have to go.

His fever was so *high*. But I always managed to get it under control before we thought we needed to take him in.

But he's okay now. Everything's okay—everything except for the fact that I'm so tired I feel like I'm walking in my sleep.

"So... Chelsea," I begin, my voice low. The last thing I want is for any of the Rowes to have come back downstairs and over-hear what I'm about to say to Mark.

"The kid? What about her?" Mark turns to me, running his fingers through my hair to push some back from my face.

"I think she has a little secret," I say, tugging on the blanket he's hogging.

"I'm sure teenagers have all kinds of secrets." He clears his throat and shifts position, allowing me to pull the blanket farther onto my lap.

"Yeah, but I think it's a big one." While I speak, I stretch, arching my back and feet at the same time. While my feet were little ice cubes when we first sat down on the sofa, they're finally warming up.

Just in time to head to bed.

"Care to share or are you going to leave me in suspense?"

I grin at him, debating whether or not I want to tell him my theory. Mark is so dang clueless, which is something I always found endearing about him.

I snort out a laugh, then immediately clap a hand over my mouth.

"Oh, Mark. I'm surprised you haven't picked up on it yet. It's pretty obvious watching her." I eyeball him, trying to see if I'm going to get a rise out of him, but he's unflustered. He's watching me, waiting.

"What's obvious?"

I can't hold it back any longer and I grab a throw pillow then launch it right at his chest. "She has a crush on you, silly!" My voice is much louder than I meant it to be, and I cover my mouth again, trying to hold back laughter.

Of course Mark wouldn't see it. He's always been clueless, always completely unaware of what's going on around him.

"She—*what*?" His eyes are wide, and he shakes his head in disbelief. "You think she has a crush on me?"

I nod, still covering my mouth. When I'm sure no laughter is going to escape, I spread my fingers a bit, allowing my words to slip through. "Yeah, don't you? It's pretty obvious, isn't it? She stares at you like she can't get enough of you. She keeps angling to sit next to you at the dinner table, and then she hangs on every word you say like they're made of gold. It's a crush. She has a crush on you."

"Oh my God," he breathes, leaning his head back against the sofa.

"I know!" I squeal. He catches me by the hips as I launch myself onto his lap and pummel his chest with my fists. I'm crying I'm laughing so hard, tears streaming down my cheeks, and I try to put a stop to it, but I can't.

"I'm sorry," I say, wiping the tears away. "I know I shouldn't laugh; it's just so obvious. I don't know how you didn't notice, but you've always been terrible at knowing how people feel about you."

"That may be true, but a crush? That's a stretch, don't you think?" He laughs, squeezing my hips before planting a kiss on my forehead. "Not a chance, Abs."

"Geez, Mark. You're such a guy. Trust me, as a past teenage girl, I know these things." I swat his chest. It's playful. "But don't worry. It's not that you need to do anything differently, and I'm not saying you were encouraging her attention or anything. But she likes you. It's obvious." I chuckle.

It's what anyone watching her would think.

"On that lovely note," he says, extracting himself from under me and slowly pushing me to the side so I can sit on the sofa and he can leave, "I think I'm going to bed."

I hop right up. "I hope I didn't upset you. I thought you'd want to know. It's harmless."

"No, no, you didn't do anything wrong. I don't know what it is, maybe the storm. I'm exhausted and going to bed feels like the only way to get over it."

Fair enough. I'm exhausted too, the weight of how busy I am pressing down on me.

"Well, I'll come with you. I'm going to check in on Henry on our way to bed."

I yawn and stretch. "Tomorrow, I think you might be able to get out before the next round of snow moves in. Do you think you'll have any jobs?"

"Oh, if I can get out, I'll have jobs," he assures me. "People always need me, no matter the weather. Taking a few days off like this isn't a bad thing, but I want to get back on track so I'm not behind on jobs."

"Sounds good." I link my fingers through his and grab the baby monitor before pulling him from the living room. The fire can die down now. Mark will have to stoke it in the morning, but that won't be a problem.

Everything's going according to plan.

TWENTY-ONE

ABBY

Tuesday 4 Dec

I can hear Mark stumbling around in the bathroom. He flushes the toilet and runs the sink and, for a moment, I think it's the middle of the night and he just got home from the bar. Groaning, I pull the sheet up over my head and roll over, my back to the bathroom, then I hear him brushing his teeth.

What in the world is he doing?

Against my will, I roll back over and blink until I can make out the clock on the bedside table. The red letters glow in the dark, making it difficult for me to see what it says for a moment. I'm blinded but only temporarily, then I blink hard again and they come into focus.

It's five thirty in the morning.

Adrenaline hits me like a wave, and I throw the covers back, hopping out of bed. A shiver runs through my body when I plant my bare feet on the floor. There's usually a fluffy rug I have here so I don't freeze when I get out of bed, but I must have kicked it off to the side when I was crawling into bed last night.

I grab my night robe from the end of the bed, wrap it around myself, and walk over to the bathroom. After rapping my knuckles on the door, I don't wait for Mark to respond before I push it open, blinking rapidly at the bright light.

"Good morning," he says, around a mouthful of toothpaste. "You okay?"

I stare at him. My brain is taking a lot longer than normal to come online today and it's difficult for me to form a coherent thought. He spits and rinses and then turns to me, pulling me in for a hug.

"I overslept," I tell him. My alarm is set for five in the morning, every morning, without fail. Why in the world it didn't wake me up, I don't know, but I don't like it. "I heard you in the bathroom and that got me up."

"I thought you were sleeping in on purpose." His fingers play in my hair then trace slowly down my back, making me shiver harder into him. "I'm sorry, Abs, I would have gotten you right up if I'd known you overslept."

"It's fine. It's not that long." The last thing I want is to step back from his warmth, but I need to get a move on if I'm going to be able to tackle this day, so I do. He gives me one more squeeze before letting me go. "But you're not usually moving around this much in the morning. What's going on?"

"I got some emails about work." He clears his throat and turns away from me while he speaks. "I was going to grab something to eat and head on out. If I hurry, I'll be able to make it back before the snow returns. The radar looks like it's going to hit around noon, so I want to get dressed and out the door in case we all get snowed in later."

Something about this doesn't ring true to me. I can't help but think about how he changed the passcode on his phone, but right now is definitely not the time to bring that up. It's not like I'd want to admit I was trying to read his texts anyway.

"You never head out this early." I'm in front of the door and

I close it behind me, leaning back on it and crossing my arms. "Is something wrong?"

I can see his expression in the mirror. He splashes a little water on his face before he answers, but even when he does, it's clear he's avoiding my question. I can see it there in the set of his jaw, in how his eyes dart around the bathroom for a moment before he speaks. Part of me wants to laugh at the thought that he'd find something in the bathroom to help him change the subject, but this is my *husband* we're talking about.

He's lied to me before. What would stop him from doing it again?

"I got a few emails late last night and I need to handle them."

That's it? That's all he's going to give me? I settle back against the door.

"From who?" I feel like that's a normal thing to ask. Wives are allowed to ask their husbands where they're headed off to work and who they're going to be with, right?

"Who?"

He sounds like an owl. I frown at him. It's way too early in the morning for us to be doing this song and dance, and I haven't had any coffee yet.

"Yeah, I'm your wife, and I'm asking where you're going to be going today? Is that a problem?"

"No, of course not. Maggie called, for one."

"Maggie Moran?"

He nods and grabs a shirt off the counter, shrugging it on and yanking it down into place. "Yep. I fixed her garbage disposal the other day but she's having problems with her toilet now apparently. I'm a little fuzzy on the details but I told her I'd head there bright and early this morning so I could take care of it."

Do I believe him? Nope. Mark isn't a great liar. He tends to fidget, tapping his fingers against the side of his leg when he's trying to lie to me. He's also terrible at eye contact.

Nobody told me that, when I became a wife, I'd have to overlook certain things my husband did. Nobody mentioned that you go from being this entire whole and complete person to someone who helps prop up your spouse, someone who has to be willing to carve off bits of yourself for other people.

I do it for Mark. I do it for Henry.

It's exhausting, but it's what I signed up for. Still, sometimes there are times when I wonder if I'm carving off too much of myself. Is there a point of no return where you give and you give until one day you look down at yourself and realize you've given so much that you're no longer who you were—you're a shell, or a stump, or something collapsed on the ground?

I don't want to ever end up like that.

"Tell Maggie I said hi," I say, and the flash of relief on his face is evident. It makes my heart hurt to see it there, so clearly, so obvious. He's looking at me though, and not in the mirror, so he can't see it, can't see the way his face relaxes like all the stress in his life is gone.

But I see it.

He thinks I bought his lie.

"I will, yeah." There's a silence, a long one, one I don't want to try to fill. He clears his throat. "If you don't mind, I'm going to head downstairs. Start some coffee. See about getting the truck out of the driveway."

The truck. Right.

"I'm in your way," I tell him, stepping to the side. As he walks past me, I turn my head and drink him in.

I love Mark. Love him more than anything. When we met, I knew right away he was the man I was going to marry. It felt like it wasn't even optional to me, like my path had been set out for me and I was simply traveling it.

Fate, I guess some people would call it. Fate that Mark and I would be together for the rest of our lives, that we would grow old on the porch of the pink B&B, that the two of us would always be together.

But now I'm not so sure. He's lying to me. Again. I see it written all over this face, just like I saw relief there that I would move out of the way and let him past. Mark was the one person I loved more than anything in the world, and I still love him, that's not a question.

But now there's one person I love more. One person I'll do anything to protect.

Mark gave him to me, but I'm the one who fought for Henry. And I'm not through doing that yet.

TWENTY-TWO

MARK

I exhale hard as I crank the key in the ignition. I'm not a religious man, not by any stretch of the imagination, but I still pray a little bit that the truck will pull free from the snow, that I'll be able to back down the driveway, that I can flee this house for one day so I can try to get my head on straight.

But there's nothing. The damn thing must be too cold to start.

"Come on," I mutter, smacking my palm against the steering wheel. It stings in the chill of the cab.

Normally I'd crank the engine and let it run for a while to warm up, but I'm more than ready to get out of the house and go to town. I just need air. It's hard to breathe in the B&B during the winter, with the windows all sealed tight against the wind's assault. It's even more difficult to breathe with guests wandering around, bumping into you, seemingly taking up all the oxygen. Oyster isn't a bustling metropolis, but there's one major draw about it right now.

It's not here.

I take a break from turning the key, holding it in my palm as I count to thirty. My breath puffs out in front of me in little clouds, and behind me I can see how the sky is starting to lighten up. It's going to be a gorgeous sunrise, the type that Abby and I used to come out onto the porch to watch when we were first married.

I rip my eyes away from the rearview mirror and stab the key back in the ignition.

Twist it hard away from me.

My truck doesn't make a sound. For a moment I imagine I hear metal on metal, the cold sound of the engine trying to warm up, but there's nothing. No sound, no light, no juice.

"What the hell?" I throw the door open, the frigid air whipping into the cab, and hop out, then walk to the front of the truck. It takes me a minute to sweep the rest of the snow off the hood before I pop it and pull a small flashlight from my pocket. It snaps to life, a thin beam of bright light bouncing off my truck's guts.

Everything looks fine. It's hard to tell when my flashlight is the only reliable illumination in the dark. Things don't look out of place—but I won't know for sure unless I get in there. My hands are starting to cramp up in the cold, but I forgot my gloves in the house and I don't want to go back for them right now.

I heave a sigh, slam the hood. When I look back up at the house, I'm struck by how warm and cozy it looks. It would be easy to go back in, tell Abby I canceled the jobs for the day, have another cup of coffee by the fire. Soon she'll have that lit and the entire building will be a beacon of comfort.

But it won't just be my wife waiting for me in there.

I scowl. Still holding my flashlight, I venture around the other side of the truck, looking for anything that will clue me in as to why it's not starting right up. Yes, it's cold. It's my fault for not running it before trying to crank the engine, but I can't even get the engine to catch.

What's up with that?

My gaze darts back and forth across the snow as my subconscious works to figure out something I just saw. There was something wrong under the hood, I'm sure of it, but I can't put my finger on what it was right now.

I'll have to look again.

But first I move the flashlight around me in an arc as I look at the snow. The storm came in from the south, which means this side of the truck was mostly protected. While the snow rests in high drifts on the tires on the other side, it's not nearly as thick over here.

Still, it's not flat. Not by a long shot. There are depressions in the snow, like you'd expect during any wild storm, but these are different.

They're spaced evenly.

They're all the same size.

They're footprints.

That knowledge hits me right in the chest, and I step back away from them like they could hurt me. Someone was out at my truck, probably messing with it last night after the worst of the snow died down. The frustration I felt at my truck not starting has increased to a dull roar in the back of my head, and I hurry back to the front of the truck and throw the hood back open.

Now I know what I'm looking for and I scan for the battery. As soon as my eyes land on it, I take a deep breath, then reach out and lift one of the battery cables.

It's cut in half, the two ends hanging ragged like a blown artery, the ends flopping uselessly when I drop it back in place.

What the hell happened? That doesn't occur without human intervention. Your battery cables don't rip in half for no good reason. Someone took my keys from where I hang them by the front door, came outside in the snow, and sawed through my cables.

"Dammit!" The wind whips the word away from me, and I

slam the hood back in place as hard as I can. The vibrations make my wrists ache even more than the biting cold, but I ignore the pain.

There's only one person who would want to mess with me like this.

Anger rushes through me and I take a deep breath, trying to calm myself. My hands are still planted on the hood, and I realize with a start how cold my skin has grown. Shoving them into the pockets of my coat, I hurry to the cab to grab my keys, coffee, and cell phone.

I'm not going anywhere until I get the battery cables repaired. No, *replaced*. There's not going to be any way to repair them, not when the ends are jagged like that.

Tim. It had to be Tim.

As I lean into the cab to grab my things, I think I hear someone calling me over the wind. Pausing, I tilt my head towards the house, trying to better hear what that sound was.

There it is again.

Closer now.

I slam the cab door and turn around. Even though I thought I recognized the voice and already knew this person would be coming for me, I'm still surprised he ventured out into the cold to talk to me.

TWENTY-THREE

MARK

"What do you want, Tim?" There's a bite to my words and I hope he picks up on it. He's not welcome here, not outside to talk to me when I'm so frustrated about my truck, but also not in my house.

Especially not in my house.

"I saw you having trouble with your truck." He turns and waves his hand back at the B&B like that will create a visual of him standing in the warmth, watching me stamp my way around the vehicle.

I glare at him. There's no doubt in my mind that this is who sabotaged my truck so I couldn't leave. Hate for him washes over me, hot and sharp, and I have to fight to keep my face neutral.

Do I mention it now? Or should I wait until I feel like I have the upper hand?

"Trouble with my truck," I scoff. "Well, that was kind of you to come out and check on me."

He smiles, showing me his pointy teeth. "That's me. Kind."

Yeah, kind of an asshole.

I start to walk past him, more interested in warming up

inside than continuing whatever discussion it is he wants to have, when he reaches out and grabs my arm. I glance down at his grip then do a double-take.

"You're wearing my gloves."

"Sure, well, you weren't, and it was cold. Now, Mark, don't you think it's time you and I had a chat? It's hard to do that with the wives and kids running around, bumping into us, listening at every door, isn't it?"

I don't respond. Whatever it is this man wants to say, I'm going to let him say it, then I'm going inside. I'll figure out some way to get off this mountain, I swear I will. No matter what he and Lottie have planned, I'm not going to wait around for it.

"I want to talk to you about payments." Tim finally lets go of my arm. When I don't make a move to run to the house, he exhales and nods. "I need more money."

"More money." The words are meaningless to me right now. I hear them, just like I hear the way the wind wails in between the woods and the house before launching right at us. His words wrap around me, but I don't let them soak in.

"Yes. Chelsea is going to college soon." He holds up his hand—in my glove—and begins to tick things off like what he's saying is the most important thing. "She's going to need money for room and board. And books. Food. You want to make sure she has a good college experience, don't you, Mark?"

I don't answer him. Hatred burns for him, a hot coal in my stomach. I *hate* this man, hate him like I don't think I've ever really hated anyone in my life before. The thought of punching him, how it would feel to connect with his skinny face, what it would be like to watch his teeth fly out, blood splattering the snow... I feel my fingers forming into a fist.

My skin is cold and the movement painful, but I grip my fist tight, staring at him. One swing. One punch and nothing would be fixed, but at least I would feel a bit more in control of the situation.

He has five fingers up now. While I was daydreaming about knocking him out, he was still talking, listing everything he wants my money for.

"Did you get all that?" He leans forward. Leers at me. Finally, he glances down at my clenched fist and sucks in a breath. Takes a step back.

"You came into my house to threaten me?" I can't keep the rage out of my voice. It bubbles in me. Hot. Acidic. "You rented out the B&B with the money I've been sending you to threaten me? Is that why you're here? That's your evil plan?"

He straightens up, lifts his chin a little like he was already expecting this rage. I see it written all over his face. His confidence is there in the set of his jaw, how he's staring at me, how he almost seems to draw himself up like he's trying to show me how tall he really is.

But I'm taller. I'm bigger.

He still has me backed into a corner.

"You weren't taking my calls." He stabs his finger right into my chest. "My family deserved a vacation and you and I needed to talk."

I don't move.

He repeats himself. "You stopped taking my calls. You weren't sending as much as you had been."

"Times are lean!" I scream at him, too furious to worry about anyone else listening. Surely nobody else would dare to be outside in this cold, right? I can't imagine a single person besides the two of us who would willingly be outside instead of in the warm. "You think I was holding back? Jesus, man, you need to get a grip! And a job!"

This makes his eyes glitter. From behind me, the sun is rising faster now, casting a peachy glow on his skin.

"I don't need a job." He moves closer to me now, almost like he wants to make sure I hear every single word he's going to say. "And do you want to know why?"

There's no way I'm responding to him. Not now, not here, not in the driveway of my home. This shouldn't be happening, any of it. None of this should ever have happened but it is, and I'm the reason. It's all my fault.

"I don't need a job because you're going to give me money. *More* money, Mark. I don't care how much you have to work or if you barely get to see your wife and kid."

I groan, the sound a whisper on my lips, and grab the sides of my head, squeezing hard.

He's right.

I will.

If I want him to keep my secret, then I'll do whatever he tells me to.

TWENTY-FOUR

ABBY

The windows in the kitchen are so old, the frames so worn, with cracks in the wood, that I can feel the cold air from outside seeping into the room. But I don't want to draw the curtains.

We're in a whiteout. The sight of it is incredible, so overwhelming that I feel smaller than I think I ever have before. There's something about a storm like this, one where the snow isn't only falling from the sky but also being whipped up from the ground and spun around the house like a cape, that makes me feel like all of my problems are insignificant.

Mark told me he cancelled his jobs because of the snow, that he took one look at the truck and changed his mind about trying to get down into town, and I'm glad he's going to be home.

Even though he was lying to me.

Still, the thought of him trying to navigate this storm, even if the wind were to die down, makes me nervous. You can be as careful as possible and bad things can still happen to you. Accidents happen in good weather.

But more of them happen in weather like this.

And now, thanks to the constant storm, we're officially

snowed in. Even if Mark's truck had cranked right up, the drifts are so high, the roads covered in layers of snow and ice, that driving would be folly. We can't get out of here, but what's worse: nobody can get up to us.

A particularly strong gust of wind slams into the side of the house, rattling the glass in the frames. I stop chopping carrots, wrap my old gray sweater tighter around my torso, then pick my knife back up. All I want to eat right now are stews and roasts, anything warm that will keep me from being too chilled.

As soon as I chop these carrots and potatoes then I can get the pork roast in the oven. It'll be delicious for dinner tonight. By then, the sun will have gone down and there won't be any light entering the house from outside. Right now, light from the weak sun still reflects off the snow. But tonight, that ends.

Besides the moon and stars, there won't be any light. We're too isolated to have neighbors' windows shining like beacons in the night, and there won't be headlights cutting paths through the thick dark. We never feel more utterly alone up here than in the middle of a snowstorm at night.

Normally, that doesn't bother me. But things are different with guests.

We'll light some candles for ambiance, but not too many.

The last thing I want is to accidentally go through our stash. We need candles if we lose power, which is very possible in storms like this.

Stuck up here with guests. And we might lose power.

The thought makes me shiver.

Next to me on the counter is Henry's baby monitor. That's what I'll miss more than lights if we lose power. I need to be able to stay in contact with my baby so I can make sure he's okay. If we lose power, then I might lose that.

The thought makes me shiver.

One last chop and I set my knife to the side, grab my cutting board, and dump the carrots in the roaster. As I'm setting the board back down on the counter, half of the lights on the baby monitor light up.

They blink to life then fade away before lighting back up.

I frown and grab it before twisting the little volume knob to the right to turn the volume as loud as possible. If Henry were crying loudly, I would have been able to hear him already without turning it up. This monitor is incredibly sensitive, which was why I chose it.

But the fact that the lights lit up without me hearing anything tells me the sound in his room is quiet. Almost too quiet to pick up.

I press the monitor up to my ear.

There's static. Crackles. I hear nothing but interference, and even though I know it won't help, I slap it against my palm.

"Henry."

The voice in my ear chills me. I freeze, suddenly feeling ice in my veins. Even though I know I'm alone in the kitchen, I turn, my heart pounding, to see if there's anyone behind me.

Someone said Henry's name.

"Henry, come here."

The voice is garbled. Whoever is in his room is whispering, the monitor trying so hard to pick it up that it's having trouble transmitting.

Henry's not alone.

I'm hot. I was so cold a moment ago and now I'm burning up. I drop the monitor on the counter and turn, racing from the kitchen, stopping only at the base of the stairs.

"Someone's in the room with Henry," I gasp out to Mark. He's holding a cup of coffee, a book tucked under his arm like he was going to go sit and read, and he frowns at me.

"What do you mean?"

But I don't respond, because doing so would mean I had to slow down and talk to him, and I don't want to waste time doing that. I push past him, ignoring how he cries out when coffee splashes out of his cup and onto his hand. My feet pound the stairs, the sound so loud whoever is with Henry will hear me coming, but I can't slow down.

I'm sweating as I throw open the door to the second floor and race down the hall to Henry's room. His door is closed, and I lean against it, my heart pounding in my ears, my breathing erratic. I need to slow down, need to stop panting so I can listen to what's going on in there, but there's another part of me screaming to break down the door and get inside, to save my son, to make sure he's okay.

I turn the knob. Fear eats at the back of my mind, but I push it away and step into the room. Cool air washes over me. It's colder in here than in the rest of the house, and that worry worms its way into my mind, but I push it away.

Of course it's cold. He's far away from the kitchen. Even with the heat working overtime, the bedrooms are always cold.

The lights are off, the curtains drawn, the room nice and dark for his nap, and I fumble my hand along the wall to find the light switch. Shadows seem to shift and move in his room while I stare, blinking into the dark, looking for him. It's almost impossible to pick out his crib, to see the lump in the middle of it.

Is it Henry?

Is someone hiding in here with him?

There's a soft click when I finally find the light switch and I blink in the bright light, shielding my eyes for a moment before dropping my hand and looking around the room.

Nothing's out of place.

Henry rolls over in his crib, his face already scrunching up like he's going to howl. His hand forms a fist, and he holds it up in the air before bringing it down on the mattress next to him. He's a ticking time bomb, sure to start screaming at any moment, but I have to find the person I heard on the monitor.

Even though I know there's not enough room under his bed for an adult to hide, I drop to my knees.

Nothing.

I stand back up and cross the room to the closet. The door is closed. Everything's right where it should be.

Not a toy or book out of place.

But someone was in here. I heard them.

Maybe inside the closet.

I throw open the door, jumping to the side as I do. Behind me, Henry has woken all the way up. He's crying, taking deep breaths as he gets louder and louder. I want to turn to him, to lift him up, but I step into the closet, swinging my arm into the hanging clothes, kicking the bucket of shoes on the floor.

Something wraps around my wrist, and I cry out, pulling my arm back, trying to free myself. Someone's in here, someone was hiding, and they grabbed me. Panic grips my throat. My wrist feels hot from being held, and I take another step back, jerking my arm away from the rack of clothes.

There's a loud clatter. A navy sweater, one I'd bought Henry for family photos in the fall, pulls from the hanger. Its soft weave caught on my watch—the pressure I felt of something pulling me into the closet was just the sleeve.

I gasp, then yank the sweater free. There's a soft ripping noise as some of the fibers catch on my watch and tear, but I leave it in a puddle on the floor.

Grab my thighs.

Take a deep breath.

Nothing.

There's nobody here.

But I know what I heard. Someone was in here with my son. They're gone now, but they were *here*. I know they were.

I'm moving on autopilot as I walk to Henry's crib and lift him up. Mark's in the doorway now, his eyes wide as he watches me. I ignore him until I have Henry in my arms.

"Shh, baby, it's okay," I say, bouncing him. His face is wet and hot, and he smears snot and tears against my cheek as I grip him, trying to settle him back to sleep.

"Nobody's in here," Mark says, his voice flat. "Are you sure you heard—"

"Someone was in here, Mark," I snap, pushing past him. I need to get out of this room. Someone was in here, I know they were, and it doesn't feel safe. "Someone was with Henry. One of our guests."

I have to get him out of here, get him somewhere I can keep an eye on him.

"Abby," he says, and I'm about to keep walking, to ignore him, but what he says next stops me dead in my tracks.

"Abs, his sliding door is cracked open."

I whip around, still gripping Henry tight.

No, he has to be wrong.

Even as I think that though, I feel the chill from the air slipping in alongside the sliding door.

TWENTY-FIVE

CHELSEA

The heat from the fireplace washes over me in waves, and even though I'm wearing a hoodie and wrapped up in an ugly plaid blanket I found draped over the chair, I'm still chilly. This place is gorgeous, four towering stories of catwalks, decks, and bright windows, but it's drafty and I can feel the wind come in the window behind me every single time it blows.

No, not blows. *Howls.* The sound of the wind whipping against the house kept me up part of the night. It sounded like someone out there, knocking, testing the windows, rapping at the shutters.

And while it's not as bad now as it was last night, the wind is still stronger than I like. Fresh snow falls while old snow is whipped up from the ground, spun around, thrown against the walls.

Shivering, I adjust myself in my chair, glad I pulled on some thick wool socks right before coming out of my room. At home I'd have turned the heat up high enough that I could walk around in a T-shirt without feeling chilled.

The blanket slips off my shoulder and I yank it back up before settling my book back on my legs so I can keep reading.

Well, so that I can *look* like I'm reading. It's not very interesting, definitely not something I'd want to read, no matter how bored I was, but having the book in my lap isn't about losing myself in a story.

It's about making sure nobody pays attention to me.

The one thing that adults don't realize about kids is that when we have our noses tucked in a book, we can still easily listen to whatever is going on around us. Books are magic. Invisibility cloaks. As soon as I pick a book up and start to read, it's like I completely disappear from sight.

I love it.

It's been a few years since I figured it out. When I was around ten, books went from being magical because they can transport you to an entirely different life to being magical because they bring to light all of the secrets of everyone around you.

It doesn't matter what I'm reading. My eyes drift across the page and, every once in a while, I reach up and turn to the next one, but when I'm listening, I don't actually pay attention to anything that's written there. I'm much more interested in learning about what's going on around me.

And now that we're at the Saltside Inn, acting like we're one big happy family, it's how I'm going to make sure I don't miss a single thing that's said around here. Kids—even teenagers—tend to be invisible to adults.

Books ensure nobody will pay attention to me.

The History of Love is open on my lap, and while I'd love to go ask Abby what in the world she was thinking even buying a book like this, I won't. It's not part of the plan. Yes, I'd wrinkled my nose when I'd pulled it free from the shelf, but it's thick and wordy and it'll do.

Mom and Abby are in the kitchen drinking tea and chatting. Dad disappeared a while ago, telling me he wanted to try to make it to the cliffs to see the ocean. He took those stupid snowshoes again since he didn't make it far yesterday before the storm hit us and promised he'd be back by lunch before the snow came, but how the hell he's going to make it ten feet from the house, I don't know.

He's insane.

And even though he'd asked if I'd like to come with him, tromping around through the snow and the biting wind was the last thing I wanted to do. I'd much rather sit here and try to get warm, *thank you very much.*

Besides, it's just the ocean. I've been there, seen it, and I don't need to see it again. That's not why I'm here.

I think it's fair to say both of my parents were surprised at how much I wanted to come on the trip. They'd hardly mentioned it, both of them obviously worried I was going to turn them down, when I started packing. Did they really think they'd be able to leave me at home?

I scoff. Not a chance. Now, if this trip was simply some "Kumbaya" bonding bullshit for the three of us to try to grow as a family, I'd still be at our house, the heat turned so high I'd be rocking shorts and a tank top. But I saw right through their little spiel about *bonding* and *togetherness* and whatever other crap they wanted to try to pretend was the inciting factor for us coming.

Chuckling, I settle deeper in the chair. It doesn't have great back support, so it's totally not a good option for someone old to sit in, but I rather like how it conforms to my body and makes me feel like I'm a cocoon. It's comfortable, cozy.

It's a great place for me to sit and wait.

No, no matter what my parents tried to tell me, this vacation isn't what it appears on the surface.

The sound of someone walking into the living room makes me pick the book up. I hold it in front of my face and peep out over the top.

Mark.

He sighs as he sits down on the sofa by the fireplace. It's a weary sigh, like it comes from way down in his toes. I stare at him, then flick my gaze back down to my book when he shifts position.

He'd tried to leave this morning—I saw it through my bedroom window. I also saw when my dad went out to talk to him and how angry they'd both been.

They don't know this about me, but I see everything.

TWENTY-SIX

MARK

God, my head hurts. I didn't get nearly enough sleep last night to be dealing with everything going on in the house today. The guests. The sudden burst of energy Henry has that somehow enables him to squawk at exactly the right decibel for me to feel like my ears are bleeding.

This damned snowstorm that's swept in, keeping me from leaving the house and escaping everything. Even if my truck were working, there's no way I could make it down the mountain.

It was stupid of me to even think that I could, but I had to try. As much as I hate to admit it, staying in is the safest option today.

Tim's out there, like a fool. I give him twenty minutes before he either comes back in, his cheeks ruddy and burning, or he freezes to death.

Not that that would be a waste, would it?

Groaning, I rub my temples. I need to go back to bed, let the sweet oblivion of sleep drag me down so I can feel better when I get up, but I'm not stupid.

Abby would have a fit if I went to bed right now. She's

already upset with me for letting the truck die, telling me that I should have changed the battery last month like she told me to.

But I did. I changed it. If I tell her someone sabotaged the battery, then she'll freak out.

Pushing that thought from my mind, I stumble into the living room and collapse on the sofa facing the fire.

"Hey." A soft voice pulls me from my thoughts, and I sit up, my eyes flicking over to the easy chair to my right. Chelsea's there, her eyes locked on me, a thick book in her lap. I hadn't even noticed her sitting there, not when she was wrapped up in that ugly blanket.

"Oh, hi. I didn't mean to bother you." Automatically, I start to rise. I want to be alone right now. The thought of having to make conversation with anyone makes my head hurt even more.

It's nothing personal.

"Oh, you're not bothering me." She closes her book and smiles at me.

I'm caught, half-standing, half-sitting. I'm wary but not really wanting to walk back into the kitchen where Lottie and Abby are talking. Right now, I'm an inmate in my own home and I have no idea how to get out of here. Freedom would require walking outside, but Tim is out there snowshoeing around like a damn fool in the worst snow we've had for a while, like he's on a dream vacation, and...

God, I need a drink.

"I was hoping to go on a walk and look at the ocean while I was here, but this storm is something else." She closes the book and sets it down on the floor, leaning forward so she can prop her elbows on her knees and stare at me. "Is it a bit of a bummer to have guests when the weather is bad and you have to be stuck inside?"

I sink back down to sit. So much for being able to exist without having to make conversation with anyone.

"It can be pretty fun," I tell her. "Just depends on the guests, I guess."

That makes her grin. "You must have some horror stories about bad guests, huh?"

"Oh, geez. You know, the last thing I want to do is talk bad about a guest, but yeah. You meet all kinds when you run a place like this." I pause. Talking to her isn't as bad as I thought it would be, if I'm being honest with myself.

I guess I don't have a lot of experience with teenagers. I find them confusing. And, frankly, a little stressful.

But Chelsea isn't so bad. None of this is her fault.

"So, what do you think you'll study in college?" *Since I'll be paying for it apparently.*

"Psychology." She straightens up a little bit and sets her jaw. "I want to know what makes people tick. Everyone is so different, right? And some people are so *weird*." There's a huge smile on her face and she reaches up to brush some of her hair back as she speaks. "I want to help them."

"That's admirable."

A shrug. "I like to help people. Mom says I'm good at it but that sometimes I get in my own way and don't think things through."

"Like the knife at gymnastics?" I offer, and she nods.

"Right. It was a mistake." Her voice is small, and I feel bad for her.

"We all make mistakes," I start, but she cuts me off.

"Right. We do. But that was stupid. I wasn't going to do anything with it, but you should have heard my parents. Off the gymnastics team, just like that." She snaps her fingers. "And grounded. I'm not allowed to do anything but go to school, to the library, and then come home. This is the first time I've been anywhere, really, since that."

"And then you're stuck inside thanks to a huge snowstorm. That's kinda lame."

"So lame." She chuckles. "But yeah, it's nicer than being in my room, let me tell you. I'm hoping Mom and Dad will see that I'm doing my best, that the knife was a mistake. I hope we can move past this."

"I bet you can."

We fall silent after that. Not only do I have zero frame of reference for dealing with teenagers, but now I feel even more out of my element. When I was younger, I never broke the rules. That only started when I got much older, and I'm not about to share that with Chelsea.

Abby's voice floats down to me. Is she coming? Now that Chelsea and I have talked a bit, I don't know what else to say to her. I wouldn't mind my wife coming in here and giving me something to do.

"Anyway, I'm headed up to my room for a bit." The tip of her tongue darts out and she licks her lower lip, then holds up a book for me to see. "As gripping as this book is, I might need a nap."

I laugh. "I'll let you get to it."

Chelsea stands, leaving the book and her blanket behind, then exits the room. She moves slowly, languidly, like she's exhausted enough to sleep for a few hours.

Abby is crazy if she thinks Chelsea has a crush on me. She's just a teenager. Sure, she's a little messed up, but aren't they all? Show me one teenager who says they don't have problems and I'll show you one that's lying to you.

Chelsea has problems, I'm sure of it. But crushing on me isn't one of them.

TWENTY-SEVEN

ABBY

I punch down the bread dough, letting my fist sink into its soft surface, then grab the bowl and unceremoniously dump it out onto the floured counter. It smells good, yeasty and sweet, and my mouth waters a little bit as I start tearing off chunks of dough to roll into balls for dinner rolls.

Thank goodness I've made this bread dozens of times before, because, right now, my body is moving on autopilot while my mind won't seem to stop racing.

There's too much going on.

Mark's been lying to me—I know he has. The lies spill so easily from his lips, like he honestly can't help himself. And even though I know men lie—*my mother told me that's what they do*—knowing it and experiencing it are two totally different things.

It hurts. Of course it hurts. We said our vows and promised to build an amazing life together. I have the B&B. I have my son. I have my husband, but not his honesty.

And, in truth, these guests are shaping up to be a lot more trouble than I thought they'd be.

Lottie falls all over herself to be helpful. Tim does everything he can to stay out of the way, to avoid spending time with me or Mark.

And Chelsea?

I scoff, then use my wrist to brush some stray hair back from my face. My hands are covered in flour, and I'll probably have a streak of the white stuff on my temple, but I'll worry about that later. There are too many other things to worry about now.

I told Mark she has a crush on him.

But it's more, isn't it? I see the way she tracks his every movement, how she angles to sit next to him at the table for every meal, how she hangs on every word he says.

There's definitely a secret there and Mark knows it. There's guilt written all over his face.

And now the baby monitor I keep in here is missing. I know I wouldn't have left it somewhere. It's important. It's my lifeline to Henry.

But then where is it? I've looked everywhere for it.

The back of my neck prickles. Before I turn around, I close my eyes. Take a deep breath. My heart is suddenly in my throat. I'm fully expecting someone to be right behind me, and I clench the dough in my hands.

Nobody's there.

A heavy sigh and I turn back around. Try to force myself to relax.

The monitor must be misplaced. Maybe Mark took it to give me a bit of a break so I'm not always the one looking out for Henry. Maybe I misplaced it.

Or maybe someone took it.

"No." The word is explosive as it leaves my lips, and it breaks the silence in the kitchen. It's so surprising, even though I'm the one who said it, that I wince, closing my eyes, and forcing myself to breathe slowly and deeply.

Nobody took the monitor. I'm on edge—and for good reason —and I misplaced it.

Henry is fine.

As for the door being open in his room earlier? This wind is out of control. As much as I want to see our home as a fortress, strong winds can rip shingles from the roof. They can throw debris through windows. And, as Mark promised me, they can open doors if they're left unlocked.

I wasn't sure I believed him at first. Wind opening doors? But he'd promised me, cupping my cheeks, looking into my eyes like we were the only two people in the world and told me he wouldn't lie about something like that, not when Henry's safety was all that mattered.

And I believe him.

I don't like that his monitor is missing, but I must have moved it and I'm so tired I can't remember where I put it. That's the only thing that makes sense, the only thing I'm willing to believe.

Because any alternative is too unpleasant to entertain.

Another scattering of flour on the counter and I start rolling out the dough balls, cupping my hand around the top to get the surface tension just perfect. I'll crowd them all in a pan, let them rise again, then brush them with an egg wash before baking.

The result will be delicious, warm and light, fluffy and golden, and I hope everyone likes having them on the dinner table.

Normally I wouldn't make every single meal for our guests because people do like to go out to eat sometimes, but the snowstorm has kicked it up a notch, turning into a raging blizzard that managed to drive all of us inside. We're all stuck here together now.

If I don't make food, we won't eat. It's as simple as that. Lottie might try to make something, but I know for a fact that Mark won't step up to help. And I doubt Tim would either. I couldn't make either one of them.

Of course, you can't make men do something they don't want to—or talk them out of what they do want to do. There was no way I could make Mark see how dangerous it was for him to be out there. Men, I've learned, like what they like, and damn you for trying to keep them from doing anything stupid.

I squeeze a perfect ball of dough so hard it squishes out between my fingers.

Men. Always doing things that they shouldn't. And then what happens? You have to be willing to clean up their mess, pick up their pieces, *fix* everything so nobody gets hurt.

"Mommy?"

Henry's voice yanks me right out of my thoughts, as rudely and abruptly as if someone splashed cold water on my face while I was sleeping. Dropping the mangled bit of dough back on the counter, I turn to him.

"Hey, Henry-boy. What are you up to?"

He has bare feet, which probably means he's going to complain about being cold, and is holding the same metal truck he takes with him everywhere. When I realized how much he loved it, I went right back to the store to buy him another one. It's tucked in the top of my closet just in case he ever loses this one.

Most kids have a blanket they drag around with them everywhere that makes them feel safe. Henry has a little yellow truck.

"I woke up. Kelsey got me up."

"Chelsea," I correct automatically as my brain tries to process what he said. "Her name is Chelsea, darling. Did you sleep well?" I don't like that the teenager got him up when I should have heard him crying. I specifically told the Rowes to stay off our floor. And she wasn't only on our floor, she was in Henry's room.

She might have been in mine.

Automatically, I look for the baby monitor.

Then I remember it's missing.

A chill dances up my spine. Is it possible that Chelsea had something to do with the missing monitor? That maybe I'm not as careless as I was imagining?

No. I have to be in perfect control.

"Chelsea." He nods, reaching up for me to pick him up. I start to do that, thinking I'll swing him onto the counter to hang out with me while I bake, but then something hits me.

"Have you peed?" When he shakes his head, I wipe my hands on my apron and grab his free hand, leading him down the hall to the bathroom. "It's always smart to do that when you first get up, okay? That way you don't have to worry about having an accident."

Henry potty-trained a month or so ago and there's no way I'm going to stand by and watch as he regresses. I'm tired of diapers and all the laundry that comes with potty-training, and if that means dragging him to the bathroom every hour on the hour during the day, I'm willing to do that.

"Okay, Mommy." He gives me a grin and holds out his truck. "Hold this."

"You got it. You want help in there?" I already know the answer, so I'm not surprised when he shakes his head and flicks on the light, shutting the door for a little privacy.

Exhaling, I sag against the wall. The problem with not keeping my body busy is that it gives my mind time to kick into high gear. I can't seem to quiet my thoughts when my hands aren't working on something, and right now my mind has half a dozen things to mull over.

I hear Henry flush and then the sound of the tap cuts on for a moment before he turns it back off. When he joins me in the hall, his hands are still wet, but I give him back his truck and then scoop him up, resting him on my hip to carry him down the hall to the kitchen.

"Okay, little man," I say, plopping him on the counter and

tossing him a towel, "dry off your hands and you can play with this piece of dough."

He does what I ask, and I give him the mangled bit I squeezed out of shape earlier.

We work in silence for a moment, then I cover the rolls with a towel and turn to set them by the stove to rise. Henry's behind me, sitting far enough back with his back against the wall that I don't need to worry about him accidentally falling off the counter as long as I move quickly and don't turn my back on him for too long.

The pan clanks against the stove when I set it down and I wince at the grating sound then turn back to my son.

But before I can look at him, my eyes fall on the shelf where I always have his baby monitor.

It's there. Turned on. The lights indicating that there's sound in his room aren't lit up, but the green one that shows that there's power to the monitor is.

I know it wasn't here before, so how the hell did it get put back?

TWENTY-EIGHT

ABBY

I stumble forward and grab the baby monitor, turning it over and over in my hands like that's all it's going to take to convince myself it's real. The plastic is cool to my touch, the unit heavier than you think it should be, just looking at it.

It's here now. But I swear it wasn't earlier.

Like I can feel someone watching me, I whip around, my heart hammering out a staccato beat, my stomach twisting with the thought of someone watching me. Laughing at me. The only person in the kitchen with me is Henry and he's so engrossed in flattening his dough out on the counter that he hasn't even looked up.

Not that I expect a toddler to be tuned in to my emotions or worry about what's going on with me, but still. Something is wrong here. Something happened.

Someone took the monitor after I put Henry down for his nap and then put it back while I was waiting on him in the bathroom.

That's the only explanation.

I put it back down, then walk over to Henry and clear my throat.

He doesn't look up.

"Hey, Hen?" I reach out to touch his knee so I can get his attention and hate how my hand trembles. "Henry. I have a question."

This gets his attention. He's still squeezing the dough in his fat little hands, but he looks up at me. Waiting.

"You said Chelsea got you up from your nap?"

He nods. His mouth forms a little bow like it always does when he's thinking.

"Were you crying?"

Maybe that's it. Maybe I didn't hear him crying on the monitor, but it was in here the entire time, and I looked right past it. *It had to have been in here.* He woke up and Chelsea must have been coming downstairs and heard him. Never mind that I don't want guests on the second floor, she still helped my son. She must have gone into his room to get him before he could really ratchet up the sound. Only—

Only we told the Rowes our floor of the house was off limits and that we didn't want them in there.

So what was she doing near Henry's room?

"Not crying." He laughs, holding up the dough so I can see it. I nod, then push his hand down so I can look at him.

"You weren't crying?"

Henry shakes his head, a serious expression on his face. "No. Sleeping. But we played."

I feel like I'm going to throw up. "What did you play?"

"Trucks. She's funny."

"You were playing trucks in your room?" I glance at the baby monitor. I would have heard him playing with someone— or even by himself, but only if the monitor had been here. It's completely out of the question for me to believe—if the baby monitor was here, where it was supposed to be—that he was awake and talking and laughing and I didn't know about it.

Only I don't think it was here, do I? I think it was gone and someone brought it back and now they're laughing at me while I go insane.

I obviously didn't misplace it.

The thought is terrible, but now that it's been planted in my brain, it's taken root. It's one thing for there to be guests in the B&B. That's what it's for—that's the purpose of it after all. I loved the idea of opening our home to new people, of getting to meet them, of learning about them.

But I don't love the idea of anyone going somewhere in my space where they weren't invited.

"You know what?" I'm making a split-second decision and I know I need to be careful, that the Rowes are scheduled to be here for a long time, that there's no way anyone can safely leave the B&B, but right now I can't seem to quiet the screaming in my mind. "Come here, Hen." I scoop him up, not even caring that he brings his dough with him.

Well, I care a little. But I don't care enough to rip it out of his tiny fist and cause the screaming fit I know that would trigger.

He snuggles against me, and I'm sure I'm going to have bread dough in my hair any minute now, but I still hold him tighter than usual as I carry him down the hall to the living room. The B&B is huge, with plenty of floors for people to explore, as well as a library and pool table, but every time we have guests it's the same thing.

Everyone wants to be in here, in the main living area. They want to crowd around the fireplace, drawing heat and comfort from it and from each other, and while I normally love that, right now I want everyone out of my house.

"Hey," I say, forcing myself to speak up before I can lose my nerve. I'm in the doorway to the room and the entire Rowe family is here. For a moment I wonder where Mark is, but that isn't the problem right now, is it?

It has been in the past—me wondering *where is my*

husband?—but right now I'm more worried about keeping Henry safe.

I'm always terrified something is going to happen to him, that he won't wake up, that I'll lose him, that's why I can't seem to bear being away from him, that's why I'm doing all of this in the first place—

And it hits me that Tim, Chelsea, and Lottie are all staring at me. All I want to do is swallow hard and melt into the floor.

But I can't. I started this and I have to see it through.

I take a deep breath and try to steady myself, digging deep to find any strength. I'm supposed to be in control. *But this wasn't how it was supposed to go.* It doesn't matter. I can fix it. I have to be careful how I handle our guests.

I don't have a choice.

"Chelsea," I say, dragging my eyes away from Lottie, "did you get Henry up from his nap?"

First, she glances at her mom, like she's looking for some kind of confirmation that things are going to be okay, then she nods, her teeth sinking into her lower lip as she looks at me.

"I did... Is he okay? He was calling for someone to get him up and I heard him, so I went down the hall to lift him out. I hope that isn't a problem—I thought he needed to get out of his crib."

Lottie reaches over. Rests her hand on Chelsea's leg. The message is clear. *You did nothing wrong.*

"No, he's fine. I just..." How do I handle this without making it seem like I'm pointing a finger, which is what I'm about to do? "He should have slept longer than he did, and I'm surprised you could hear him calling."

There. That says more than the actual words. If they can't pick up on the fact that I don't like the idea of Chelsea on our floor of the house, then I don't know what to do. I don't want to spell it out for them, don't want them to see the little cracks I feel forming in the edges of my sanity, but maybe I'm going to have to let it all out.

Maybe I need to be as transparent as possible with them, but that's not the goal here.

The goal is—

"I'm sorry." Again, Chelsea glances at Lottie before looking back at me. "You're right. I know you told us not to go to your rooms, but I was coming down the stairs and heard him freaking out, so I went to his room to get him. Your monitor must not have been working or something because he was carrying on."

I shift Henry on my hip. She's lying to me. I know she is. But I can't argue with her, and I can't seem to tear my eyes away from her. Chelsea is good at this; she's spinning her web of lies so expertly, so tightly woven, that I don't think I could easily poke holes in it without coming across like I'm crazy.

Or like I'm out to get her.

And that wouldn't end well.

"So, you got him right out of his crib and brought him downstairs?" I'm fishing for another lie. The line is cast, the bait is *right there*, and even though I think she's onto me now, that she knows I'm looking for her to dig her hole even deeper, she holds my gaze when she nods.

"That's right. I brought him right down the stairs and then he wanted you, so I put him down. Really, I hope I didn't overstep—I thought getting him up when he was so upset was the right thing to do." She dips her head, letting her red hair fall like a curtain over her face.

Before she does though, I think I see something there.

A smile.

No, a smirk.

"You did the right thing," I say, staring at her. She doesn't look back up at me until I continue. "Thank you for taking care of him."

"It takes a village." Lottie clears her throat. Stares at me.

"You know, if we didn't have help from other people raising our children, what would we do? How would we manage everything? You're obviously juggling a lot, Abby, and I know running this place is a crazy amount of work. I'm glad Chelsea was there to help Henry out when you weren't."

Bitch. For a moment I allow myself to think about what it would be like to lunge at her, tossing Henry to safety as I do. I'd wrap my fingers in her hair, slam her head down into the coffee table. She'd scream and fight, but she can't win all the time, can she? I have to be able to win once in a while.

I'm counting on it.

"It sure does," I say. "What would we do without our village?"

Henry shifts on my hip, but I refuse to put him down. I've been pretty lax with him running around with our guests, but that ends now.

"Well, don't let me disturb your family time."

"Oh, you couldn't." Chelsea grins at me. "I feel like we're all family here, don't you?"

I see the look Lottie gives her. Tim, for his part, hasn't said anything. He stares at me, and I give him a nod, then back away, down the hall, back to the kitchen.

My mind won't slow down. I can't seem to focus on a single thought; it's like there's a hurricane in my brain, whipping up my thoughts and swirling them together into a thick soup I'm mired in, but I have to keep my wits about me.

I knew this wasn't going to be easy. I knew when the Rowes signed up for three entire weeks at our B&B that tension might be high and that people would butt heads, but I never once —*never once*—thought that Henry might be in danger, and that changes the entire game for me.

TWENTY-NINE

LOTTIE

Leaving Chelsea in her room, I make my way down to the first floor. There's no way she heard Henry crying in his room unless she was already on the second floor, and Abby made it quite clear when we first got here that she didn't want us up there.

So what in the world was she doing?

I feel like things are spinning out of my control. Chelsea lied to Abby, that much is clear. She's been sneaking around the house. For all I know, Tim hasn't even approached Mark about more money. Everything seems to be falling apart. Coming to the Saltside Inn was supposed to be the best way for me to fix everything, and yet now it feels like things are even more out of control than before.

At the bottom of the stairs, I pause, my ears on high alert, listening for where everyone else is in the house. Since he tried to snowshoe to the cliff this morning, Tim has barely left the room. He goes on and on about how cold he is and how much he wants to be home, but then why hasn't he pushed Mark?

If he would, then we'd at least know what we were going to do next. We couldn't leave right away of course, but things would be set in motion.

Abby's in the kitchen. I hear her humming as she cooks and the sound of Henry hitting a pan with a wooden spoon. Wincing at the noise, I turn in the other direction, following the sound of the crackling fireplace. Dinner tonight will probably be quiet as we all try to figure out how we can share space without getting on each other's nerves, but some quiet time in the living room will help me prepare.

Mark looks up as I walk in. He's sitting right in front of the fire, scrolling on his phone, and he clicks the side button, turning off his screen, as I walk in. He watches me, his eyes never leaving mine, and I snuggle down on the sofa, grabbing an ugly blanket and wrapping it around myself as I do.

"How are you doing?" I'm the first to break the ice. "I'm sure having guests here helps break up the monotony, but you must get bored in bad weather. At least you get to go out, meet new people. Do new things. But what about Abby and Henry? Do they get a little stir-crazy when they're left behind?"

"Well, sure. I think it's normal that they'd feel a bit claustrophobic. We love it here and Abby doesn't mind staying around the house for weeks on end when the weather is bad, but we're always happy to get out when the snow melts," he tells me, then clears his throat. "It's hard getting snowed in anywhere, especially with people you don't know very well."

I watch as he shifts on the sofa, then reaches up and rubs the side of his nose with his finger, then quirk an eyebrow and wait for him to continue. When he doesn't, I speak up. "Well, for what it's worth, I think it's kinda fun to be locked in somewhere and not be able to leave. I can't do laundry, I can't sweep the floors, I don't have to worry about my neighbor stopping by. This place is starting to feel like home, just like I hoped it would."

He doesn't respond. It's only when I feel like I'm about to come out of my skin waiting that he gives a little nod.

"I'm glad you're enjoying your stay, but I think it's best that we all have boundaries and understand what's allowed while you are all here. Everyone will be happier if we're not accidentally stepping on toes."

"Right. You're right." I shift position. The sofa is lumpy and there's a spring shoved right into my thigh, but I'm warm for the first time in a while and I'm not interested in shifting too much and letting cold air in. "Abby went over the rules with us that first night at dinner, but I don't think anyone thought we'd all be snowed in like this. Since we can't even get outside without risking frostbite, it makes sense to give us a little leeway on where we can go and what we can do."

"As long as your family has a nice time and you stay off the second floor." He moves to turn his phone back on, but I want to keep talking to him.

"So what do you like to do when you're not working?" I ask and shift position a little bit, tucking the blanket farther up under my chin. "I already know you spend a lot of time away from home."

He looks wary. "Well, Abby and I love to hike, so we spend a lot of time outside. And Henry takes up a lot of my free time, but I wouldn't have it any other way. I make sure I'm home as soon as possible when I get done with a job."

"Is that so? No dilly-dallying in people's houses and taking your time getting back?"

He doesn't respond so I continue. "That's great. It's so nice you're able to be around for Henry. I imagine he's worth coming right back up the mountain to see every day.

"Yeah, I'm blessed. I wouldn't want it any other way."

There's a slight pause before he continues. "What about you, Lottie? What do you like to do?"

"Bake." I lean forward before I catch myself and settle back into the sofa. "I don't know that I'm as good as Abby, but I'm pretty handy in the kitchen. And I love to read too. I've got more time for that now Chelsea is older. Before, I spent most of my free time hanging out with her. Tim tries to be a good dad, but he's always out working, always has his fingers in lots of pots."

Silence.

"You know about that, don't you?"

"Lottie." His voice takes on an edge I haven't heard before. "I don't want to talk about your husband or the *pots* his fingers are in. The bad weather is unfortunate, but the place is big enough that we can all be under the same roof without any problems."

"Hey, I'm sorry. I didn't mean to push buttons. Didn't know Tim was such a sore spot for you, not when you two share such a history. And, you know what, I'm not even mad about Abby getting a little short with Chelsea. I get it." I'm just talking now, like Mark and I are old friends, but even though the words flow freely, I do see the way he stiffens a bit at what I said.

"She wasn't *getting short* about Henry. She was being a good mom."

He stands up, stretches. Even though I know I shouldn't, I look at the way his shirt pulls up, how I can see a sliver of skin right above his waistband.

When he continues speaking, I have to force myself to look up at him.

"Abby is a great mom, Lottie. If she wants Chelsea to stay out of Henry's room, then you need to make sure that happens. She's your daughter."

I bite back a response. There are so many things I want to say to him but nothing good can come from me arguing or snapping at him. Instead, I nod.

"I'm glad we're on the same page." He's walking away from me now, and even though I know I blew it and I should get up, try to fix it, try to calm him down, the only thing I can do right now is stare at him.

I drink in his wide shoulders, the set of his jaw. How big his hands are as he palms his phone and then slips it into his pocket. He's the complete opposite of Tim.

"Hey, Mark," I say, suddenly filled with regret at how this conversation went. This isn't how any of it was supposed to go. I thought for sure I could get things back under control, but maybe I was wrong. Maybe things are too far gone for me to be able to fix them. "Hang on a second—I want to talk to you. Really talk to you, okay?"

But he doesn't slow down. I feel my foot catch in the blanket, and I swear, yanking hard on the top of it to try to free it and untangle myself. Finally, my foot is free, and I stand, unwrapping the blanket, ready to try to run after him and catch him before he reaches Abby, but before I can do that, everything goes dark.

It sounds like the entire B&B is holding its breath. All of the sounds that were playing in the background, the heat running, the electric bulbs buzzing, the way the stove clicks on and off, it's all quiet.

I suck in air, filling my lungs, then exhale, closing my eyes for a moment. Maybe, when I open them, the power will be back. The lights will be back on, and Mark will have turned around so the two of us can talk. He'll realize that I want to hash things out with him, that the best option he has to make the rest of our time together as pleasant as possible is to talk to me.

But when I open them, Mark is gone.

The power is still out.

And I can't help but wonder which one of my family members figured out how to turn it off.

THIRTY

LOTTIE

"Well, I checked the breaker box and it definitely wasn't user error. There's no cell service either because our Wi-Fi got knocked out. It sure would be great if cell service extended up this way and we didn't have to rely on Wi-Fi." Mark walks into the kitchen, a flashlight bobbing in his hand. I know he sees me because the beam sweeps over me, but instead of talking to me, he walks over to Abby.

She's at the stove, dressed in an apron, Henry at her feet. I watch as he takes her by the hand and gives it a squeeze.

"I wish we could afford a whole-house generator. I know it's been on the to-do list for a while, but we might need to make it top priority." She pauses, chewing her lower lip for a moment. "I wonder how long we'll be out this time." She sounds worried. In fact, the entire kitchen feels on edge. Even though I know I should be relieved that Tim or Chelsea didn't turn off the power, maybe it would have been better if it had been one of them.

At least then we'd be able to turn it back on.

Even in here, with the stove going and the oven still hot from baking, I can feel the chill. This place is going to be downright cold soon, and I'm hoping we can all stay warm in our rooms without having to move downstairs to be by the fireplace.

"Oh, it could be a week." Mark runs his hand through his hair. His back is to me, and I can't take my eyes off him. "I'm grateful you're so on top of the grocery runs. I don't know what we'd do if you didn't keep us all stocked up. And you already got out the blankets, right?"

"Right." Abby nods. "We keep extra long underwear around if anyone needs to borrow it. Worst-case scenario is everyone moving into the living room, but I'd rather avoid that if possible. I guess they could sleep in there and we could sleep in here with the oven and stove if there wasn't any other choice. Thank goodness we have a gas stove."

"Let's hope it won't come to that. You ready to set the table?"

Mark doesn't give her a chance to respond. Instead, he steps to the side and opens the oven, sending a wave of heat through the kitchen, along with the delicious scent of whatever Abby was baking. He carries the dish over to the table and sets it in front of me before turning back to his son.

"Do you want to ring the bell, Henry?"

He could have easily asked me to get Tim and Chelsea myself. Instead, I sit and watch as he hands a giant bell to Henry, who grins as he shakes it. Abby walks over to the table with a lighter.

"Do you mind lighting the candles?" She offers it to me, and I reach out without thinking, taking it and clicking it on. "I figured they'd be best for dinner tonight. It's not like they'll put off much heat, but they will make it possible for us to actually see what we're eating."

"You got it." I move quickly, lighting them all the way down the table. Just when I'm about to take the lighter back to Abby, Chelsea and Tim walk in. She stalks in front of him, her head down, the glow from her phone lighting up her face.

"Do you not have internet if the power is out?" Chelsea's voice is loud. Grating. "How am I supposed to keep in touch with my friends if I don't have internet?"

"No internet, no landline, and no cell service," Mark tells her, walking past her to the table with a basket of dinner rolls. "Welcome to the Dark Ages, Chelsea. Population, six."

She doesn't laugh.

"Well, it won't be such a terrible thing to be cut off from the rest of the world for a while, will it?" Abby asks my daughter. "Now, if everyone will join us at the table, we can eat while the food is still warm."

She scoops Henry up from the floor and brings him to sit. Unlike any other meal we've had together before though, she pulls his chair as close as possible to her.

I don't know if anyone else notices, but I do.

"This smells amazing." Mark sits across from me but addresses his wife. "Pork roast, right? And roasted veggies and fresh bread. You outdid yourself, Abby. As always."

"It does smell great." Tim serves himself without waiting for anyone else to reach for the food. "And I'm starving, so don't mind if I do." He piles food high on his plate and shovels in a mouthful while Chelsea reaches for a roll. "You're a hell of a cook, Abby, you know that? No wonder Mark sticks around."

I freeze.

"Mom."

Chelsea lightly taps me on the shoulder. When I turn to her, I'm surprised to see she's holding the bread basket out for me.

"Pay attention."

"Sorry," I mutter, grabbing the basket and dropping a roll on my plate. I have to lean to the side to hand the basket over Henry's head to Abby. She takes it from me without remark.

"Well, I'm sure my cooking isn't the only reason Mark sticks around," Abby says, glancing first at her husband, then at mine.

"After all, we promised each other to be together forever. And we have Henry."

I shift in my seat. Without turning completely to the left, I'm not going to be able to get a good look at her or the expression on her face. Instead of risking it, I keep my eyes on the food as it's passed.

"Ahh, yes, Henry," Tim says. The flickering flames between us cast strange shadows on my husband's face. "I can only imagine how much you love him. Haven't you ever been worried about his safety, inviting strangers into your home the way you do?"

"This was the life we chose to live together, and we've never had a problem with our guests," Mark says with a shrug. "Right, Abby?"

Abby laughs. "Right. Well, except for people staying with us when they don't feel great and bringing their germs, we've never had a problem. I love it. Love meeting new people." She leans forward, resting her chin in her hand. "You don't think you'd like it, Tim?"

"No, not a chance. All of those people coming in and out all the time and you not knowing who they really are?" Tim holds his hands up like he's surrendering. When he speaks again, he's looking at Mark. "I know how much you love Henry. How much you love your family. How far you're willing to go for them. That's all I'm saying. It's strange to me, knowing the lengths you'd go to in order to protect your family, that you'd be willing to let strangers in your house. I don't think I could do it. Put Chelsea in danger like that?" He chuckles, shakes his head. "Not a chance."

Chelsea snickers. If I were closer to her, I'd stop her. I'd put my hand out, try to make her be polite, be quiet, but she's too far away for me to do anything but sit and listen.

"Why is that funny?" Abby turns to look at my daughter, her brows knit together.

"She laughs when she's uncomfortable," I blurt out, trying to draw attention away from Chelsea.

It works. Both Mark and Abby turn to look at me.

"I'm sorry," I say, not wanting to be the center of attention but also not wanting either of them to look back at Chelsea. "This is a lot more stressful than I think any of us thought it would be. Getting snowed in here? And everyone is so tense." I shiver.

"It is stressful."

Mark's agreeing with me, and I can't help but feel a flash of pleasure at that fact. Still, when I turn back to look at him, I'm not surprised to see he's staring at Abby.

"Having guests here can be stressful. Do you not remember when the McKenzies came to stay with us? It felt like pure chaos every moment of their stay."

Abby relaxes a bit. Next to her, Henry is studiously stuffing his face full of bread.

"You're right," she finally says. "I think we're all a little tired of being stuck inside, and now that the power is out, things are going to be even more tense. I think it's best if we all finish our dinner and then retire to bed. That way we can get under the covers and try to stay as warm as possible."

"Sounds like a plan," Tim replies. "This is delicious, Abby. And let me be the first one to apologize for the way things have gone since we got here. I promise you, we don't normally bring the chaos with us wherever we go."

"It's fine." Abby sounds like she's smiling. "Let's all remember that being locked in a house together can be more stressful than you realize. We'll eat, clean up down here, gather what we need to take upstairs, and head to bed. Sounds lovely."

It doesn't though. The only thing I want to do right now is try to hash things out with Mark. I want to know where the two of us stand. If he's talked to Tim and if he's going to do what my husband wants.

I have a thousand questions to ask him, but in order to do that, I'm going to have to get him on his own. Without Abby knowing what I'm doing.

And without him trying to run away from me so he can avoid our talk.

I'm running out of time. One of us is going to walk away from this with the thing we want.

And it's going to be me.

THIRTY-ONE

MARK

You know what I hate? Clichés. I hate the way they're used whenever people can't think of a better way to describe what's going on around them. They're lazy, they're messy, and they're overused, but I can't seem to come up with a better way to think about how terrible things are here:

The tension is so thick you could cut it with a knife.

Abby's so cold she seems frozen.

Company that stays longer than three days smells like bad fish.

That last one might not be right, but I can't seem to get my mind working any better to come up with a nicer way to explain it all. I'm exhausted, Abby looks haunted, and the only people who seem to be enjoying themselves are our son and our guests.

Nothing is good.

Dinner was terrible, all of us around the table, each of us talking around our secrets as the wind roared outside. From time to time, it rattled the shutters so hard Abby would wince. I knew she was thinking about how much she loved painting them and having them hung to give the house a more welcoming look.

Now I can only imagine the amount of damage we might find when the snow melts. I want to get out of here, but to do that I need new truck cables and possibly also a new battery. I can't walk to town, not even with the snowshoes Tim tried to use, and there's no way I'm asking to borrow his Jeep.

He'd come with me. The two of us locked together in a vehicle, no way to get out and free myself without sinking up to my knees in snow... That's the stuff of nightmares right there, I swear it is.

It's even worse than being trapped with him in the house without power.

I'm in the living room putting more wood on the fire so it'll burn through the night. Every time I hear a noise behind me, I jerk around, looking for which of the Rowes might be coming in here to talk to me before we all go to bed.

Tim wants more money than we have on hand, and while I could have gone to the bank to talk to them about a loan, the damn storm blew in worse than anyone thought and here we are, all of us locked together in our own personal hell.

There's a soft knock on the doorframe, which is laughable considering how I feel like any privacy we had in the house is gone. I turn to see who it is, fully expecting it to be Tim telling me he wants the money, but it's Lottie.

She wrings her hands as she walks into the room. Her eyes are downcast and shadowed, but there's an expression on her face I don't like.

"Hey, are you busy?" Her voice is low. Down the hall I can hear Abby thunking around in the kitchen.

"I put Henry to bed and now I'm keeping the fire going." I'm wary of all of the Rowes, but part of me is worried for Lottie. I don't know if I've ever seen her looking this nervous about anything.

Maybe when the blackmail started.

He just asked for money, didn't he? *Demanded* it. And I,

like an idiot, handed it over, desperate to do whatever it took to keep Abby from learning the truth.

He said it was a one-time thing and I was stupid enough to believe him.

This is all on me.

"I'm scared." She looks up at me then away again. It's long enough for me to see the tears glistening in the corners of her eyes. "Mark, I'm sorry to drop this on you. I know it isn't fair, but I'm scared."

"Of what?" I keep my voice low. "What are you scared of?"

She doesn't answer at first and I'm about to ask her again or maybe leave the room, or *something*, but she gives her head a little shake. Clears her throat.

"Tim."

"You're scared of Tim?"

A nod. "I don't know what he's going to do to me when he gets this money." Her fingers twist against each other so hard her knuckles turn white. "You know how he gets, so angry and focused on something. He wants the money, and as soon as he gets it..." Her voice trails off.

"As soon as he gets it, what? What is he going to do?" Without thinking, I cross the room and take her by the shoulders, giving them a little squeeze so she'll look at me. "What are you trying to say to me, Lottie?"

"I'm scared, that's all." She pulls back so my hands drop from her shoulders. "You get that, right? I mean, you know Tim."

Not the way she does. I know Tim, the man coming at me for money, always with his hand out, always wanting to make sure I don't forget to pay him so he won't *accidentally* tell Abby about our deal. I deal with him and then return home to my wife, my son, and I try to forget he exists until he reaches back out to me.

"Does he hurt you?"

A long pause. "Yes."

Oh my God. I knew he was a terrible person, knew he couldn't be trusted, but to hurt his wife? That's worse than I thought. I reach for her, my hand shaking, then instead clench it into a fist at my side.

I can't turn my back on her. She needs help.

But what choice do I have?

I have to protect my family first.

"What are you going to do?"

She stares at me, her eyes searching my face like she's not entirely sure she heard me correctly. "What am *I* going to do?"

I nod.

"You're not going to help me? Mark, he's..." She pauses, giving her head a little shake. "Tim isn't safe. You don't think he's going to stop, do you? What did he tell you he wanted?"

"More money."

"How much more?"

"He hasn't given me a number. But it's a lot."

She sighs, exasperated, letting her hands fall down by her sides. Her palms smack against her legs, and I wince at the sound.

"Do you see what he's doing? He's leading you on, like he always does with people. What, you really believe him when he says that this is going to be the last time he comes to you for money? Are you that naive?"

I don't answer her, not because I don't want to, but because I honestly don't know what to say to her. She's so intense, staring at me like she'll be able to see through to my private thoughts, and all I want is some space, some time to try to figure things out.

"Mark. Do you believe him? Because if you do, you're—"

I cut her off, not wanting to know what she thinks I am. "I want him out of here, Lottie. I want him to go. Do you really think I'm enjoying this? That I find this, what? Fun? No." I scoff, rubbing my hand down my jaw. I need to shave and the sound of my skin against my stubble is loud.

"I don't know if you're taking it seriously. He's never going to stop. That's not who he is. I know you think it'll disappear, that *he'll* disappear, but you're wrong. Tim isn't going anywhere until he gets what he wants." She grabs my hand, clinging to me like she's drowning.

When I move to pull away, she tightens her grip. Her eyes are locked on mine, watery and wide as she stares at me like I'm the one who can fix everything.

And I guess, in her mind, I could.

But I'd lose so much doing that.

I need to smooth this over.

"No. No, I'm not saying that. What I'm saying... shit. What I'm saying is that I'll figure out how to deal with Tim. I don't have the money now, but I'll get it."

"You think it'll stop him? You think it won't all come back to haunt you?"

There's a threat there, very thinly veiled. I stiffen.

"What have you done?"

Lottie takes a step back, shaking her head. But it's not convincing.

"Lottie, what are you going to do?" There's desperation in my voice, and I hope she doesn't pick up on it, but the expression on her face tells me she has.

There's triumph there, in the way she arches her brow, how she purses her lips together. Lottie is a smart woman, even though she doesn't always make the best decisions. She knows when someone has messed up, when they're weak.

And I have no doubt she's willing to take advantage of the situation.

"I don't know. But I know what I want. I need to be free from Tim." She stabs her finger into my chest. "You see that, don't you? Chelsea and I need to get away from him. You can help us; I know you can." She pauses, chewing her lower lip. "Figure it out."

With that, she turns away and stalks out of the living room. Her perfume floats behind her, dusky and rich, like wet earth in the woods, like cinnamon sticks and chai, and I breathe it in, suddenly unable to move. My life as I thought it is falling apart, the ground tilting under my feet, everything I thought I knew and had planned no longer sturdy, no longer safe.

I have to get this family out of my house.

Resolution pours through me and I follow Lottie from the room, grabbing her arm and pulling her back.

She gasps, spins in my grip. Her eyes are wide, locked on mine, her breathing shallow. When I loosen my grip, she steps back, her hands clenched into fists.

"Leave Abby alone," I say. "And Henry. Lottie, don't push me. Let me figure out what to do. I'll figure out how to handle Tim. I'll get out of the mess I made and make sure he doesn't hurt you again."

Her eyes light up.

Good. Make her think I've got this under control. If I can keep her happy, keep her thinking I'm going to help her, then maybe I'll have enough time to figure out how to protect my family. *And how to keep my secret.*

Because right now I'm not sure how to do either.

THIRTY-TWO

ABBY

I plunge my hands into the soapy water, doing it as quickly as possible so I don't chicken out and jerk my hands out of it. It's freezing.

But at least we have water. The pipes haven't frozen, thank goodness for that, and while I didn't think that was going to happen with this storm, it's happened before in the past. And I'm not looking forward to all of us stumbling around in here together, reeking.

So, the water is cold, but I can wash our dishes. We can wash up, even if it's just a fast sink shower.

I shiver at the thought.

"I'm going to put Henry to bed, okay?" Mark drops a kiss on the top of my head, but I don't turn around for another one. "You got things under control in here?"

"Sure do. Hey, lock the second-floor door, okay?"

"Are you sure that's necessary?" I hate the surprise in Mark's voice.

"I think it's a good idea," I tell him. It's almost impossible to keep my voice light and happy, but I don't want him to know how bothered I am by what's going on. It's obvious to me that

Tim and Lottie came here with ulterior motives, but it's impossible for me to read Lottie. I see the way she watches Mark though.

Just how I see the way Chelsea watches him.

So why haven't I confronted them? They're guests in *my* house, right? Sure, but I need to come across unruffled, in control. It's the only way I'll get what I want out of this. Me confronting them doesn't get me what I want in the end.

Even though I *know* the door didn't lock on accident. Someone here is playing games with me.

"Night, Mama," Henry says, his little voice heavy with sleep, and this time I do turn around, to give him a kiss. He plants one in return on my cheek, and I watch as the two of them walk out of the kitchen. It's quiet down here. One of the Rowes already went upstairs, but I heard someone in the living room a bit ago.

After the uncomfortable dinner, I'm glad they're out of my kitchen. They all wanted to help clean up, the hustle and bustle in the kitchen too much for me, and I had to step out until the table was cleared. Now I've kicked them all out so I can get it cleaned up. As uncomfortable as it is having them here, I keep reminding myself that it's almost over. That it will all be worth it in the end.

I wash the dishes quickly, leaving them to dry in the drainer, then package up the leftovers to put outside on the porch. They'll keep just fine out there, and I won't have to open the refrigerator and risk spoiling the food inside. Maybe the power will come back on tomorrow and this will be a distant memory, but judging from the way the wind slams into the side of the house, I doubt it.

I wipe my hands on a towel, then pick up a candle and walk over to the coffee station. In the morning I can boil some water on the gas stove and then make coffee in the French press. It won't be quite the same thing as turning on the kettle and letting the machine do the work, but I'll take any and all caffeine I can get.

So, to make it as easy as possible, I figure I might as well measure out the grounds. That way, when I do stumble downstairs bright and early, all bleary-eyed and dying for something to wake me back up, all I'll have to do is boil the water and pour it in the press.

The smell of coffee grounds makes me smile when I open the canister and reach for the scoop. The candlelight is flickering and not very bright, but I can still easily see what I'm doing.

That's when I see what's written on the notepad.

For a moment, I freeze, then I drop the scoop back down in the coffee. My hands feel like they're on autopilot as I push the canister out of the way so I can get a better look at the note. When I pick it up, my hand trembles, and I have to grab the candle and hold it up as well so I can get a better look at what's written on the paper.

My stomach turns and I press my knuckles against my lips.

I won't throw up.

I'm already cold from the heat in the house turning off when we lost power, but now the chill that races through me is far worse. I feel it deep in my bones, the kind of chill that you only get when something is terribly wrong.

You made a huge mistake inviting us in.

That's what the note says. I don't know who wrote it, don't know which of the three guests in my house would have the guts to scrawl something like that on the notepad when I'd stepped out of the kitchen for a moment, but I do know one thing.

I'm in trouble.

THIRTY-THREE

LOTTIE

Maybe everything is going to work out. I can't help but feel excited about that prospect. Tim will get what he wants, or maybe I'll finally be the one to get what I want. I'll be the one to come out on top, which is something that's never happened in my life. Maybe I'll—

The soft glow of a phone screen makes me stop short.

Chelsea's walking towards me from the front door, using her phone as a guide. She moves it back and forth in front of her, looking around her like she's trying to memorize the space. As soon as she reaches me at the bottom of the stairs, I loop my arm through hers and pull her close, yanking her down the hall away from the living room, towards the stairs.

Why is she so cold?

"What were you doing?"

She whips around to face me. Though her clothing is too big for her, I can tell from her stance, from the way she squares off against me, even from the set of her chin, that she's annoyed.

If there's one thing about Chelsea that I know she hates, it's that she's easy for me to read, no matter what's going through her head. She's always been terrible at hiding her emotions.

"I was exploring for a bit. Now I was going to go hang out by the fire."

"You don't need to be *hanging out* anywhere right now. We're all supposed to go up to our rooms."

She shrugs. "What's Abby going to do, Mom? Kick us out? Lock us up? Please. The power is out, it's cold, and I want to warm up. It's not a crime."

"God, Chelsea," I groan, letting her go so I can massage my temples. There's a monster of a migraine coming on—I feel it. It's pounding right behind my eyes, and the longer I stand here arguing with my daughter and trying to talk some sense into her, the worse it's going to get.

"What? You want to act all high and mighty now? You're the one letting Dad blackmail Mark. You think I don't know where the money comes from?" She's whisper-yelling at me, each word aimed like a bullet, but I guess I should be grateful that at least her voice is low.

What?

The ceilings here are high, the foyer mostly empty. I'm worried about our words echoing in the space, but Abby hasn't appeared yet. Maybe she won't for a minute. Maybe she's still cleaning up after dinner or putting the leftovers in the snow like she mentioned she would. Outside, wind batters against the front door, sending cold fingers of air around its frame.

"I want you to stay away from Mark. And Abby. Your dad and I have a plan; we've got this all under control. He's—"

"Oh, stop, Mom. I know. I know it all."

When I stare at her, she grins right back at me. How did I never notice the way she stares at me, like she's looking through me? How have I ignored the sick flip-flop my stomach makes when I see this expression on her face?

"You and Dad need to figure out a better place to talk than in the kitchen. I can hear everything through the vent. It comes right up into my room." She mimes something floating through the air and I can picture her now, her ear pressed against the floor vent, her eyes greedy, soaking up everything Tim and I were saying.

"You should have told me you knew." My voice is flat.

"Why? So you'd leave me at home? Not a chance, Mom. I wanted to come. I wanted to be here for everything."

"You'll ruin your dad's plan. Don't you see how careful we have to be, Chelsea? Don't you want things to be better than they are now?" Maybe if I convince her of that, if she understands what's really at stake here, she'll back off.

"Have some faith in me, Mom." She reaches out, pats my shoulder. "You want me to have faith that you and Dad are making the right move for our family, right?

I nod, unable to say anything.

"Well, I want you to trust me that I'm making the right move for me. Everyone will get what they want, okay? Relax."

Relax, right.

She brushes past me, knocking hard into me with her shoulder. Typical. I can't help inhaling to stay calm as I turn to see her go, watching how she wanders down the hall to the living room. I saw the drive in her face, how she obviously isn't going to back down from this.

She thinks she's in control.

Only one person in our family can be in control and right now it's just Tim and me vying for it. If Chelsea thinks for a moment she's going to come out on top, then who knows what she'll end up doing.

Tim and I came with a plan, and I have no doubt in my mind that Chelsea could easily screw it all up.

Then it hits me.

I know exactly what she wants.

I exhale hard like someone punched me and reach out, resting my palm flat on the wall for support.

Maybe she and I can both get what we want.

But I can't let her screw this all up.

I have to rein her in. But when someone knows your biggest secret and can destroy everything you've worked for, how in the world do you manage that without that person taking you down with them?

THIRTY-FOUR

ABBY

None of this is going to plan. None of it—from the creepy note left on my notepad, to the power getting knocked out so we're all stumbling around the B&B in the dark—is how I thought any of this would go.

And even though I want to scream at how unfairly this is going, I have to remain calm.

I have to make Mark think nothing is bothering me. He can't know about my plan or the fact that it's getting closer and closer to coming to fruition.

He just has to see me as Abby, the stupid but loving wife, completely oblivious to everything going on around her.

That's the only way this will work.

I could confront them, could point fingers and kick them out, but this is something I've been working towards for so long that I don't want to ruin it now. I'm so close.

So, instead of freaking out or jumping the gun to put my plan in motion, I stay the course. Pretend to be normal. I had a load of laundry in the dryer right when the power clicked out, and now I have to dig it all out, find places to hang it up, hope nothing will be too wrinkled, because it's not like I'm going to have access to an iron anytime soon.

When I get this taken care of, I'll check on Henry, then head to bed.

I squat down and pull a bath towel from the dryer. It's damp, the fabric heavy and wet, and I groan as I yank it free from the tangle of other laundry. Holding it in my hands, I turn in a slow circle as I look for a good place to hang it up. Even though I asked him a few times, Mark never got around to installing indoor clotheslines in the laundry room for me. I guess I could take it into the bathroom and loop it over the shower curtain.

With a sigh, I drop it into the laundry basket and squat back down, digging out two more towels. There's no way there will be enough room in the bathroom to hang all of this up, but luckily there are plenty of other options in a place this big.

I grab the basket, tuck it against my hip, then pick up the flashlight waiting for me on the dryer. After our first winter here, I learned the value of having flashlights scattered throughout the house. Most of them are in the kitchen, but I had this one tucked up in a cabinet with the laundry supplies. Even Henry has his own in his room, one he loves to use when we turn off the lights and play hide-and-seek.

The beam of light is weak, but I know this place well enough to walk around in the dark without it. Still, I don't want to scare anyone by sneaking up on them.

The memory of the note I found eats at me. I keep turning it over and over in my mind, trying to decide who might have left it for me, but it's impossible for me to come to a conclusion. Rather than allowing it to paralyze me, I keep working. If I hurry in here, I can sit in Henry's room for a few minutes before going to bed myself.

If I could only sit by his crib and watch him while he slept, I would. But I have things to do. Mark will take care of him.

Mark locked him on the second floor at bedtime. At least, I hope he did.

Worry chews at the back of my mind. Mark seemed frazzled when I asked him to put Henry to bed, and what if he forgot to lock the door?

No. He wouldn't.

I adjust the basket on my hip. It presses into my flesh, hard, but I barely focus on the pain.

I'm thinking about when someone locked me in my room.

Of the creepy note on my notepad.

Of how the power is out and how anyone could be watching me without me knowing. Cold trickles down my spine and I pause in the door, shining my flashlight around, cutting through the shadows, hoping I don't see any movement, any proof of someone staring at me.

There's nothing. The house is still, hushed. Even the wind has quieted down for the first time in days. It feels like time is suspended here.

I'm acting insane.

The thought makes me scowl.

"Abby!"

Mark steps out of the shadows right in front of me as I'm about to head up to the second floor to hang up these towels. Henry can help me hang up his underwear tomorrow; I think he'll find it funny.

"Hey, have you seen the monitor so we can keep an ear out for Henry? He went down okay, but I couldn't find it." He rubs the back of his neck.

"You just put him to bed, didn't you? Henry's fine." I eyeball him, trying to figure out if he's been drinking. He blinks as the light lands on his face. As soon as I do, I hate that I had to. What kind of mom needs to worry about whether or not her husband is sober all the time?

"Of course I did." He exhales like he can't believe I'd question him. "But I couldn't find the monitor to turn it on. Do you have it?"

"Yep, it's right here." I have to put the laundry basket down on the floor to dig into my apron pocket. "Hang on—these pockets are deep."

I pull it out, feeling vindicated, then turn it so Mark can get a look at it.

He snatches it from me. "It's not on."

"Let me see it." I fumble the knob for a moment before giving it a twist, back and forth, clicking the monitor off and on. It's a satisfying noise as the knob twists, one I've heard hundreds of times by now, and the sound of it must be like a hit of heroin is to an addict.

Relaxing.

Comforting.

Just bliss, the pure knowledge that someone somewhere might have thought you messed up, but you salvaged it and there isn't anything wrong with how you're handling things. It's on, it's on, *it has to be on*, and since there's no sound coming from it, I'm more than confident that Henry is fine.

But the lights across the top of it aren't flashing. It never turned on. There's no sound not because that's proof my son is fine, but because it's didn't turn on in the first place.

I flip it over, my fingers trembling as I pop open the back. Mark moves to my side, shining his flashlight into the empty battery compartment.

They're gone.

My breath catches in my throat, and I reach up to massage my neck, like that will help me breathe. They're gone, the batteries are gone, but where would they be? How would they be missing?

Who took them?

"Why would you take the batteries out?" Mark stares at me like he's trying to read my mind.

"I didn't." My voice is low, cold. A chill races through my body and I shiver, turning the monitor over once more in my hands, like that's going to make the batteries suddenly appear. "I didn't, Mark; why would I do that?"

He exhales. "Okay, it's no problem. Everything's fine. But I'm still going to check on him."

He spins away from me, moving erratically, and I wonder again if he's drunk. Before I realize what I'm doing, I reach out and grab his arm, yanking him back so he can't leave me.

"Who the hell would take the batteries out?" My throat is tight. I choke out the words as my fingers sink into his arm. "Mark, what happened to them?"

"I don't know. The batteries? I don't have any idea, Abby. Just... I'm going to go check on him."

"I'm going with you."

Leaving the basket of damp laundry where it is and sticking the monitor back in my pocket, I shine the flashlight down the hall and hurry towards the stairs, well aware Mark is right behind me.

"Abs, let me look." There's a worried tone in his voice that I don't like.

"I've got it." I'm hurrying up the stairs now, my feet pounding into them. "Henry!" I'm too far away for him to hear me yet and I know that. "Henry!"

"Abby, let me go. I'll go down there and make sure he's okay, make sure the missing batteries were an accident."

Mark's hand is on my shoulder. He's pulling me back. We're right at the top of the stairs, poised to turn down the hall to our private wing, but I don't want him to beat me there. If something is wrong with Henry—and dear *God* don't let there be anything wrong with Henry—I'm not letting Mark see it first.

"He's my son, Mark. Let me go to him." I'm frustrated with him now, the flashlight bouncing in my hand, an erratic circle of light as I push Mark out of the way, not worried one bit about the grunt he makes when he slams his shoulder into the wall. I'm running now, even though the hall isn't very long, well aware that I need to get to Henry now.

Before. Something. Happens.

My lungs feel like they're going to burst as I throw his bedroom door open and run inside. Without thinking, I reach for the light switch. Click it up. Back down.

I swear, then use my flashlight to hurry across the room to where his crib is set up, right between the two windows that overlook the front yard of the property.

I know he's old enough to be in a toddler bed. I've known that for a while and considered moving him from his crib, but there's something safe about the slats, about the memory of laying him down in it to sleep, that prevents me from swapping it out for a bed.

But maybe now I will.

Maybe a race car. Rocketship. Something all boy, like Henry. He loves his Spider-Man flashlight, the one he keeps by his crib and uses when the two of us are playing hide-and-seek in the dark. It's one of our favorite games—his because he gets to be sneaky, mine because it's quiet.

The slats of the crib cast strange jail-cell shadows onto the mattress as I cross the room, the flashlight in my hand bouncing even more now. I'm crying, hot tears running down my cheeks even though I don't know *for sure* that anything bad has actually happened.

Except I do know, don't I? I knew it the moment I saw the empty battery compartment.

The crib is empty.

Henry is gone.

I made a mistake inviting the Rowes into our home.

"Abby."

I whip around, not wanting to see Mark but needing to know for sure if he's feeling the same stabbing, terrible pain I am. Without remorse, I shine the light right in his eyes, and even though he lifts his hands to try to block it, even though he can almost stop the light from burning his irises, I don't care, and I don't drop the flashlight.

"Where is he?" My words are pure venom. I imagine them as arrows, aimed right at my husband's heart, all of them hitting him where it hurts, where maybe he can understand why I want to kill him right now.

"Abby, let me—"

"You were supposed to lock the door! Keep them away from him! Where is my son?" I scream at him now, not caring who hears, not caring if Chelsea and Lottie and Tim hear me screaming because they need to hear me; they need to hear my rage and my torment and know that I'm coming for them.

Someone did something to my baby boy.

And even though it's my fault, even though I'm the one who set this all in motion, who took the steps that resulted in my sweet baby being taken from his room, even though judge and jury would convict and I'd deserve every last thing they decided to do to me, I'm going to find him.

And then they'll pay.

THIRTY-FIVE

ABBY

I feel like I'm flying as I run down the stairs. Mark is behind me, so close I feel like his breath is *right there* on the back of my neck, but I don't turn around and I don't slow down, not even when my heel slips off a step and I hover there in midair for a moment, my heart in my throat, gravity grasping at me, clawing at my weight, trying to pull me down to the ground, before I find my footing.

"Henry!" I'm screaming for him, my throat raw.

Maybe somehow he got out of his crib and decided to hide. I didn't see his Spider-Man flashlight, so he could think we're playing a game. *It's possible, right?* But even as I try to convince myself of that, I know what I saw in the baby monitor.

Missing batteries.

And then there was the note. Someone locking me in my room.

Besides that, there's no way he got out of his crib on his own. He hasn't tried, not once, not even when I got busy with bread dough in the kitchen and could hear him calling for me but knew I needed to finish what I'd started before heading up the stairs to him.

That's my Henry. He's a good boy.

And now he's gone.

I stumble as I reach the bottom floor. "Where is he?" The words leave my mouth in a screech.

Lottie's walking through the hall and I clutch at her, the flashlight falling forgotten from my hand to the floor. I hear the dull thud it makes when it hits the ground and I know I need to pick it back up to resume my search, but I can't let go of her arms, can't walk away from her when she might know something.

"Who?" She grabs me back, gripping my arms tight.

Mark's right behind me. I feel his presence there and I turn to him, my mind whirling as I try to figure out what to do.

"Henry's missing." Mark's voice is tight. There's something there, some hint of knowledge that I don't want to admit to hearing.

He knows more than he's letting on.

"Did you take my boy?" I turn back on Lottie, who steps away from me. She's faster than I am, and even though I reach for her, my hands close on empty air. "Did you do something to him? I trusted you, as a mother! I thought you would leave him alone! What is wrong with you?"

"No!" The word is explosive. "No! I didn't do anything. I wouldn't."

Is that a lie? I can't see her face, not in the dark like this, and I bend down to grab the flashlight, then shine it at her.

"Then help me find him." I'm appealing to her not as the woman I know she really is but as a mother. I have to hope she'll see the pain on my face, hear it in my voice, help me, not because she likes me and not because I like her, but because we're both mothers.

"Please." I'm panting. When she doesn't immediately respond, I groan, clutching at my throat. "Please help me find him."

"I'll look in our rooms." She gives a little nod and brushes past me, grabbing the handrail as she practically runs up the stairs.

I whip around to look at Mark. "You," I tell him, fighting the urge to scream. "I want you looking on our floor. Look in all our rooms, under the beds, in the closets. He has to be here somewhere, and we need to find him."

Mark pauses, for just a moment. But then he nods and turns, hurrying up the stairs behind Lottie. I wait as they go for a moment then turn around, my mind racing as I try to picture where Henry might be.

Where would someone have put him? What would they want with him in the first place?

There's still a tiny bit of hope that Henry got out of his crib and left his room, the soft glow of his flashlight bouncing ahead of him. We only put older batteries in his flashlight so he can still see but so he won't accidentally hurt his eyes with a super bright light if he looks into it. Maybe that's what happened—he does love playing with me in the dark. Even though I'm sure, in my heart, that's not what happened, I still cling to the hope.

There's a pit in my stomach and all I can think is that something terrible happened to my little boy.

Either he was taken from his crib or escaped on his own, but my question remains the same.

How the hell am I going to find him?

My knees threaten to give out, and I have to fight the desire to sink to the floor and let someone else handle this.

Because they won't. Nobody here loves my little boy the way I do. Nobody else in this house will go out on a limb for him like I will.

The kitchen.

Last week he thought it was funny to hide in the pantry, tucked between the big container of flour and a box of canned goods that I never got around to putting on the shelves. I only found him thanks to the soft glow from his flashlight clueing me in when I opened the door to peek in there.

Maybe he's there. Maybe someone put him in the pantry and he's tucked in there, stuffing his face with cookies or chocolate chips in an act of two-year-old defiance.

But even as I hope that, I know it's not true. Something about that doesn't feel right.

Still, I turn to the kitchen. The alternative is much too scary for me to consider.

As I'm walking into the kitchen, Chelsea appears. She has her phone out in front of her, the soft glow illuminating her path so she doesn't knock into anything.

"My phone's battery is going to die pretty soon," she says, her tone accusatory. Like I'm the one who knocked out the power.

Like I'm the one who got us all stuck in this house together.

Like I'm at all happy about this turn of events and the fact that these people are in my house, breathing my air, while all I want is Henry.

"Henry's missing," I blurt, ignoring her complaint. "Have you seen him?"

Just saying the words *Henry's missing* carves a hole in my chest, making it hard for me to breathe. I can't catch my breath, can't seem to inhale deeply enough to keep from feeling like I'm going to pass out.

"Henry?"

Is that amusement in her voice?

I tilt the flashlight so it's shining right in her eyes. She scrunches her nose and blinks as shadows play across her face, and for a second I think I see her laughing.

No. She wouldn't laugh about something like this.

She's got her own issues but she's not a monster.

"Have you seen him?" I take a deep breath and exhale, my

hand starting to cramp around the flashlight from how hard I'm gripping it. "He has to be here somewhere, but I can't find him."

One deep breath.

Another.

My hand drops, the light now shining mostly on her feet.

"Haven't seen him."

There it is again, that little quirk of a smile, but it's gone before I can train the light back on her face and see if it was even there in the first place.

But I think it was. I really think it was.

"Will you help me look?" I'm desperate now and I wonder if she can smell it on me, the way I can feel my terror seeping out through my pores. "Please. I need to make sure he's okay."

She stares at me. Takes a deep breath. Exhales. "I'm sure he's fine." Then she turns, obviously dismissing me even though I can taste my terror now.

Without thinking, I reach out and grab her arm, pulling her back. She stumbles a bit.

"Hey!"

"I'm sorry. I just—"

"He's fine. I'm sure of it."

She did something to my son.

But before I can make sense of that thought, she yanks her arm from my grasp. There's something about her tone, about how she spits the words at me, rapid-fire, that gives me pause, but this is not my child. She's not my family. There's literally nothing I can do to her to make her help me. I feel like I'm drowning and she's sitting there in a boat, the life preserver in her hands, her eyes locked on me, and she won't. Throw. It.

Throw the damn thing.

I wheel away from her and hurry through the kitchen. It takes me a moment to pause and glance under the table, the mass of chair legs confusing, but there's no bulk there, no Henry tucked away, waiting for me to find him. In the pantry it's the same, boxes of food there for the winter, but no Henry.

Everywhere I look, no Henry.

He has to be upstairs. I hesitate, then hurry to the stairs, wanting nothing more than to hold my little boy, to know he's okay, to make sure nothing terrible ever happens to him.

But before I can even grab the stair rail to help me ascend, I realize what I saw in the hall.

Snow. Kicked off on the floor. Someone was outside.

THIRTY-SIX

MARK

The sound of Abby crying reaches my ears. Even from the second floor I hear the way her voice rises and falls, warbling, like she can't catch her breath, like she can't get enough air in her lungs to stop the keening pouring from her lips.

I stumble to the stairs and look down into the black void that is our first floor. Henry wasn't up here. He wasn't hiding under beds or in the closets. He wasn't tucked away in the tub, the shower curtain wrapped around him like a shroud, his little flashlight creating a soft glow around him.

And I never heard him giggling as we searched for him. He's pretty good at being quiet, but he's never totally quiet. He's two.

But he's not here.

Where's my son?

Fear eats at me as I try to reconcile where my little boy could be, and the sound coming from Abby. I've never heard her make this sound, not when we were pregnant before and lost the baby, not when her doctor told her she wasn't sure if her body would even be strong enough to carry a child to term.

She's stoic. She keeps all her emotions locked deep in a box inside her, the threat of what would happen to her if she opened it so real, she's willing to refuse to show emotion about certain things.

And now she's almost screaming.

"Abby! I'm coming!"

I'm halfway down the stairs, Lottie right behind me, before I can make out what she's saying. Her words run together, all expelled in one long breath rather than in individual syllables, and I actually have to pause to be sure that I'm hearing her correctly.

"He's outside! He's outside! I know he is!" She's gasping for air, and I skid to a stop in front of her. "Someone took him! They got into the house and took him!"

"What do you mean, he's outside?"

Tim joins Lottie to watch me, but I grab my wife by the shoulders anyway, giving her a little shake. "Abby, take a breath! What do you mean, *he's outside*? Why would he be outside?"

She sobs and points past me, her hand shaking.

Immediately, I turn, unsure of what I'm going to see. What could be behind me that would have her so upset?

At first, I don't see anything.

My light illuminates the foyer. Shoes on the floor. A coat, slipped off and left in a puddle. And then—

"Oh my God."

I release Abby and run over to the front door. There's snow on the floor, snow on a boot. Without thinking, I bend and grab it. "Abby, it's your boot. This is your coat."

Abby thinks someone came in from the storm and took Henry, but that's not what it looks like to me.

She groans, squatting down on the floor, her head in her hands. "You have to find him, Mark." She looks up at me, her face pale when I shine my flashlight at her. "Promise me you'll go out there and find him."

"I'll go with you." Lottie steps over to the closet and yanks open the door, grabbing a coat and shrugging it on. "Chelsea, you too."

"Mom." Chelsea's voice is soft, but then she sighs. "Right, I'm coming."

"I'm staying in the house with Abby. To make sure she's okay." Tim sounds calm. In control.

Did he do this to my boy? Where has he been this entire time?

When I shine the light at him, he winces, reaching up with one hand to block his eyes. The last thing I want is for him to stay with Abby, but she's in no condition to go outside. He's got to stay here to keep her from doing anything stupid.

And maybe Henry is still inside the house. Maybe, even though I think I already know the truth, he'll appear while I'm outside stomping around in the snow, his little flashlight clutched in his hand, tired of playing and not being found.

Besides, Abby could easily follow us outside and get turned around in the storm. Losing Henry would be horrific, but losing them both would put me over the edge.

Right now, I don't know who to trust. But I do know I have to find my son.

It feels like a minute goes by before I'm able to find my voice.

"Okay," I say, grabbing a coat and tossing it to Chelsea. "Okay, we'll all go out. Split up but keep the house in sight. The last thing you want is to get too far away and not be able to find your way back. Snow is dangerous when it's coming down like this."

As if on cue, the wind picks up. It howls around the house, tapping at the windows, rattling the front door like something trying to get in. Already I feel the chill in my bones, and I know it's only going to get worse once I'm outside.

My zipper sticks for a moment and I yank it up, then swing my flashlight back to the others. "You two have a light?"

"I have my phone." Chelsea taps the screen a few times

until a thin glow appears. "It's not like I can use it to make calls or anything."

"I'll stick with her." Lottie swings her arm around Chelsea's shoulders.

I'm ready to argue with them, to explain that we'll have an easier time finding Henry if we split up and cover more ground, but the set of her jaw tells me to drop it. The sooner we get out there, the sooner we can bring him back in.

The better the chance he'll survive this.

"Okay. Remember, don't lose sight of the house. He's out there, and we have to get him back as quickly as we can. If you two find him, start yelling for me and we'll meet back here. I'll do the same for you."

There's a terrible feeling in my gut. Something about this is wrong, something is *more* than wrong, but we have to find Henry, and if that means relying on these two women to do that, then I don't have a choice.

But what if one of them did something to my son?

I push that thought away. I might be able to find him by myself, but the odds will be better if we have more people looking for him.

"Mark, hurry." It's Abby, and her plea is the thing that finally propels me forward. The door feels alive when I turn the knob. It flies open at me, cold air rushing in around me, making me brace my feet and lean forward into it so I don't get knocked over.

How in the world would Henry have managed this door on his own?

The snow on the floor. The strong wind. If Henry's outside, someone put him there. *Maybe someone came in from outside and took him.*

The thought hits me and I pause for a moment, horrified at what that might mean for my son.

"Let's go," I call to Chelsea and Lottie. I gesture to the open door, and they hurry past me, hoods up, thick coats obscuring any identifying features. It would be impossible to tell who was who if Chelsea weren't holding her phone, the flashlight casting a pale glow in front of them.

I follow, slamming the door hard behind me to ensure it sticks.

As soon as I'm outside, the wind tears around me, howling its way into my hood, whipping it back, choking me. It's freezing, and cold flakes bite into my skin. Holding the flashlight with my teeth, I pull my hood back up and yank the bungees to hold it in place.

Lottie and Chelsea have already made their way down the porch. Henry's name makes its way back to me on the wind as they call. I grab my flashlight again and follow them, turning to the left where they turn to the right.

We have to find him. The thought of him freezing to death out here, his little face blue, his heart stopping—

No. I won't think about that.

I also won't think about leaving Abby alone with Tim.

Right now, the only thing that matters is finding Henry.

THIRTY-SEVEN

LOTTIE

Stepping out into the storm with Chelsea, I'm terrified. The wind wails around us, throwing snow into our faces, and even though turning and running back into the house to let Chelsea find Henry by herself won't win me any medals of honor or valor, I want to do just that. My goal now is to walk away from this in one piece. Before I can do that though, we need to find Henry. Tim and I came here under false pretenses, yes. But that doesn't mean I want the little boy to die.

"Come on, Mom." Chelsea takes my hand, yanking me down the steps away from the B&B and also out of my thoughts. "We need to get him before Mark does."

What does she mean by that?

That doesn't make any sense. If Henry escaped and is outside in the cold, then why keep Mark from him? The only thing that matters is someone finding him before the unthinkable occurs.

I slip in the snow and grab her arm, carefully picking my way down the steps. Even with the light from Chelsea's phone and the flashlight I yank from my pocket, it's not easy to see.

Thank God there's a full moon, although, with the thick storm clouds overhead, it's difficult to make out much more than dark shapes.

"Here—he's over here." Chelsea sounds eager, even though it's difficult for me to make out her words. She's walking a little ahead of me, speaking back at me over her shoulder. "Come on —I think I hear him over here."

How can she hear him?

"Oh God, how is he?" I push forward, coming up next to her. "Chelsea, is he hurt?"

"Let's go see. He must be hiding under the truck, out of the snow. He must not have been able to find his way back to the house."

She turns, walking a few yards away from me, then bends, pulling something out from under the truck. I hear her murmuring but can't make out her words.

"Chelsea, we need to get him inside." I grab her arm, trying to turn Henry towards me so I can get a good look at him and tell if he's alive. "He needs to warm up, and we have to make sure he's okay. Trust me, it will all work out, okay? It'll be fine. We have to go. Now."

"He won't stop wiggling!" she cries as the child on her hip slips from her grasp. "Mom, can you grab him?"

Henry stumbles forward away from her—*almost like he was pushed*—and takes off, running in the other direction. He's wearing his PJs and has little hiking boots on, but that's not enough to keep him warm out here. He slips and falls, and I stare for a moment, almost unable to believe what's happening.

This is insane. This isn't why we came.

I need to intervene. I need to get to Henry and stop this madness, this running around outside. He has to be freezing—I know how cold I am, and he's been out here longer.

Chelsea turns and runs after Henry. She scoops him up and I exhale hard, sure that we're out of the woods, that the worst is over, but he slips free again, a scream ripping from his throat as he dodges her grabbing for him.

"You have to keep a grip on him!" I feel insane shouting at my daughter like this, but if she keeps letting him go, then we'll never get him back inside. Mark and Abby will never know how we tried to save him.

Why Chelsea can't just grab Henry and stop him from running, I don't know, but he keeps slipping from her grasp. I need to move, need to help. Snowflakes burn my cheeks, and I take off running after the two of them.

This is harder than it looks. Each step is a battle, and my lungs scream as I run. The light from my flashlight bobs ahead of me. A gust of wind knocks me off-balance.

"I got him!" Chelsea's voice floats back to me, and I pause for a moment, bending over and grabbing my thighs as I suck in huge breaths of freezing air. I'm not in shape to run like this, especially not when the air is so cold. Everything is whited out so it's impossible to tell exactly where we are, but I know one thing.

We're close to the cliffs.

But she's got him. He's okay.

"Stay there," I manage to call. "I'll come help!" They're so close to the cliffs now that if she were to let him go, he could run the wrong way, he could—

No, he's fine. Chelsea has him. We'll get him in, get him warmed up.

There's only black night in front of me, peppered with swirling white. Then, finally, a glow of light, and that's what I head towards.

The roar of the ocean grows louder as I chase after my daughter. I'm wary with every step, afraid that I'm going to get too close to the edge and go over, but I have to stop her from doing something stupid.

I have to save that little boy.

When I reach Chelsea, she has a tight grip on Henry. I shine my light into her face, but she doesn't wince away from it. Henry lets out a muffled cry.

"Honey, you're holding him too tight. You have to let him breathe." I reach for Henry, fully intending to pluck him from my daughter's grasp. We'll get him inside. He'll be fine.

"I have him!" Chelsea jerks away from me. She's shaking with rage, but her hand has slipped from Henry's mouth.

And then two things happen at once.

First, I reach for the little boy again, desperate to get the three of us away from the cliffs. It would be so easy to slip, and there's no way to undo a mistake like that.

And Henry inhales hard, breathing like his life depends on it, which I guess it does, then he screams.

Chelsea fumbles him and he slips from her grasp, sinking down to the ground at her feet.

"Shit! Come here, Henry!" I grab at him, snagging him by his arm and pulling him back from the edge. Before I can pick him up though, Chelsea is there, swinging him into her arms.

"You have to keep him in your arms!" I gasp, bending over to brace my hands on my thighs as I suck in a breath. "We have to go back to the house. We have to get him warm, and we don't want to have to explain that he kept getting away from you."

She doesn't answer.

I reach for her, take her by the arm. "Chelsea, come on. We need to get inside, not stand out here at the cliff."

The relentless pounding of the waves on the rocks makes me nervous.

"He's cold, Chelsea; he's been out here too long, and we still have to make it back to the house. Come on."

But then she laughs. "Mom, don't worry." She takes a deep breath and then screams. "Over here! I have him over here! By the cliffs!"

No. Why won't she just bring him to the house with me?

Mark's going to hear her. He's going to wonder why we have Henry so far from the house.

And if he jumps to the conclusion we had anything to do with Henry going missing, he's going to be livid.

THIRTY-EIGHT

MARK

The beam of light from my flashlight is barely strong enough to cut through the whirling snow. I feel like I'm trapped in a snow globe and someone has violently shaken it. It would be so easy to get lost out here, to wander out to the barn or the woods and not be able to find your way back.

The thought chills me and I stop to turn. Behind me, I can barely make out the B&B. The windows are dark—candles aren't bright enough to illuminate the building—but the bit of light from the moon is enough to outline the hulking building. If it starts snowing again though...

We have to hurry.

Being out here any longer than necessary could be deadly.

Henry.

"Hen!" I scream my son's name and take a few steps forward, leaning into the wind. "Henry, where are you?"

Nothing in response but the sound of the wind. I close my eyes against the biting snow and try to focus as best I can. Keeping Henry alive is the only thing that matters, and the only way I can do that is by finding him. I stand still, letting my body be buffeted by the wind, and listen.

There.

There's something there. It's difficult for me to make out what it is.

Someone screaming.

"Henry!" Even as his name leaves my lips, I feel silly. There's no way he'll be able to hear me, not when I can barely hear whoever is calling. "I'm coming!"

Down the driveway. Each step is more difficult than the last thanks to the snow caking my boots. I struggle to lift them high enough so I don't have to break my way through the deep mounds of the stuff. At my truck, I pause, leaning on it, then kick the tires, trying to break off some of the snow weighing me down.

"I'm coming!" My throat is already sore from how loud I'm screaming.

There's an answering cry and I push off the truck, pumping my arms now. I warned Chelsea and Lottie not to go too far from the B&B, that they might get lost and not be able to find their way back, and now I'm doing just that.

But I heard someone.

I know I did.

Across the road, there's only a small bit of land before the cliffs. In clear weather, Abby and I love to come out here to watch the waves crashing against the giant rocks below. It's not a beach with sand, not a pleasant place to stretch out on a blanket and drink a fruity little thing with a paper umbrella.

It's dangerous. The maw of a beast, dark and wild, the stormy sea forever lurching against the rocks before being sucked back out to the ocean.

Henry knows not to come out this far. He knows it's dangerous—I've told him that time and time again. But if he ended up outside somehow and then got turned around, if he thought he was headed to the front porch but was instead moving towards the cliffs—

Then he might go over.

The terror of Henry's little body pitching over the edge of the cliff to batter on the rocks below spurs me on.

"Henry!" Wind rips his name from my lips, and I try again. "Henry, I'm coming!"

"Over here!"

It's not Henry but I turn anyway, adjusting course, one hand gripping the flashlight, the other trying to block some of the snow from my face.

"Over here! Mark! Help!"

It's Lottie. Or Chelsea. I can't tell, not when the wind keeps ripping sound away like this, not when everything is so distorted, when the sea sounds even louder and angrier than usual. I see the person, the heavy jacket, the hood up. Then I see the other person. Holding Henry.

Henry, without a coat. He's writhing, trying to slip away from whoever's holding him. His cries reach my ears and, instead of listening to my screaming muscles and slowing down, I run faster.

He's there, he's right there, and I reach him, reach *for* him, but before I can get my hands on him and get him out of here, the person holding him speaks.

"I got him." Chelsea steps forward and around me. "It's okay. Trust me! I had to save him, because Mom wants to kill him. She was going to throw him over—she was going to kill him so you would leave Abby!"

"Mark! Look at me!"

Before I can try to make sense of what Chelsea said, Lottie calls for me, and I'm suddenly back in bed with her, hearing her cry out my name, feeling her under me, but I shake my head and clear the vision.

Now is not the time to think about what happened between the two of us. I need to keep my head in the game, need to pay attention. If Chelsea is to be believed, her mother wants to kill my son.

But I don't know who to believe.

Lottie holds her hands up, panting. It's difficult to make out the expression on her face. I wish the snow would stop swirling, that it was brighter out. I need to know what she's thinking, because what Chelsea said terrifies me.

"Mark. She's lying! You have to listen to me—I wouldn't ever hurt Henry." Lottie reaches out, her fingers dragging down my arm. Even through the thick coat I have on, I swear I can feel her touch, feel heat from her body. I jerk my arm away and square off on her.

Behind me, Henry sobs. I turn to take him, but Chelsea is right there with him, her arms around him, his face buried in her shoulder.

"Henry?" My voice is strangled as I call for my son. "Henry, are you okay?" I don't realize I'm moving until I reach him and touch his shoulder.

"He's fine. I promise, he's fine." Chelsea blinks up at me. "I'll keep him safe. I won't let Mom hurt him."

Oh God.

What have I done?

What am I missing here?

Who do I trust?

Chelsea? Or Lottie? The disaffected teenager who seems more interested in reading than anything else? Or Lottie, who knows my darkest secret, who helped her husband blackmail me? Who would throw me under a bus to get what she wants?

Lottie's wanted something from the moment they came here.

I turn back to her, not wanting to look away from Henry but needing to finish this.

"You were going to kill my son?" Even to my ears, my voice is low. Dangerous.

Lottie blinks at me like she's surprised to hear that tone in my words, and she takes a step back. It's difficult to tell where the edge of the cliff is.

When she doesn't answer my question, I repeat it, screaming the words at her. "You were going to kill him? Is that why you're here, Lottie?"

"I'm here for you." She shakes her head like she's trying to convince herself of something. "I wouldn't hurt Henry—you have to believe me!" She steps closer to me, dropping her voice to ensure I'm the only one who can hear her. "Don't you see that, Mark? Tim wants to blackmail you, to hurt you, but I wouldn't let him."

"No. Don't say that." My head hurts. It feels like someone is pressing an ice pick right between my eyes, making it impossible for me to think straight. I want to pop some pills, maybe have a stiff drink, then pass out for a few hours. That's what I want to do, what I need to do. It's the only thing that will keep me from doing something I regret.

Instead, I take a step towards her.

She moves back from me.

"You came here with your family to destroy mine." Anger flares in my chest, burning hot. I should try to temper it, but I can't. My hands clench into fists, my grip so tight I feel cramps in my fingers. "You knew what you were doing when you came, and you came anyway. To hurt me. Hurt Abby. Hurt Henry."

"You hurt Abby years ago!" she shrieks and flies at me, her fists pummeling me in the chest. "You think I did this? *You* did this! And then you left me to live with Tim to try to survive, and all I ever wanted was to be happy."

"Stop it!" Without thinking, I grab her shoulders. Shake her. She gasps but she stops flailing against me. I need her to shut up, need to make her stop saying these terrible things. My mouth is by her ear, my lips brushing her skin before I pull back a bit. "Don't you dare blame this on me, Lottie.

What we did was in the past. You're dragging it into the present."

My fingers sink into her flesh. I want to hurt her, want to make her see she can't ruin my family like this.

"Daddy?"

It's Henry.

Without thinking, I drop my hands from Lottie's shoulders and turn to him. He's got his thumb in his mouth and screams around it. Even with the wind whipping around us, the sound is so loud it's hard for me to concentrate. It makes it hard to think —his screaming has always made it hard to think—and I can't focus on what to do.

I need a moment to think.

Chelsea's got him on her hip. She's hugging him—*no, she's holding him back*—but he's safe, he's safe, he's safe. His eyes are wide, and he's screaming, but he's okay.

"Hey, Hen, it's okay, bud. You're okay. It's okay." I reach for him, wanting to pull him to me, but before I can touch my son to comfort him, there's a hand on my arm.

"Mark, please." Lottie squeezes my arm, her voice a whisper. "I love you."

"How dare you?" I whirl back around, Henry all but forgotten. "How *dare* you pretend to care for me when you're so willing to do whatever it takes to hurt me? Lottie, you need to go. You all need to leave!"

"Mark, no, I—"

I act without thinking, throwing my arm out, catching her across the collarbone. She's so little, just a slight thing, stress and poor diet making her skinny, keeping her from putting on muscle, and I hit her just right.

She trips backwards and, for a second, I picture myself reaching for her and pulling her back up. I see myself grabbing her around the waist, by the arms—*hell, around the neck if that's what it takes*—and yanking her back to safety, but before I can do that or even try to think about taking a step towards her, she's falling, her arms windmilling as she tries to catch her balance.

I see the moment she realizes she isn't going to be able to catch herself, that gravity has taken over now, that it's heartless and cruel, and—

She screams, the sound ripped away from her, and I step forward, unable to stop myself, even though I know what I'm going to see. I can barely make out her body twisting as it falls— before it's swallowed up by the dark, open nothingness of the ocean.

I wince. *Was that a thud?* Freezing ocean spray blows up from the water, carried by the wind, and I stumble back, losing my balance.

What the hell did I just do?

THIRTY-NINE

CHELSEA

"Mom?"

The wind whips the word away from my lips, and I step forward, closer to the edge of the cliffs, still gripping Henry to me. I should let him go, should push him back to Mark so he can take him, but I want to see where my mom went.

Over, then down, down, down, and then sucked deep into the black water. Even if she were alive when she hit the water, there's no way she'd last for very long. It's freezing out here, the rocks are huge, and bodies are so soft, so breakable—

"Chelsea." Mark's voice wraps around me like a scarf and he grabs me, pulling me back from the edge. I'm still holding my phone, and I angle the light up at him, taking in the fear on his face, the lines around his eyes, how he looks from me to Henry and then back again. "Oh God, Chelsea, I'm so sorry."

"You killed my mom." I choke out the words, then step into him, letting him pull me into a hug. I'm still holding Henry—*I kept him from going over the edge*—and Mark grabs him from me, hoisting him onto his own hip while he pulls me closer at the same time.

Smart. That was smart. I don't know what I might have done if I was allowed to keep holding Henry.

"I'm so sorry, Chelsea. I didn't mean to. I—oh God. She was right there, and I knocked into her and she fell, and I would have caught her, *should* have caught her, but it happened so fast and she was gone. I'm sorry."

There's pain in his voice, and fear, and anger, and it's all mingled together.

"You didn't mean to. It was an accident." I don't know what else to say. He killed my mom, but now he has to protect me, like I'm going to protect him. He has to be my dad—*he has to*. There's no way he can kill my mom like that and then turn his back on me, not when I need him now more than ever.

And if he doesn't want to? I'll make him. I'll tell everyone what he did. I'll blackmail him into staying with me, just the way my dad was going to blackmail him for more money. "It's okay, you're here, you're here, it's okay."

He shudders. Henry is shivering and Mark turns away from me, angling his body towards the house. "We need to get inside, Chelsea. Henry's freezing. We're all cold. I have to tell Abby that he's okay. I have to tell Tim..."

His voice trails off. He's ahead of me now, by a few feet, and I hurry to join him, slipping my hand into his. He doesn't pull away.

My mind races as we walk. I don't know what my dad will do to him. I have to protect Mark, have to make sure Dad doesn't hurt him.

I should have pushed Henry over the edge.

But I wanted Mark to think I was on his side, and then it was too late. I was going to blame my mom for it, tell Mark that she pushed Henry over the cliff—*that was the plan; that was what I was hoping to do in the first place*—but then Mark showed up and there wasn't any way to do it without him seeing exactly what happened.

But could I have done it? I look up at Mark, the way he's clutching Henry to his chest, and a bit of remorse shoots through me. It was easy to think about killing Henry to get what I wanted—*to get Mark*—but could I have actually gone through with it?

I think so. But now I don't have to find out.

The trudge to the house seems to take forever. Coming out here to get Henry was fast because I knew where I'd left him. I figured he wouldn't be able to get very far from where I'd left him by the cars, and I was right. He'd been right there, huddled against his dad's truck, like that was going to be enough to save him.

And then all Mom and I had to do was scoop him up. But no. She wanted Mark to love her, and she thought the best way to make that happen was by saving Henry.

But I knew something she didn't. Mark loves Abby. There's not enough room in his heart for all of us. That's why I knew I needed to get rid of his son. But he has Henry back.

For now.

"Up the stairs and we'll get warm. The fire will still be nice and hot, Chelsea. I want you in the living room right away, and I'll talk to your dad." Mark's voice catches when he says that, but he holds the front door open for me. I don't bother turning and telling him that *he's* my dad, that Tim is nothing to me.

He can't hear it right now, but he will soon. Soon enough I'll be able to tell him the truth—that I need him as my father, not Tim.

"Thanks," I say, stepping into the foyer.

A wave of heat washes over me, and I kick off my boots before shrugging off my coat. Mark closes the door behind us, the sound loud in the quiet of the dark house. A beam of light cuts through the foyer as Abby runs towards us.

"Henry! Is he okay?" She brushes past me, her elbow knocking into me, but she doesn't slow down to look at me; she grabs Henry from Mark, pulling him to her and squeezing him. "Give me my baby. Oh, he's so cold. So cold! What in the world happened out there?"

I'm silent, ready for Mark to speak up, to defend me.

"How did he end up out there in the first place?" Her words have an edge to them.

Henry starts wailing as he presses into her, his arms flailing, his body squirming against hers like he can somehow get even closer to her, but she doesn't take her eyes off me. She doesn't drop the flashlight from my face.

"My mom," I say quickly, my voice tight. "It was my mom. She was going to hurt Henry, but I saved him. He's okay because I saved him."

Abby gasps. Shakes her head. I think for sure she's going to turn away from us and take Henry to warm up, but she does the opposite, stepping closer to me, her lips right by my ear.

"I want you to stay the hell away from my son."

Anything I would have said in response freezes in my throat, and before I can try to figure out how to speak, she hurries away from us, her flashlight tucked under one arm, Henry held close to her chest.

Mark sighs next to me, pressing his hand into my lower back.

"Get warm, Chelsea. We all need to warm up."

I'm about to do what he said when Dad hurries towards us. He has a flashlight too, and he shines it in my face before turning it on Mark.

Was he not worried about me?

I stiffen, well aware that I should walk away right now but not willing to do that. I want to stay, make sure Mark is okay. I don't think Dad would hurt him, but there's no way to know for sure.

Not when he finds out about Mom.

"Where's Lottie?" His words are clipped, his voice tight.

I move to the side as he walks past me, his hand already out for the door. He's going to go out and find her, only there isn't any Mom for him to find.

"She... fell over the cliff." Mark's so quiet I barely hear him.

But Dad does. He turns, almost seeming to grow taller as he advances on Mark.

"What did you say?"

I have to intervene. "She was going to kill Henry." I move quickly, getting right between the two men. "Dad, she was going to kill him. She told me so herself." My heart races as I stare up at him. His flashlight is trained over my shoulder, on Mark, so I can't make out the expression on his face.

"She wouldn't."

"She would. She did." I nod furiously to try to get my point across. "You have to trust me, Dad. She was going to kill Henry. I stopped her." I conjure up a sob. My voice catches. "Please, don't make it any worse than it already is."

For a moment, the three of us stand still. I don't want to move in case Dad takes a swing at Mark. Even though I'm terrified of what he might do, I stay right in front of him, looking up at him, waiting for him to realize there's nothing for him to do here.

When neither of them responds, I turn a little bit to the side. What's Mark doing? What's he thinking? Is he grateful I'm willing to get between the two of them to try to keep Dad from attacking him?

"This isn't over." My dad flicks his wrist to angle the flashlight, the light now right in Mark's eyes. "Don't think for a second, Mark, that this is over."

Then he turns and storms off. His feet pound on the floorboard, and I shiver.

"You should go upstairs," Mark says, lightly touching me on the shoulder. "I'll see if I can calm everyone down."

I don't want to go upstairs, not without him, but I'm willing to do what he asks.

This is just the beginning.

FORTY

ABBY

Mark's footsteps are slow and heavy as he walks into the living room where I'm sitting with Henry. My son is alive, thank God, but he's shivering and cold, his skin pale and waxy, not warm like it should be.

He's stopped screaming but he's hiccupping now, gasping for little breaths of air as I coo in his ear, trying to calm him. *Is he hypothermic?* He's so, so cold, and I rub my hands up and down his back, holding his little body as close to mine as possible. I'll never forgive myself if something bad happens to Henry, if something irreversible might have happened and all because of my husband.

This is on him. I want so badly for this to all be Mark's fault.

The cushion sinks when Mark sits. He pulls off his hat, his red hair sticking up from his scalp. I scoot away from him, not wanting him to think I can draw comfort from him. I need my space. More than that though, I need Henry to be okay.

"How is he?" Mark reaches out to brush the blanket back from Henry's face, but I jerk to the side, blocking him with my shoulder.

"He's fine. No thanks to you."

"Me?"

The hurt in his voice is rich after all he's done. He's the one who put us in this situation in the first place. He's the reason I almost lost Henry.

Some part of me screams that that's not true. That this is my fault. I'm the one who came up with the idea of the promo.

I'm the reason the Rowes are here.

But Mark's the reason I had to put my plan in action in the first place. If he hadn't been screwing around, if he hadn't fallen into Lottie's bed, Henry would be fine. *We'd* be fine.

I refuse to think about that.

"Tim hates you." Turning to get a good look at him, I'm pleased to see the way he grows pale at my words.

He looks sick. Shifting Henry in my arms, I turn my body to get a better look at him. I have to admit, after all the lies and sneaking around, it's nice to see him like this. I want him to suffer. I didn't realize he was draining us dry and sending Tim money every month until he'd made a huge dent in our account. I could have left then, but I wanted a baby. I didn't want to have to start fresh with someone else. I wanted Henry, and I stuck around until I got him, until I could come up with a plan to make Mark suffer. If he hadn't stolen our money, if he hadn't...

I shake my head to clear it.

"What? Why are you shaking your head?"

Why are you shaking your head? Not an apology. Not an explanation, even though I don't think I'd give him the time of day if he tried to offer one.

I have no answer for him.

"I don't know what to do."

He sounds tormented. *Good.*

"You brought this on us, Mark, and you need to fix it. How are you going to do that?"

"I'll keep them away from you. From Henry." His answer is immediate, like he was waiting for an opportunity to make himself out to be the good guy. "In fact, Abby, I'm kicking the two of them out. Tonight. Now."

I close my eyes. Inhale. Exhale. Do it again. Against my chest, Henry shifts. He's going to be okay; I have to believe he's going to be okay.

But Mark can't kick them out.

I'm not done with them.

Or him.

I've been waiting for this moment, when I can show my hand. Tell him everything I know, prove to him that I'm not the stupid wife he thought he had, that I've been in control since I found out the truth, since I sent that social-media post to someone to speed things along.

"Mark." My voice is steady. Strong. Clear. I've never felt more in control than I do right now, and even though it takes a moment for him to look me in the eyes, I'm not worried. This is working out how I wanted it to.

Finally, he turns to look at me, guilt written across his face. I shift, sitting up a little taller, holding Henry a little tighter. "Mark, I know everything."

He freezes, his eyes locked on me. Shadows from the fire dance across his face. I see a host of emotions there as he tries to figure out exactly what to say to me. He gives his head a little shake.

"I don't know what you're talking about."

"Stop lying. Tell me how you know the Rowes. I want to hear you say it."

"I met them here, with you. I met them—"

"Bullshit."

His mouth snaps shut. Muscles dance along his jaw as he grinds his teeth together.

He's caught and he knows it, but whether or not he'll fess up... I don't know. There's something about the set of his jaw that makes me think he's going to fight having to tell me the truth for as long as possible. It's the same way he holds it when he's working on a particularly challenging repair job around the house.

Finally, he speaks. "How do you know?"

His voice is quiet, and I hate him for it. When a marriage dies, it's not supposed to be with a whimper. I want to rage against him, but he's meek, barely able to look at me.

"I checked your phone, Mark. You thought you could hide something like that from me. Now tell me. Tell me about Chelsea. Tell me why she has your red hair, why she's obsessed with you. Tell me what it is about you that she's so interested in. Tell me why, when I look at her, I can't help but think that I'm looking at a reflection of you. I want to hear you say it." My voice is rising and I'm getting louder. Henry shifts against my chest but doesn't make a sound.

I should try to be quiet, should temper how I'm talking to him, but I can't. Months of rage and hurt have been building up, the pressure almost too much for me to bear, and it's all coming out now.

Mark exhales hard, drops his head. Buries it in his hands. When he speaks, his voice is strangled, like he's not able to get a full breath of air in this position.

And I don't care.

"She's my daughter."

God, finally.

It feels good to hear him admit it.

I sigh, lean back. Henry stirs with me, but he still doesn't try to get up. He'd probably let me hold him for hours. He's traumatized and warming up, and the only person I have to blame for that is Mark.

And myself, if I'm being honest.

"You slept with Lottie." I know everything.

I found it all out when I started checking his phone, even though I felt insane doing it the first time.

I've known the truth for a long time now, but I still want to hear him say it himself. I want him to have to tell me what he did.

He nods.

"She didn't come back with you and Chelsea, so where is she, Mark?"

No response.

My stomach sinks. I need to push him on this, find out the truth of what happened out there, but I have other things to worry about.

"And where has all the money been going? The money we've been making here at the B&B, the money you work so hard for taking care of other people's problems when you could have been at home with us, not having to pay it to someone. Does it go to Tim?"

I know the answer. Of course I know the answer. There's no way I would have invited the Rowes to stay with us if I didn't know the truth about everything, if I hadn't caught on to where the money was going, but Mark has no idea. He's so clueless, just like he's been for years.

I'm never going to get an apology from him. But I want him to know that I know everything. Then, when it all falls apart, he'll see that I did this to him.

"It goes to Tim." He sounds like he has a cold; his throat is closing up. I have no sympathy for him. I want him to hurt right now, like I've hurt since I found out the truth.

"Hush money?"

"Yes."

"And now you want to kick your daughter out into the snow to freeze to death because you couldn't keep your pants on and it all came to a head? You're a piece of work, you know that? They're staying."

I'm on thin ice.

But this has to work. I don't have any other plan. He has to suffer for what he did to me. To Henry.

The expression on his face almost makes me laugh. He's frowning, his mouth still pressed in a flat line, his eyes furtive as they dart around the room, refusing to land on me.

"You want them to stay?"

"I want her to never have existed," I correct him. "But I'm not going to be the reason three people are dead. They go to their rooms, Mark, and they don't leave. We'll put food outside their doors. As soon as the roads are scraped and passable, they're out. Make that clear. I don't want to see any of them again."

I stand, then hesitate. This has to work. Mark and I have been together for a long time and I'm fairly certain he won't take their side over mine, but that already happened once, didn't it? It happened and he ended up with a daughter he was willing to pay money for every single month, just to prevent me from knowing the truth about what he did.

And now, if I want everything to work out the way I hope it will, I have to rely on him not messing up.

Again.

"Tell them to go lock themselves in their rooms. Tim will make sure Chelsea listens to him, I'm sure of it. I'm going to Henry's room with him. Once I know for sure he's okay, I'll come down and make him something hot to warm him back up. You ruin this and I will..." My voice trails off. I have no idea what I'll do to my husband if he ruins this for me, and it's clear from the expression on his face that he wants me to finish my threat.

"Abs," he says, reaching out before I can step around him. His fingers circle my wrist, and he tugs me closer to him.

I step towards him, unwilling, but afraid that if I pull back or fight him, I'll drop Henry.

"What, Mark? What do you want? You've gotten what you wanted for years now and it's time to pay up."

"I love you." He stares up at me, his eyes wide, unblinking. "You know that, don't you? I love you, Abby. I'm sorry this is happening, but I want you to know I never meant it to. I love you."

I should respond to him. If I want to keep him calm, complacent, willing to follow my commands, I should answer him and tell him I love him too. I should look my husband in the eyes and lie to him.

But that's what I've been doing for so long now. I'm exhausted.

"Take care of it, Mark," I tell him, tugging my wrist away from his grip. He lets me go and I adjust Henry so he's more comfortable, then sweep out of the room.

Even as I go, I know one thing.

Mark won't take care of it. But I'm not afraid to move forward with my plan.

This ends tonight.

FORTY-ONE

ABBY

Henry settles down easily. I hold the thermometer to his forehead for another moment, listening for the soft beep and flashing green light to let me know it's finished.

97.8°F.

Still cold but warming up. He's going to be okay. *He has to be okay.* That refrain plays through my head as I tuck another blanket under his chin and touch my lips to his forehead. If the power weren't out, if our cells worked, if the roads were clear...

I want to get him to the hospital, but how am I supposed to do that when I'm trapped here? I always thought being so far from town was part of the charm of this place, but now I'm seeing how dangerous it really is.

"I'm going to get you some hot chocolate," I tell him, kissing him again then tucking the blanket tightly around his body. "You hang out here, okay, little man?"

He's already nodding off. I was terrified he'd start screaming again, but he's exhausted, completely worn out from what happened to him. When he whimpers, I pause, stroking his head and pushing his hair back from his face, and he settles back down.

I have to leave him. It's part of the plan. Even though it makes me feel sick to leave him here by himself, that's my only option for a little bit longer. My plan went a little off the rails, but that's not my fault. I can still fix this, but not with Henry on my hip.

I need to leave, but I pause, pulling the baby monitor out of my pocket and clicking the button to turn it on.

Nothing. No lights shine in the dark, no little buzz lets me know it's working.

The batteries.

I'll need to grab some from the kitchen junk drawer while I heat up his hot chocolate. Leaving him alone right now is the last thing I want to do, but I don't have a choice, not when this is all so close to being finished.

I hit the staircase at a run and hurry down it, breathing hard as I hurry into the kitchen. The gas stove clicks when I turn the knob, and I light a match, holding it to the gas for it to catch. When it flares to life, I turn the flame down, plunk a pot on it, and grab milk from the refrigerator.

We'll have to be careful about how often we open the refrigerator so the food doesn't spoil.

Frustration fills me as I yank open the junk drawer. How much crap do we need to keep in the junk drawer? I guess that's why it has its moniker, because there are rubber bands, broken wheels from one of Henry's cars, three toothpicks, an empty box of matches, and finally, tucked in the back like they're the least important things in the drawer, some AA batteries.

"Thank you," I mutter, grabbing them and slipping them into my pocket. Maybe I won't need them. If I can get this plan back on track, then this will be over sooner rather than later.

It'll be over tonight.

I head back to the stove to stir the milk and keep it from scalding. My back is to the door when I hear footsteps behind me.

Mark.

He clears his throat. "They're upstairs. Do you think that's okay? That it's the best option?"

A pause, and during that pause, I discover the truth, something I've wanted to keep hidden and ignored for years.

I hate my husband.

Then: "How's Henry?"

He should have led with that. Henry should be the most important thing to him. So why was it the second thing he asked?

"He'll be fine." I speak slowly, carefully choosing my words. Mark has to know I'm more upset than I'm letting on, but what am I to do? Scream and throw things? Yell at him to try to get him on my side? He knows I'm at my wit's end—he has to.

This isn't how any of it was supposed to go.

He doesn't respond and I turn back to the stove. The milk is starting to simmer already, one of the perks of cooking on gas and not an electric stove. Just another moment and I'll stir in some hot chocolate mix and take it to Henry. He loves it, packed full of sugar and chocolate the way it is.

I'll be glad to have something warm in him. It kills me to be away from him right now when I know he needs me, but I don't have a choice. Not when the end is so near.

I wipe my hands down my pants, feel the batteries in my pocket.

I need to get up there.

"Abby, are you even listening to me?" Mark's voice cuts through my thoughts, through the litany of things I'm telling myself I need to do.

Slowly, I turn to him. "What?"

"I asked you what you think is going to happen. How you think this is going to end. Someone put Henry outside, someone—"

"Henry's fine! He's fine because I'm taking care of him, not because you're doing anything helpful!" I cut him off. He needs to stop talking, needs to listen to me. Henry is okay, and it's because I was there to help him. If I don't keep him warm, then something terrible could happen to him, yes, but I won't let it.

I'm his mom. I'll protect him.

"Abs, you're being too calm about this." He holds his hands up like he's surrendering. "I think we need to talk about what's going to happen now that the Rowes are upstairs. Are we going to call the police when the power's back? Do you want to press charges? Are we going to kick them out as soon as possible? Someone's to blame for what happened, Lottie is probably dead, and you're being way too calm about it all!"

I take a deep breath before responding.

"Mark. What happened to Lottie?" It's been bothering me since everyone else got back, but nobody's brought it up. "Where is she?" I stare at him, daring him to lie to me.

"She... fell. At the cliffs. Abby, it was terrible, it—"

"Stop lying to me!" My voice is loud, too loud. I need to calm down, need to keep my head on straight, but that's hard when Mark is lying right to my face. She fell?

No. I don't think she did. Not without his help, anyway.

He opens and closes his mouth like a fish. Useless.

"You want to know who's to blame for all of this?" The stove turns off with a satisfying click and I carefully pour the hot milk into a bright red sippy cup. There's a picture of a race car on it. Henry's favorite. "You're to blame, Mark."

"I'm to blame?" He gasps like something physically hurt him. "*I'm* to blame? You're the one who thought you could twist everything around instead of coming to me to talk about what happened! You wanted to be the puppet master and control all of us. If you had come to me, if you had—"

"If I had come to you and asked you about Lottie, you would have lied. You would have doubled down on the lies, because that's the type of man you are." My words are measured, slow. While my mind had been racing a few minutes ago, making it almost impossible for me to think clearly, I can think clearly now. I see it all, especially how Mark is trying to deflect any blame away from him.

"And you think inviting them here instead of talking to me was the better option? That doesn't make any sense, Abs."

"Right, because you're always so honest when you're confronted with something you did wrong." I let the words hang between us.

"You're going to blame me for something I did sixteen years ago?"

"When that *something* tried to kill my son, yes."

The more I think about it, the less I trust Chelsea. Mark may have bought into her lie that Lottie was going to hurt Henry while she saved him, but I don't. Call it a mother's instinct, if you will. While I talk, I pat my pockets to ensure I have what I need. Batteries? Check. Mark and I are done here.

Mark and I have been done for a while.

He hasn't realized it, but this is the moment I've been working towards since I found out about Lottie. Just leaving him would have been easy, wouldn't it? But I didn't want to make this easy on him.

I wanted him to suffer for what he did to me. To Henry. To our family. And I needed time to stash away as much money as possible, to ensure Henry and I could start over. I lost control there for a bit, when someone was running circles around me. Moving the baby monitor. Locking me in my room.

But Lottie is gone now and everything's going to work out the way I planned. There were some bumps in the road, but that's over.

"*Our* son. Henry's our son, Abby."

"Right. Our son." I sigh and gesture to the door. "Take this up to him, will you? I'll be up in a minute."

Mark eyeballs me, the distrust evident in his eyes. He knows something's up, but he doesn't know what. I sigh, holding out the hot chocolate, practically pressing it into his hands.

"Please take this to him." My voice sounds thick, even to my ears. "I need to take a moment to calm down. I don't want him to see me so upset."

"Oh, Abs." Mark takes the hot chocolate from me.

I stand still as he lightly traces his fingers over my cheek.

"I love you. We'll get through this."

No, we won't. I have to fight to keep from shivering away from his touch.

Then he's gone and I hear his heavy footsteps ascending the stairs.

I wait a moment. It's killing me to stand still, to wait for what's coming next, but I don't have a choice. The plan got off track, but it's going to work out now.

It has to.

Just as I'm about to leave the kitchen to look for him, I hear Tim coming towards me. I see the jumping light in front of him.

I take a deep breath.

This is it. I have to hope this goes the way I need it to.

FORTY-TWO

ABBY

"Scream again." Tim sounds lazy, like we're watching football on a fall afternoon, like he's just asked me to pass the corn chips because I didn't hear him the first time. "Louder."

I do what he asks and clap my hands over my ears as my scream rips through the silence of the house. We're both in the kitchen, both of us leaning against the counter.

Sweat breaks out on my brow. I wipe it off.

"He's not coming," I say, turning to look at Tim. "He's not going to come and then what are you going to do? How are you going to make this work out?"

"Oh, Abby." He chuckles and my skin crawls. "This isn't only my problem to work out. You know that. We're in this together."

He has a heavy kitchen knife in his hand and keeps adjusting his grip on it like he can't get comfortable holding it. It's my favorite knife, one Mark bought me on our tenth wedding anniversary. He hadn't chosen it of course. He wouldn't know what makes a good kitchen knife in the first place.

I picked it out, showed him the link online, dropped so

many hints I was almost afraid I'd overdone it and he wasn't going to buy it. But then, the morning of our anniversary, while I was making pancakes and frying bacon and mourning the fact that we *still weren't pregnant*, he appeared behind me, looped his arms around me, pressed the box into my hands.

It's my favorite knife. I sharpen it regularly, making sure it will cut through anything.

And here Tim is, holding it like he's afraid he's going to break it.

"He's coming." Tim turns to me, holding the knife up, looking for all the world like he's going to stab it right into my eye.

I blink.

Scream again.

Now there are feet pounding on the stairs. Heavy steps, like a man, not like Chelsea.

I exhale, grateful. *It's him.* Before I can sag against the counter in relief though, I remember what's happening and I stiffen, wrapping my arms around my body.

"Abby!"

"In the kitchen! Hurry, Mark!" When I glance at Tim, he nods. It's not light in the room, not by a long shot. The candles I've lit cast barely enough light for me to make out some of his features.

He looks like a rat.

I shiver.

Mark runs towards us. I see Henry on his hip, my son bouncing around like a sack of flour, and I take a step forward. Tim stops me. His free hand closes around my arm and I freeze.

"Not too close!"

When Tim yells, Mark stops too. Slowly, like he's afraid of moving too quickly and upsetting Tim, he lets Henry slip from his hip. My son clings to his father's leg, and Mark puts his hand on the top of his head, pushing him behind him. Now both of his hands are free.

He doesn't have to explain why he put Henry down for me to understand what's going through his mind.

But why did he bring Henry down here in the first place? I don't want my son anywhere near this. That's why I left him in his room.

"What the hell are you doing, Tim?"

There's exhaustion in Mark's voice. I search his face for what emotion he might be feeling, but it's so hard to tell with the flickering candles.

I can't take my eyes off Henry. He's everything to me, the whole reason I'm doing this in the first place.

"I want my money." Tim's grip tightens on my arm. "It's all I wanted in the first place, and you could have given it to me, you know that? You could have paid me what I wanted and none of this would have happened."

"Let Abby go." Mark takes another step closer.

Tim shifts, moving behind me. I feel heat from his body, he's so close. Sweat breaks out on the back of my neck, coating all of my skin. Do I smell? Can he tell how terrified I am?

Yes, I know the plan. We've gone over it and over it, making sure both of us are on the same page. But can I really trust this man?

I feel the press of metal in the side of my neck. For the first time, a wave of fear washes over me.

This is fake, this is fake, this is fake, this is—

"I swear to God, I will gut your wife if you don't give me what I want."

Mark doesn't respond.

This isn't how it was supposed to go.

Why isn't Mark acquiescing? Why isn't he responding? Why is he making it so much more difficult than it has to be? I want to scream at him to help me, to end this, but my tongue feels fat and thick in my mouth, and even if I could speak, I have a very good feeling Mark is going to dig in his heels.

He always does this.

"I killed Lottie." Mark's voice is quiet, and he takes a step closer to us, then another. "I pushed her off the cliff. You have nothing, Tim. Let my wife go."

"Why the hell would I do that when you ruined everything?"

His grip on my arm tightens. I squirm away from him a little bit, but he dips his head to mine, and I catch the dark expression on his face, knowing immediately what he's trying to say.

Don't. Move.

His breath smells like old coffee and I wrinkle my nose, pulling a bit farther away from him, but there's nowhere to go, and he's right. I need to remember the plan, but this isn't how I thought it would go.

I thought Mark loved me more. I thought he'd be willing to do whatever he had to in order to keep me safe. It never once crossed my mind that this would turn into a battle like this, that I'd be the bait, that I'd—

The knife presses harder into my neck.

I know enough human anatomy to know that if he cuts my jugular, it's all over for me.

Surely he won't. He wants to stick to the plan as badly as I do.

Behind Mark, Henry whimpers. He's exhausted and I want to go to him, but I can't move, not now.

"Mommy?" Henry cries out for me, and Mark turns to him.

"Mommy's fine," he says. "Wait here, Henry."

His jaw is set when he looks back at me. I see how he holds his hand out behind him a little, keeping Henry out of the way.

At the same time, Tim tightens his grip.

"Please no," I squeak out. My voice is quiet. It's not for Mark. It's for Tim.

"You want money?" There's resignation in Mark's voice and I tense. "Fine. Just don't hurt Abby."

I tense. He's doing exactly what I knew he would. Lying. Acting.

We don't have more money unless he has a stash somewhere, and I'm sure I'd know about it. Mark will do or say whatever it takes to get what he wants. I've seen it time and time again.

"Don't hurt me," I whisper, my voice tight with fear. Mark can hear me, I know he can, but that's okay. He needs to stay panicked, needs to struggle to think things through or he's suddenly going to get the upper hand.

"Let her go," Mark says, drawing my attention away from Tim. "Let Abby go. I'll give you the money."

Tim stiffens. "How do I know you won't turn on me?" His eyes are locked on Mark.

You don't. Just finish this.

"You'll have to trust me." Mark takes a step forward, then another. He's stepping in and out of shadows from the candles, the expression on his face almost impossible for me to read. "Do you trust me, Tim?"

Tim doesn't answer. Time seems to stand still for a moment, a terrible cliché, but that's exactly what happens. All I can do is stare at Mark. Henry's behind him, crying now.

For a moment, I can't breathe, then Mark's running at the two of us, his hands outstretched.

"Shit!" Tim jerks his hand back. The tip of the knife cuts into my neck, just a bit, just enough to hurt and draw blood. I swear, then drop to the floor, desperate to get away from the two of them.

The floor is freezing. The hard wood cuts through my pants and into my knees, and I inhale hard, tucking my chin to my chest as I crawl away from the two men.

Towards Henry.

Screaming. He's screaming now, and I need to get to him, need to scoop him up and get him out of here. He's behind the kitchen table; I see him through the chair legs, then he darts to the side.

Mark hits Tim at a full run. There's a loud thud as the two of them slam into the counter then Tim swears again.

I close my eyes, moving faster now, doing everything I can to put as much space between them and me as possible.

This isn't working out the way I planned.

"I'll kill you!" That's Mark, and seeing how angry he sounds, I don't think he's lying. He sounds feral, his words all clipped like enunciation is too much effort. There's the sick sound of flesh hitting flesh.

Then my husband screams.

Thank God.

My neck is bleeding, but only a little. The smell of copper coming from my cut is nothing compared to the sharp, hot scent of it that immediately fills the air. It rolls over me like a storm cloud, filling my lungs, making it almost impossible to draw a breath.

I swear, feeling the smell choking me. It doesn't make any sense, but it's in me, filling me. I glance over my shoulder at the men behind me, then I look back for Henry.

Where is my son?

"Abby, run." Mark chokes out the words. It sounds like he's drowning and I'm instantly terrified, unsure of where Tim cut him, of how much damage he must have just caused my husband. "Run."

Instead, I stand, turning back to the melee, squinting against the dark to try to determine what's going on. Both men are on the floor but then one stands, taller and taller as he unfolds.

Tim.

He turns, his hair hanging around his face, then he drops

the knife. It thuds dully on the floor. He takes a step back, then turns, fleeing the kitchen.

My heart pounds in my chest.

We're back on track.

I can fix this. I can make sure I get what I want. I'll grab Henry and end this.

I'll make sure Mark pays for what he did to me.

FORTY-THREE

MARK

The pain in my shoulder is so intense I have to fight against waves of nausea. The scent of my own blood turns my stomach, the feeling of it soaking my shirt to my chest enough to make me close my eyes, turn my head.

Count down from five.

Five. Four. Three. Two. O—

"You're going to be okay."

Abby leans over me, her brows knit together. When I make eye contact with her, she frowns, pressing her mouth into a thin line. She moves quickly, pressing something against my chest.

Pain radiates out from the pressure, hot and bright, and I suck in a breath. Close my eyes.

"What happened?"

"He stabbed you." She pulls her hands back from my chest. There's the sound of something ripping and I know she's going to apply a bandage. I reach for her.

She scoots away from me.

"Are you okay?"

There's silence for a moment and I open my eyes. She's lit more candles and placed them around me on the floor so she can see what she's doing. Behind her sits Henry, his eyes wide, his thumb in his mouth. Tears stream down his cheeks and he yawns, then starts crying.

"I'm fine." I can see the cut on her neck. Part of me wants to reach for it, but I'm afraid she'll move away again. I don't want her pulling away from me. "Is Henry okay?"

"He's fine." Her voice is stiff. Unnatural. She glances over at him, then steps away from me.

I grab her arm before she can escape. "Hey, are you really okay? What happened with Tim?"

The glare she shoots me makes me let her go. I swear, my fingers are still warm from touching her skin, but if she doesn't want me to touch her, then what the hell am I to do?

She's stressed. She needs time to decompress. Tim almost killed her, for God's sake—if she weren't upset, I'd wonder what the hell was wrong with her.

Henry almost died.

And I killed Lottie.

A long exhale and she pushes some of her hair back from her forehead. "I need some space right now. I need to be with Henry, and I need some time to think."

My stomach drops. "Abby, that's not what we need right now. It's not what *I* need. I need to be with you and our son."

She's shaking her head before I finish speaking. "No, Mark. No. Listen to me. Everything is out of control and the only thing that matters to me right now is making sure our son is safe. You're going to let me do that."

I nod. "Right. I can do that."

"Good." She stands, but when I reach for her hand for her to help me off the floor, she jerks it away from me. Rubs it on her leg like she needs to wipe off my touch.

I watch as she turns, scoops up Henry. She nestles him against her side and his little arms go right around her neck.

"I'll give you some time to take care of Henry," I say. I'm

desperate for Abby to listen to me and hear my side of the story. It isn't fair for her to put all the blame squarely on my shoulders. "I'm sorry, Abs. But I want you to know that I'm not giving up on us and I don't want you to either."

She bounces Henry. "Right now, you need to make sure Chelsea is okay. She lost both of her parents, Mark. You need to comfort her. I can't.

Right. And she shouldn't have to.

"I'll do whatever you say. But I want you to know I never meant to hurt you."

"Well, you did. And you hurt Henry." She swallows hard, like there are more things she wants to say right on the tip of her tongue but she's doing everything in her power to keep them from being said. "That's something we're going to have to work hard to get through."

I know.

"I didn't mean for any of this to happen to you. Or Henry." It hurts when I shift position and try to sit up. How the hell Tim stabbed me right in the chest, next to the armpit, but apparently didn't hit anything major, I don't know. But I guess I should be grateful for that. "I made a mistake, but I need time to fix it. To fix us. You have to believe me, Abby."

She exhales hard, then brushes her hair back from her face again.

"Henry and I are going upstairs. I'm going to lock our bedroom door. I don't want you there, do you understand me? I don't want you anywhere near me right now. Stay away from the two of us."

"Abby, wait."

Pain rips through me as I force myself to stand. The edges of my vision go black, and I waver on my feet, but I manage to hold on to consciousness.

I reach out and brace myself on the counter. "Please. I'm sorry. Let me make it up to you."

"You can make it up to me by keeping Chelsea away from me. She's your daughter, Mark; you figure out what the hell to do with her."

And then she's moving away from me. I want to cry out for her or follow her or try to stop her, but I feel rooted to the floor. She's fuming, and she has every right to be.

I guess, in a way, I did bring this on us. I had no idea how dangerous Lottie and her family could be. The lengths they would go to. I should have known, when I saw how willing Tim was to blackmail me, but I never realized how dangerous he really was. I never knew my family would suffer this much because of what I did.

Abby leaves the kitchen. She has Henry on one hip, a candle held in her other hand. I watch as the light disappears as she walks down the hall. She's safe, but Lottie isn't.

Oh God. I feel my stomach twist at the memory of how Lottie disappeared over the cliff, how small she felt as I hit her, how she was there and then gone.

I killed her. I didn't mean to, but I did, and she's gone, and I can't stop picturing her face as she went over.

Abby knows what happened, but she doesn't know how bad it was, what it was like to see Lottie's expression change as she realized what was happening, how quickly everything ended for her.

Suddenly, more than anything, I want my wife.

What if she runs into Chelsea?

I want to stop her, to try to warn her of what might be waiting right around the corner, but she's already hurrying up the stairs—I can hear it.

Pain shoots through my body as I struggle to take a step.

I pause, resting for a moment to try to catch my breath. This is a side of Abby I don't think I've ever seen before. She's angry and cold, and has every right to be. No, she's livid. There's something going on that I must be missing.

But my head hurts too bad to try to figure it out.

I need to sit. If I can't go upstairs with her, which Abby made insanely clear to me, I need to sit, I need to rest. Honestly, I don't think I'd even be able to make it up the stairs in the first place, but hopefully I can make it down the hall.

It takes longer than I'd like to admit, but I finally reach the living room. The fire is dying down, but I don't have the energy to try to stoke it. Someone needs to put some more wood on it, but not me.

I can't.

I just can't.

With a groan, I collapse onto the sofa. There's a soft chenille blanket next to me, and I yank it with my good hand, pulling it up over my body and trying to tuck it around my shoulder for warmth as I lie down.

I take a deep breath, then another. Each time I breathe in, I feel like I'm being stabbed again. I need to rest. I need to heal.

As I let my body relax, I swear I hear movement behind me. There's a little voice in the back of my head telling me to wake up and pay attention, that I need to remember Chelsea, that I don't know where she is.

I don't know how dangerous she might be.

But there's no way I can open my eyes.

"Daddy?"

FORTY-FOUR

MARK

Dear God, how does she know?

"Chelsea," I croak, my throat dry like I haven't had anything to drink in weeks. Adrenaline crackles through my body like lightning, and I brace myself on my elbow, wiping my hand across my eyes to try to clear my vision. My head feels like it's in a vise, and even though I'm still in pain, my daughter's presence snaps me out of dozing.

Clearing my throat, I try again. "Chelsea, what are you doing?"

She smiles, curling up next to me. I feel the way the sofa cushion sinks down a little bit under her weight and I try to move away from her, but I can't make my body work like that. My muscles are all tight and refuse to move, so I'm stuck next to her, feeling her rest her head on my good shoulder.

"Are you okay? I wanted to check on you."

"I'm fine. Help me up."

For a moment, I think she's going to refuse, but then she stands, grabbing my good arm by the elbow and yanking me up to sit. I cry out, the feeling of fire burning through my flesh, but she doesn't say anything.

There's a pause, long and pregnant, and I think she's going to leave, but what comes out of her mouth shocks me.

"Do you want to play a game?"

"A game?" I blink up at her, trying to make things make sense. "No, I don't want to play a game. My wife is angry at me, I was stabbed, and—"

"And you killed my mom." Her voice is curious, not sad.

Why the hell does she sound like that?

I can't respond.

"Don't forget that. You killed her." She looks me right in the eyes as she speaks.

"I didn't mean to." It sounds weak even to my ears.

Chelsea stares at me, the expression on her face like she's trying to figure out what to say next to me.

I shift, uncomfortable. The memory of the past hour or so hits me like a ton of bricks, and I swallow hard, trying to keep from letting it pull me under. It's horrible, what I did. I should hate myself for killing Lottie, but what was I supposed to do?

I had to save Henry.

But I think I made a mistake in trusting Chelsea.

Guilt rips through me when I think about what I've done to my family. Abby loves me and I love her and I... I threw it away to be with Lottie. Then I kept lying instead of trying to fix it.

Groaning, I grip my head and squeeze it tight. Pain rips through my shoulder at the movement, and I stop, dropping my hands into my lap. Tears stream down my cheeks, but I don't bother wiping them away.

I should be in the bedroom with Abby and Henry. Tim disappeared into the night like the snake he is, leaving his daughter here to fend for herself, and I... No, Chelsea isn't *his* daughter, is she? And now he doesn't have to deal with her.

Smart man. He ran when he had a chance, and now I have to clean up everyone's mess.

"Were you going to sleep?" Chelsea interrupts my thoughts,

stopping me from spiraling any more than I already was. I nod, lock eyes with her, try to focus on her.

Damn, my shoulder hurts. The pain is exquisite, hot and bright, and unlike anything I've ever experienced before. Part of me wants to tell Abby how much it hurts. Part of me knows there's no way I'd ever be able to make it up the stairs to talk to her.

"Dad? Are you tired?"

God, I wish she wouldn't call me Dad.

Instead of saying that, however, I nod. The movement makes my head hurt. Everything hurts. I'm trying to think through what's happened since the Rowes got here. Lottie wouldn't have told Chelsea the truth, would she? That I'm her father?

But she knows. Whether Lottie told her on purpose or not, Chelsea knows the truth.

"Do you want to play a game?" She repeats the question like the two of us didn't just talk about this.

"No, Chelsea, I don't want to play a game." Even I can hear the irritation in my voice. I brace my good hand on the sofa and shift my position, trying to relieve some of the pressure on my chest. "I want this night to be over. I want to go for help, to call the police, to—"

"So they can send you to jail for killing Mom?"

Her eyes are bright and locked on me. Shadows dance across her face.

"You'll go to jail, you know that, right? I'll tell everyone what happened. That you pushed her. That she didn't do anything wrong. I'll send you there. I'll make sure the police know how you screamed at her that she deserved to die." Her voice is hard. There's an edge to it that terrifies me.

I swallow hard.

That's not how it happened, but who would the cops believe?

"Or I can make sure you don't go to jail." She reaches out, runs her finger across my bandage.

"What?" It's almost impossible to think straight right now.

"I'll tell them you were protecting me. That Mom was going to hurt me, hurt Henry. You think they'd send you to jail for murdering her if they thought she was crazy like that?"

I don't answer. I can't answer.

Her brows knit together. "But that's only if you're willing to finally be my dad. If you aren't, then I'll tell them you killed Mom on purpose, that you were going to kill me. I'll tell them you laughed when you pushed her over the cliff, that you said she had it coming. That I was next."

"None of that is true." I'd been so cold earlier, but now I'm hot. My armpits itch with sweat, and I feel more breaking out on my brow. "I was saving Henry. She was going to kill him— you said so yourself."

Chelsea leans forward. Her eyes are locked on mine, and she doesn't speak until our foreheads touch. "I lied, Dad. Mom wasn't going to hurt Henry. I was."

Oh God. I've made a terrible mistake. My stomach turns, twisting hard, and I force myself to sit up, then I turn and vomit on the floor, the smell of it immediately making my eyes water.

But Chelsea appears unbothered.

"All I ever wanted was for you to be my dad, and now you get to be," she crows like I didn't just get sick, like she isn't admitting to me that she's going to blackmail me. "I put Henry outside to get rid of him, but then Abby noticed, and we had to get him back. Still, it all worked out in the end, didn't it? You get to be there for me forever; isn't it great?"

No. What is she saying?

"You did what?" I feel like I'm choking, and even though I don't want her to explain again what she said, she has to repeat it. I have to make sure I didn't mishear her.

"I put him outside." She grabs my hand and squeezes it,

making bile burn my throat. "I came with Mom and Tim to try to get you to love me, to be my dad. Mom and I wanted you to leave Abby for us, but she didn't know I knew the truth. I've known for a long time that you're my real dad."

"Chelsea, no." I have to try one more time. It's difficult for me to think straight right now. My stomach hurts from being sick, and my head aches from everything that's happened. There's a thick fog in my thoughts, and I try to push it away so I can get my point across to her. "This isn't how it's going to go. I love Abby and Henry. I won't lose them. You almost killed him! How could I love you after that?"

She jerks away from me, her skinny arms folded across her chest. The gentle tone she's been using with me is gone, and she watches me like she isn't sure who I am.

"You don't get it, do you?"

There's venom in her words. I can't tear my eyes away from her.

"If you don't step up as my dad, I'll tell everyone you killed Mom on purpose and that you were going to kill me. I'll do whatever it takes to ensure you never set foot outside a cell again, do you understand? Don't think I won't. This is serious, Dad. You're my dad now. You can't turn your back on me and think you'll get away with it."

"No, you can't do that. You just can't." My mouth is dry, and I look around desperately for a glass of water. I need something to drink to get this sick cotton feeling out of my mouth. "That's not how the world works. You don't get to blackmail someone into doing what you want. Nobody will believe you. Besides, Tim is your father. He's raised you. No court would take you from him to live with me."

She grins. "He's not here right now, is he? He's gone, and who knows where he went? Besides, everyone will believe me." She leans forward, her face looming in front of mine. "And you want to know what I can do to make sure nobody believes you?"

No, I don't. I don't want her to say another word. But I know I'm going to have to listen to her tell me whatever terrible plan it is she's come up with, and I don't think I can handle that. I need to sleep. My eyelids are heavy and my head feels like it's full of rocks, but I can't give in to the urge to rest my head and close my eyes until I know what her plan is.

"I'll kill Abby and Henry." She whispers the words in my ear even though it isn't like there's anyone else around to hear. "But I'll tell everyone you did it of course. That's how you got stabbed, isn't it? You were fighting to kill your wife and your son, and she fought back, but in the end, it was too much. My dad and I were only saved because we ran. And *you. Can't. Do. Anything.*" She pokes me in the chest with every word.

My heart hammers under her finger.

Pain flares in my chest.

"You can't hurt them." My mouth is dry. "Please, Chelsea, you can't hurt them."

"See, Dad, that's the problem you're facing, isn't it? I can do whatever I want, and you can't stop me."

Before I realize what she's doing, she reaches out and presses down on where I got stabbed.

"Holy shit!" Pain shoots through me. The edges of my vision go dark and fuzzy, and I gasp for air, trying to hold on to consciousness. As I scream, I claw at her hand, finally yanking it away from my chest. "Fuck, Chelsea!"

I'm dizzier than I was now. All sounds feel far away, like I'm swimming through a river. I can't seem to focus on the fireplace to my side or her face in front of me. I'm woozy and weak, and even though I'm sure she'd love to continue this conversation, I can't.

I pass out.

FORTY-FIVE

ABBY

Henry doesn't fight me when I pop a sucker in his mouth. His eyes widen and he reaches up, grabbing it and holding hard to the white paper stick like he's sure I made a mistake and I'm going to take it back from him before he can finish it.

"Enjoy that, okay? I want you to stay nice and quiet."

There hasn't been a peep from downstairs since I brought Henry up here. I'm not staying. Henry and I are out of here as soon as possible, but I had to grab my go-bag. As long as Mark and Chelsea stay downstairs, everything will be fine.

This has to work.

"Okay, I have my wallet," I say, patting my pocket. "And keys to my safe box. Keys to the snowmobile." While checking to make sure I haven't forgotten anything, my eyes fall on the bed. My cell phone sits there along with my credit and debit card.

None of those things are coming with me. This is a fresh start for Henry and me and I'm not going to let something as stupid as using my credit card to get gas foil my plans.

Of course, there are some things in the house I'll miss. My grandmother quilted the coverlet on our bed, and I run my fingers along the binding. For a moment I stand still, my eyes closed, remembering the perfume she wore and how it burned my nose when she hugged me.

She wouldn't care one bit about me leaving behind the quilt. I know my Oma, and she'd love that I left Mark and his cheating ways in the past.

Quickly, to comfort myself, I unzip the smaller pocket on my backpack. There are the water bottles I brought.

"Okay, Henry," I say, bending and scooping him up. He's bulky in his winter coat and I'm glad he'll be warm. As soon as we step outside, we're going to be hit with high winds. Luckily, the snow's stayed off.

I move as quietly as possible across the bedroom and then click off my flashlight before shoving it in my pocket. Even though I know I have everything I'll need, I'm still nervous. It doesn't matter that I've thought through every little thing that could possibly go wrong.

It doesn't matter that I've made this trip out to the barn dozens of times while Mark was at work so I would know exactly how far I had to go, or that I think Henry will be quiet as we walk through the house.

Suckers work magic with little kids.

None of the practice the two of us did counts, does it? The only thing that counts right now is whether or not I can make it all the way down the stairs, through the house, and out the door to the barn without Mark knowing about it.

Or Chelsea.

I shiver when I think about Mark's daughter. She's evil, I know that now. At first, I'd thought she was an innocent party in all of this, but I look at her and see the evil within. She's determined to do whatever it takes to have Mark to herself, and while there are some women who might want to keep fighting, I'm done.

I just want my son.

But I also want to make Mark suffer. That was the goal. That's why I needed him alive. I could have left when he was at work, just disappeared, and he would have missed us. But I wanted him to know that he brought this on himself, that he shouldn't have ever slept with Lottie, that I took Henry from him and left him with his other family, that he could have avoided all of this.

"Be very quiet, buddy. If you can make it outside without making a sound, then I have a special surprise for you."

My hand is on the doorknob, and I wait for him to respond before I open it. He's a little kid, and there's no way he'll be able to ignore the allure of a surprise.

"What prize?" He has to shift the sucker to the side of his mouth to be able to speak around it.

"A puppy."

He gasps, pulls the sucker from his mouth. "A *puppy*?"

"Yes, but you can't make a sound. This is a game we're playing with Daddy and Chelsea, and if either of them hear us, we lose, and there's no puppy."

I hold my breath. Surely he's going to argue with me or call out loudly about the puppy, but he nods, settles against my shoulder. I feel his hot breath on an exposed patch of my neck, and I hold him tighter before unlocking the door and opening it.

Nothing moves.

There isn't anyone waiting for us in the hall. I exhale hard in relief, then hurry down the hall, making sure to stay on the middle of the runners in a bid to keep my footsteps as quiet as possible. I'm not worried about Mark hearing me walk around, but when I'm on the stairs, that's when I might make more noise than I'd like.

On the landing I pause again.

"No noise." I barely breathe the words into Henry's ear. He nods, tightening his arms around my neck.

The first step is fine. The second, third, fourth, fifth...

I pick up speed, knowing full well that I need to slow down a little bit in order to be as quiet as possible, but I'm so eager to get out of the house that I can't seem to pump the brakes.

There's a squeak from step ten and I freeze. Goosebumps break out on my arms, unhindered by the thick coat I have on. I take a deep breath and hold it for a moment before slowly exhaling.

Nobody's coming for us. I'd hear them; I'm sure I would. Just like I'm sure they can hear me if I'm too noisy, there's no way Mark or Chelsea can sneak up on me.

Another step. Another.

I'm holding my breath as I reach out with my foot, tapping, looking for the right place to step that won't result in me putting my weight on a squeaky board.

"Come on," I whisper, then freeze as the sound leaves my mouth.

Nothing.

I scoot to the right of the stair, still reaching out with my foot, still tapping.

There.

I'm careful walking away from the stairs. I'm faster than I mean to be.

Louder than I mean to be.

There's light at the end of the hall. The fire. It hasn't died out, not by a long shot, and that tells me exactly where Mark and his daughter are. For a moment, I stand in the hall, right in the middle of it, where either one of them could probably shine a flashlight out the door and see me.

But they're not going to. I'm confident about that. I can hear them talking, and even though they're being so quiet it's impossible for me to tell what's being said, it doesn't matter, does it?

My husband had another child and now he's choosing that child.

Like I hoped he would.

I didn't give him the option, did I? I made him choose, and I was prepared for him to make a stupid decision. Chelsea ensured he chose her. She thinks she's winning.

Henry stirs, pulling me back to the present. Tucking him closer to my body, I turn from looking down the hall and hurry to the front door.

This is where things are going to get tricky and where I'm going to need to move as quickly as possible. As soon as I open the front door, cold air will shoot into the house. It's freezing in every room but the living room thanks to the fire, but Mark and Chelsea might still feel the chill.

They'll come running to see who opened the door. Mark will think it's Tim, back to fight him again, while Chelsea... well, I don't know what she'll think, and I don't care.

Bracing myself for the cold that's about to wrap around my body, I grab the handle, hold tighter to Henry, then throw the door open.

Wind whips into my face, blowing snowflakes onto my skin. They're freezing, little pinpricks of ice, and I wince as I try to close the door behind us. For a moment I don't think I'm going to be able to do it. A huge gust of wind blows towards me, catching the door and launching it back open.

I lunge, Henry almost slipping from my grasp. He cries out, the sound loud in my ear, but I manage to hang on to him. My fingers brush the doorknob.

They're going to hear me. *They're going to come.*

One more time I lean into the house, and this time I grab the knob and yank the door shut. It slams, rattling in the doorframe. I want to stand still and calm down, try to slow the beating of my heart, but I need to get going.

The pitch-black almost gives me pause.

If I hadn't practiced this trip to the barn as many times as I had, I'd be terrified. Instead though, I slip the flashlight from my pocket and shine it ahead of us. There are eight steps down from the porch and I walk in the depressions Tim left when he fled the house.

Exactly as we planned.

The wind has been blowing so hard most of his tracks are covered. I stop, squinting ahead, and confirm what I thought.

Mark is going to have a hell of a time following me.

Another step, then another, and now I'm off the stairs. The snow shifts and crunches underfoot as I hurry away from the porch. My heart pounds hard in my chest, not only out of fear but from exertion. This is harder than I thought it would be.

I've practiced our escape regularly over the last few months, carrying Henry as I ran over to the barn, preparing for the day Mark gets what's coming to him, but now we've had almost two feet of snow. I'm wearing heavy snow boots that threaten to drag me down and enough layers that it's difficult to get full range of motion when I move.

But I can't stop now.

My flashlight is weak, but I keep it trained ahead of us. The barn is so, so far away, and the air is frigid. I would turn back, but then I remember Henry and how hard I've worked to make this plan happen. I have to do this.

For me. For him.

Suddenly, my flashlight grows stronger. I pause, confused, then hit it against my palm.

It's then I realize I can see my shadow stretching out ahead of me.

Someone's behind me.

FORTY-SIX

MARK

I can't reconcile what I'm seeing with what's been happening.

The person running away from me is bundled up, a thick coat and heavy snow pants making it difficult for me to tell who it is. There's a lump on their side like they're holding something there, balancing it on their hip. I stare at the figure in the snow, trying to wrap my mind around who it is.

I stumble out onto the porch, a flashlight clutched in my hand. I need to be closer to see what's out there, what's happening in the snow.

And then I see the thing on their hip for what it really is.

Henry.

"Henry! Abby!" I scream into the wind. It whips against me, blowing me back into the house. My wife is dressed for the weather, obviously prepared to be out there, but I can't follow without putting something warmer on.

"What's wrong, Dad?"

Chelsea plucks at my sleeve. I can't see her face, not without shining the flashlight right in her eyes, and I refrain from doing that. I turn, panic gripping my heart, and I have to gasp out my response.

"Let me go! Abby's out there. With Henry."

Without thinking, I push her to the side. She stumbles back from me, and I walk to the hall closet, opening it and shining my light inside. "Where are my boots? My coat?"

My voice rises in pitch with every word. All of my things are gone. They were here—of course they were here. I wouldn't have them anywhere else in the house, not when I might need to go outside at a moment's notice. Having them easily accessible for when I need them is important.

There's movement at my side and Chelsea grabs the flashlight from me. She moves so quickly I don't have time to try to yank it back from her.

"Your things are gone?" Her voice is slow, maddening.

I close my eyes. Grit my teeth. Try not to scream.

"Chelsea. Did you take them?"

It's insane, isn't it, the thought that she might have snuck in here, taken my things, gotten rid of them or hidden them, but what's the alternative, that Abby did it?

Abby wouldn't. She wouldn't do something like that.

But she's taking Henry out of the house. She's running. And I never would have thought she'd do something like that either.

"Did you take my boots?"

Chelsea hasn't answered me, and I turn on her, grabbing her by the shoulders and shaking her.

"Let me go!"

She hits me in the side of the head with the flashlight. Stars explode in front of my eyes, and I gasp, stepping back from her and leaning against the wall. My mouth opens and closes soundlessly like a fish, my knees shaking. Every cell in my body screams for me to sink to the floor.

To close my eyes.

To sink into the darkness fuzzing the edges of my vision, as I did for that brief moment in the living room.

"I'm sorry, Chelsea." It takes me a minute to catch my

breath enough to talk to her. For a couple of minutes, well, I didn't *forget* about being stabbed. But the pain had become less as I focused on finding out who'd opened the front door. "I'm sorry, I didn't mean to do that."

"I know," she coos and then is next to me. I don't fight it when she loops an arm around my waist and starts to lead me away from the front door. "I know, Dad."

She leads me back through the house to the sofa, and I drop down onto it, crying out as I do.

"Are you okay?"

When she shines the flashlight in my face, I wince, turning away from her.

"Sorry." She drops the light, keeping it trained on my lap. "Are you okay?"

"I need to go after them. Need to make sure they're okay."

She tsks, shaking her head. "No, I don't think so, Dad. You need to stay here with me."

My stomach sinks. Bracing my right hand on a pillow, I push myself up to sit better.

"Chelsea. Please. I have to go after them. Help me."

Now she clicks her tongue. "We need to make sure you're okay first, Dad."

I don't respond.

"Are you okay?" There's a note of fear in her voice, and she shines the flashlight in my face again.

I blink, reaching up to shield my eyes with my hand.

"No. Not in my eyes."

There's warmth coming from the wound that wasn't there before. I'm not a doctor, not nearly smart enough to have gone to medical school, but that doesn't mean I'm stupid either.

She tsks again but adjusts the flashlight away from my face. "You're bleeding. A lot. I can see it through the bandage."

"I can feel it." My words are clipped, and she inhales hard at my tone.

Five, four, three, two, one.

"I'm sorry, Chelsea. It really hurts. Do you think you can go to the kitchen to look for the medical kit? It should be under the sink."

"Sure." She stays for a moment, the light still trained on my shoulder. I don't want to look, but I do, and I'm not surprised by the red bloom growing there.

"Chelsea."

"Yeah, I got it, Dad. Don't you worry—I'm going to take really good care of you, okay? You won't have to worry about a thing. I'm here now."

She leaves the room, the flashlight bobbing ahead of her.

"Yeah, you're here now," I mutter and lean my head back on the sofa. Chills race through my body, and I'm sure that isn't a good sign. But are they because I got too chilled with the door open? Or am I going into shock?

Moaning, I rub my good hand across my eyes. Now that Chelsea is gone, I should be able to think things through. It's almost impossible for me to make sense of what's happening though.

And I don't have a single idea of what I need to do next. If I thought I could get out of the house and find Abby, I'd do it.

But where the hell is she going? The barn isn't heated, so I can't imagine she'd take Henry out there and try to wait out the storm. She knows as well as anyone does that doing so would put both of them in danger.

But then why did she leave the house?

Did she take my winter gear with her?

There's no way to start the truck. There are snowshoes in the barn, but the thought of her trying to snowshoe with Henry on her hip isn't just laughable, it's scary.

I shift position, wondering what's taking Chelsea so long.

Abby leaving me in here, alone with my daughter? That's something that bothers me. She loves me, I know she does. We can get through this. I'll do anything to work things out with her, even though I don't know what that means will happen with Chelsea.

But I can't lose her. Or Henry.

So where the hell is she going?

"Okay, I found the kit."

Chelsea's back, yanking me from my thoughts. She's carrying the huge first aid kid Abby put together when we bought this place. At least twice a year she goes through it and replaces any supplies that might be out of date and makes sure we have enough bandages to care for a small army.

I've told her repeatedly it's overkill, but right now I'm grateful for it.

The first aid case makes a loud thud when Chelsea puts it on the coffee table.

There's an answering one from outside.

"Did you hear that?" My head is dizzy, and I don't trust myself right now to know whether or not I did hear a sound from outside. Still, I think I did. I think I heard a thud, like something being dropped, something hitting another thing.

Or something in the barn roaring to life.

FORTY-SEVEN

MARK

"Help me to the window." I claw at Chelsea, who's still peering into the first aid kit, finally snagging her sleeve and making her stop to look up at me. "I need to look outside. What was that?"

"It sounded like an engine." Her voice is flat. Emotionless. She grabs my wrist, her grip surprisingly tight as she yanks me hard and pulls me to my feet. "You want to see, Dad? Maybe it's someone come to help. But I doubt it."

I doubt it too. There are only a few people who know what's going on in here. No way would there be help coming, not without someone being able to call out. The phones are down, the cell towers out of commission, the streets are impassable.

But I swear I heard an engine.

It's louder now, a roar that cuts through the silence of the storm, making it impossible to think about anything other than the way I can feel the vibrations in my body.

Chelsea loops her arm around my waist. Leaning on her, I force myself to walk, pain shooting through me with every step. We stop twice but I push on, desperate to get to the window, to look outside.

"A light!" I'm excited—I can't help it. I point at the window, leaning against the frame. Chelsea could let me go now if she wanted to, could let me lean against the frame on my own, but she doesn't loosen her grip on me. "Do you see it? Someone's coming to help us!"

I wave even though there's no way whoever is outside will be able to see me through the window. Still, I can't help myself. "Hey! In here!"

The light turns and I blink hard, realizing it's not on the road.

"Where are they coming from?" Cold floods my body. "Where are they going? Aren't they on the road?"

I'm turned around. My head is fuzzy and thick from being stabbed, and I hate that I can't put my finger on the direction the sound and light are coming from.

"The road is that way." Chelsea thumbs over her shoulder.

I turn to look at her, trying to wrap my mind around what's happening.

"So where did that come from?" I ask.

"The barn." Still, her voice is flat. "It came from the barn, Dad."

I hate that she's calling me *dad*. I hate even more that I think she's right.

The light is turned away from us now. I can see the path it's illuminating. The engine roars but, even so, it's quieter now. Whoever is driving away from us is leaving.

"That was the barn, right, Dad?"

I don't answer. *She's right.*

"Do you have a snowmobile?"

I nod, my mouth numb.

How could I forget about the snowmobile?

Abby wanted it. Abby, not me. She'd scrimped and saved and bought one three winters ago, right before Henry was born, but I always told her I thought it was ridiculous. If there was ever an emergency, we'd take the truck.

That's what I told her. And she never argued. She must have gone out there from time to time when I was working to make sure it was still running, because I've never worked on it.

What other secrets does she have?

The heavy realization of what happened lands on me, and I stagger backwards, my knees giving out. Like I'm a rock, I sink to the floor. Drop my head in my hands.

"She took the snowmobile." My words come out as a groan. I can't believe it. Abby... Abby took Henry and left. She left me here and didn't say anything, and now I have no way to reach her, no way to find out what she's doing, what she wants.

"It's going to be okay." Chelsea drops to her knees next to me and loops her arm around my shoulders. "Seriously, Dad, you have me. I'm not going to leave you like she did. I love you."

I'm silent. I have nothing to say to her right now. How the hell did I not see this coming? Abby had to have had this planned. She had to have known what was going to happen when she invited the Rowes to stay here.

She's been planning this.

"We need to follow them." I struggle to my feet. My head swims and I lean against the wall, but before I can push off it and try for the front door, Chelsea is there again.

She won't leave my side.

"Dad, you can't go anywhere. You have to sit down."

"We have to go! Let me go—I need to get to my wife. To Henry. What if something happens to them?" Even I can hear the desperation in my voice, but Chelsea doesn't move.

She either doesn't hear how worried I really am. Or she doesn't care.

Abby didn't take me with her. She could have. Or she could have told me what she was doing, but she didn't.

How long has she been planning this? She said she's known the truth about Lottie and Chelsea for a while now, but that doesn't tell me how long she's been working towards taking Henry from me.

Then it hits me what we can do so she doesn't leave me here with Chelsea. "We'll take Tim's Jeep! Come on! You can drive, can't you?" I never heard him start the Jeep after he stabbed me. I might have been too out of it to hear it, but maybe not. Maybe he didn't take it, and we can. Hope washes over and I grab her arm, shaking it a little in a bid to make her look at me. *Why won't she answer me?*

She does, but the expression on her face makes my heart drop.

She's grinning. It's the biggest smile I've seen on her face since she got here.

"They'll be fine. Dad, don't you see? This is perfect! My parents are gone. Abby and Henry are gone. She did us a favor. We finally get to be together, and nothing can stop us."

The joy in her voice sickens me. I have to force myself to look at her. Even though I can't see all of her features, I don't want to see her at all right now.

"I don't want to be with you." It makes my head swim, but I jerk away from her, stepping back and relying on the support of the wall to keep me from falling down. "Don't you see? I want Henry. I chose him before, and I will continue to choose him every single day."

I take a step towards the door. Something terrible could happen to Abby and Henry and I wouldn't be able to stop it. I know she planned this, that she had a role in this just like I did, but she still has my son. Even though I hate her for what she did to our family, I have to hope she's okay as long as she has my son. I have to get Henry back.

I won't let her take him from me.

Another step. I feel weak and I need to rest, but I won't be able to until I get to Abby. I messed up so many years ago, but it's not fair of her to hold it over my head. Doesn't she see? I killed Lottie to protect Henry. I'll do whatever I have to so I can get my son back.

I think I've left Chelsea behind, that maybe she's finally given up on what she wants, but she's suddenly in front of me, her arms out to the sides like we're playing a sport, playing red rover, and she's ready to keep me from breaking the line.

She's faster than I thought.

"Where do you think you're going?"

I'm panting for breath and can barely see. She doesn't sound stressed; doesn't sound like she's struggling. If anything, there's a note of joy in her voice.

She's really happy.

Oh God. My daughter is crazy.

"I've got to go after them."

"No, you don't. I'm your family now."

Again, her arm is around my waist and even though I want to push away from her and flee the house, my legs are so, so tired. My heart beats hard, but it feels like it's barely pumping any blood through my body.

I sag into her.

"There you go, Dad. Now let's get you back on the sofa where I can make sure you're okay. I'll keep an eye on you, how does that sound? It's you and me now, and I promise, I'm never going to let you leave me again."

FORTY-EIGHT

ABBY

The girl at the front desk stares at us before finally pushing herself up out of her chair and walking over to the large glass doors. She has on an oversized zip-up hoodie that obscures her company-issued T-shirt and a pair of jeans that have seen better days. There are half a dozen candles burning on her desk. Tim shines a flashlight through the glass, lowering it as she approaches.

She carries a flashlight lamp and holds it up to the glass, peering through like she's unsure what to make of us standing at the door. For a moment, I don't think she's going to let us in. The roar of the generator around the side of the building is almost deafening, but after being on the snowmobile for an hour, I'm grateful for the change of sound.

"We need two rooms," I say, holding up two fingers. My gloves are thick, and it looks comical, the way I'm pressing my hand up against the glass to get her attention, but I don't care. We need to get inside. "Please, my son is cold and tired. We don't have power at home. We need help."

"I only have one." She gives her head a little shake as she moves to unlock the front door.

Beside me, I feel Tim stiffen, but right now I don't care what he thinks. It's got to be warmer in the Airbonne Hotel than it is out here, and I want to make sure Henry is okay. This night hasn't gone how I wanted it to, but I can still salvage it.

The best thing to happen so far is that we're out of the house. We're more than halfway to the freedom I want for my little family.

"Our credit-card machine is down," the girl says as Tim and I file past her into the lobby. "But if you have cash, I can get you a room."

"We have cash," I answer quickly, not wanting to give her any reason to kick us back out into the cold. "Thanks."

The girl nods, gesturing for me to step out of the way with Henry so she can shut the door. I do, holding my son close.

She locks the door and shivers to herself. "Brrr, it's frigid out there. You three must have been pretty desperate to drive a snowmobile in these conditions."

Moving faster now, she takes her place back behind the counter. "That'll be eighty."

"I'm going to put you down, Henry," I say, carefully slipping my son from my hip. He leans against me, his face crumpling, and I know it's not going to be long before he has a meltdown. The sucker worked magic for a while, but now I'm running on borrowed time.

My fingers feel like ice as I shove them into my pocket and pull out my wallet. They cramp and I take a deep breath, forcing myself to peel off each bill.

"Great." The girl hands me a key. "Last room on the right. No hot water of course, and don't mess with the heat. If we have guests fiddling with it, then everyone will be cold. We have enough gas to keep the generator going until tomorrow when my boss can bring more. If you stay past ten in the morning, it'll be another eighty."

"Thanks." I pause, then ask the questions that are on my

mind. "What about the roads? Do you know when they're going to be plowed?"

She barks out a laugh and then covers her mouth. "Sorry about that. Roads? I mean, the ones in town will be plowed tonight, but there's another band of snow coming in tomorrow early morning, so they won't stay cleared long. But anywhere outside of town is out of luck. Where are you trying to go? Back home?"

I shake my head. "No, we just want to get out of Oyster."

"Oh, then you should be able to do that tomorrow if you leave early enough." She nods like she's more confident now. "This is my first winter here. It sucks. My boss told me that by tomorrow morning they would have some streets plowed and a few businesses open. Grocery store, gas station. The bank. Nothing cool though, like the mall." She scrunches up her nose in disgust.

"That's fine, thanks. Can you give us a wake-up call at six?" I pick Henry back up.

Tim shifts back and forth on his feet, obviously ready to get down to the room where the two of us can talk without eavesdropping.

"Well, the phones are out." She drums her fingers on the desk. Her nails are all bitten to the quick, and when she sees me look at them, she stops, shoves them in the front pocket of her hoodie. "But I can come knock on your door, if you want?"

"Yep, we want that. Thanks. Six a.m."

Without another word, I turn and lead the way down the hall. Henry starts to cry, and I walk faster, only pausing long enough to shove the key into Tim's hand once we reach the door. "Hurry up. He's about to fall apart."

Tim does what I ask, and we all pile through the door. It's not quite as warm in here as it was in the lobby, but the bed looks comfortable and there's a pile of blankets on the foot of it.

"Let me get him settled," I say, setting my flashlight down

on the bedside table. It has a feeble glow, but I have fresh
batteries and more flashlights packed in the bag we brought in
from the snowmobile. "Grab some more flashlights from the
pack, will you?"

Tim is wordless as he slips the straps from his shoulders and
starts digging through the pack. I ignore him and give Henry my
full attention, first unzipping his coat and removing his shoes
before tucking him in to the bed.

There's more light in the room now. Tim found the flashlights and is turning them all on, setting them up around the
room so we can see.

"Mommy," Henry says, clinging to my neck. "I'm cold."

"I know, buddy. You're so brave, you know that?"

Pulling back from him a bit, I dig his favorite stuffed bunny
out of my coat pocket and press it into his hands. "Mr. Bunbun
is cold too, but I bet you can warm him up if you snuggle him.
Get some rest, okay?"

"Where's Daddy?" His little voice is sleepier now and I
exhale in relief. I'll do whatever it takes to get him to sleep.
There's a box of Benadryl in my backpack waiting for me to use
it if he fights falling asleep.

"Daddy had to stay home but we'll see him soon, okay?"
The lies are easy. I've been lying to Mark for so long about what
I know about his past that this is just an extension of those lies.
"But I talked to him, and he said he loved you and to get some
rest."

"You talked to Daddy?"

He's fading fast. I brush hair back from his forehead and
marvel at him.

He's perfect. Henry is everything good in this world. If
there was any doubt in my mind that I was doing the right thing,
it would be gone when I look at my son.

"Yep. He texted." I drop a kiss on his forehead. Pull the

covers up farther under his chin. "Get some sleep, baby. Tomorrow's an adventure."

"An 'venture," he says, murmuring as he snuggles his bunny closer. The poor little rabbit has seen better days and is missing its right eye, but Henry loves it almost as much as he loves his favorite cars.

Now that he's settled, I dig in the pack for two bottles of water. Keeping my back to Tim, I twist them both open. My fingers tremble as I crack open Benadryl capsules and shake the powder into his bottle. My fingers are finally warming up, and I slip the empty caps deep in my pocket as I work. Five pills should do it.

My heart races as I close the bottle and shake it. If Tim looks too closely, he might see how some of the powder didn't fully dissolve.

I have to hope he won't look.

The sound of his chair squeaking makes me pause. I hold my breath, trying to hear whether or not he's going to get up and walk over here.

No. He'll ruin everything.

But he doesn't come, and I finally turn to him. He's sitting in the chair across the room, and I walk over to him, perching on the end of the bed so the two of us can talk. He looks exhausted, and the beams of light criss-crossing the room to create a soft glow aren't doing him any favors.

I chuckle to myself. Honestly, I'm probably not looking much better.

"Care to share what's so funny?" he asks, reaching out for the water I'm offering him.

I shake my head. "We did it. I can't believe we did it. Honestly, it all worked out better than I thought it could. You didn't have to cut me though." I reach up and touch my neck. The fear I'd felt when Tim pressed the knife against my skin... I don't know if that's something I'll ever be able to shake.

He shrugs. Opens the bottle. Takes a large drink. "I wanted it to look real. Mark bought it, Abby, and that's all that matters. Now, let's run through tomorrow's plan again. I don't want there to be any mistakes. I can't let this come back to haunt me." Another sip. This one smaller, but still more.

I don't mention that everything might come back to haunt him. When the police find out about Lottie's death, they're going to crawl all over the B&B looking for proof of who killed her. Mark will try to spin it as an accident, I bet. Or he'll try to pin it all on Tim, but I'm not telling him that.

If I tell him anything other than what he wants to hear, then he might doubt the plan. I don't think he'll try to go back to the B&B and smooth things over with Mark and Chelsea, but I can't risk it. The desire to pat my pocket and make sure the snowmobile key is still there is almost overwhelming, but I don't move.

I'm so close to getting what I want.

FORTY-NINE

ABBY

Tim's watching me, the water bottle in his hand now almost empty. He glances at Henry, and I take a deep breath to try to stay calm.

"Wake up is six," I say, doing my best to sound exhausted. It isn't hard. I roll my shoulders and yawn. God, I need some sleep after this terrible night. "We'll get up, get dressed. There's food in the pack you brought in from the snowmobile." I gesture to it at the side of the bed. "After we eat and things are open, we can go to town."

"To the bank."

He leans back, finishes his water. Burps. I watch as he caps the bottle and then tosses the entire thing on the floor. It's what I would expect from a man like him.

"Yep, to the bank."

We'll go to the bank alright. If things don't go as planned, then the bank here in Oyster has a small account I set up a year ago with about ten thousand dollars in it. I'm going to hand it to Tim, wish him good luck. He'll be out of my hair.

I hope it doesn't come to that. Henry and I can use that money. If things go the way I want, I'll get my hands on it later.

Either way though, then Henry and I will leave Oyster and go to the bank where I have my other account, the one Tim doesn't know about.

"I just want my money and to be free from Chelsea. She was never mine." His gaze is searching, like he wants me to agree with him. "She was a means to an end after I found out Lottie cheated on me. We were over then, you know. When she cheated. But I used the affair to get as much money from your husband as possible. And now that Lottie is gone, Mark can have his daughter."

I don't answer. Hearing it spelled out like this? It's dark. I'm glad Henry is too young to follow the conversation. And I hate this man for taking so much money from us. Money that should be mine. Should be Henry's.

Tim continues. "And then we're done with this, right? Done with each other? I never want to see you again."

I guess if someone were listening in to our conversation they'd think his words were cruel and unnecessary, but I don't see it that way.

Tim and I agree about that, at least. I never want to see him again either.

"That's right. You'll go your way, I'll go mine. I get the snowmobile."

"Yeah, I have a friend coming to—"

I hold up my hand. "I don't want to know. Don't tell me your plan and I won't tell you mine. We'll go our own ways and then we won't ever hear from each other again."

I'm going south, away from this cold. Maine wasn't what I thought it would be. It will forever be the state where my husband cheated on me, where he killed his mistress, where his secret daughter tried to kill my son. The only thing good to come from my time in this godforsaken place is Henry.

He's the only reason I stuck with Mark for as long as I did after I found out about the affair.

I glance over at him. He's a lump under the covers and hasn't moved since he passed out. Will he miss Mark?

I guess, at first. But he's young enough that I don't think it will last for too long. Kids are more resilient than we give them credit for, and I have a pretty good feeling I'll have him forgetting his dad before his next birthday.

"Time to get some rest then." Tim yawns, stretching his hands high above his head. "Can you hand me a blanket?"

Standing, I grab one from the pile on the bed and toss it to him. He snags it out of the air with one hand and grins at me.

"Thanks."

The smile on my face is fake. I don't trust Tim one bit. He's not a good person. To blackmail Mark like he did for years, to take so much money out of our pockets when we needed it? There's nothing good about the man. I need him right now though, like he needs me. The two of us have an uneasy truce.

Or he thinks we do.

"Sleep good."

"Thank you."

The Benadryl I put in his water should have him passed out within the half hour; he's already almost dead on his feet. I can keep my eyes open until then to make sure he doesn't try anything stupid.

I'd hoped, of course, that the hotel would have more than one room and we could have our own, which would make it easy for us to leave. But they didn't, and I'm glad I was prepared. That's one thing I've always tried to be: prepared. Nobody can catch you off guard if you're looking out for yourself and taking steps to protect yourself.

I let my guard down years ago with Mark and look where that got me. Every move since then has been carefully planned out. I wasn't about to let anyone else take advantage of me.

Adrenaline courses through my veins as I pretend to go to bed. That's good though. It will ensure I don't accidentally pass out before Tim does. The only thing I take off before getting into bed is my heavy coat, and that I put on top of the blankets for a little extra warmth.

My feet feel uncomfortable and tight in my shoes, but it's more important to me that I can get up and get moving without a lot of delay if I need to. Who cares how uncomfortable I am when all that matters is keeping Henry safe?

My son doesn't move as I lie down next to him. He's passed out thanks to the excitement of the day, and I have to hope the same will happen to Tim. Rather than snuggling down into the pillow and closing my eyes, which is what I want to do, I keep my eyes slitted and sit halfway up.

It's uncomfortable but I can't risk falling asleep.

He stares into the corner for a while, then gets up and turns off most of the flashlights, leaving one angled across the room to provide some light. It takes my eyes a while to adjust but they finally do, and I watch as he sits, his chin on his chest.

He nods.

He snores.

I start counting. It takes forever to get to a thousand, but when I finally do, I get up.

The bed squeaks and I freeze, but Tim doesn't move.

He keeps snoring, the sound steady, like an engine, and I shrug on my coat. Put on the backpack. Tighten the straps across my chest and hips, then pull Henry from bed. He moans, the soft sound so surprising I stop dead.

Still, Tim doesn't move.

Out the door, closing it carefully behind me. Down the hall. The same girl is sitting behind the counter, the same light on her desk, the same bored expression on her face. She perks up when she sees me.

"Where are you going?" There's accusation in her tone, and I don't blame her. I'm sure I look suspicious, but I don't care how I look.

"I have to leave." After throwing a quick glance over my shoulder to ensure Tim isn't coming, I look back at her. "Please cancel the wake-up call. Let him sleep."

She frowns, then the realization of what's happening hits her and she nods. There was confusion on her face, but her jaw tightens. "Okay, yeah, I won't get him up. I can't guarantee how long he'll sleep, but that should give you two plenty of time to get away."

"Thanks."

"Yeah, my lips are sealed." She looks over my shoulder and shakes her head. "What a bastard. My dad hit my mom. I'm glad you're getting out of there."

I exhale hard. She thinks Tim is my husband and that he's abusive and I don't care. The only thing that matters is getting away from him. Saving Henry. "Just pretend you never saw me, okay?"

I have to wait for her to unlock the front door for us, and the entire time I feel like I'm going to come out of my skin. I gave Tim an overdose of Benadryl, but I have no idea how long it will knock him out. Will he wake up when he hears the snowmobile start up? Will he figure out what happened as soon as he realizes I'm gone?

"Good luck."

She presses something into my hand as she pushes open the door. Freezing air dances around us and I brace against it.

"If he comes looking for you anytime soon, I'll tell him you two are sleeping in the office. That his snoring was ridiculous. I don't know how much time I can buy you, but I'll do my best."

I grin at her. "Thanks." Pocket the money she gave me.

"Good luck." She gestures for me to leave, and I do, dipping my head against the cold. Henry settles against me on the snowmobile. It's scary not having Tim here to drive—now I have to do that and hold my son—but I'll have to make do. Saying a little prayer, I crank the key.

The snowmobile roars to life and Henry shifts, but I loop my arm tighter around him, leaning with all my weight into the snowmobile to turn it, to start moving, to get the hell away from here.

I won.

It's over.

FIFTY

CHELSEA

Wednesday 5 Dec

It feels strange to be making breakfast in a kitchen that I'm not used to. Strange but not terrible. I'll admit, I did fumble around for a bit looking for candles and the lighter, but I remembered seeing the lighter in the kitchen last night when I wrote Abby that little note on her notepad.

Once I found that and lit a few candles then I lit the stove. The flame burst to life, warming up the kitchen. I don't want to say it's comfortable in here, but it's warmer than it is every-where but the living room. Sleeping on the sofa in front of the fire last night has given me a bit of a crick in the neck, but it was better than the alternative of going upstairs and sleeping in my bedroom.

And I had to keep an eye on Mark. *Dad.* I had to make sure he wasn't in a lot of pain during the night. Twice I got up to check on him when I heard him moaning and shifting position in the chair, and I wouldn't have been able to do that if I'd been upstairs.

Light streams in through the windows. It's bright, reflecting off the thick banks of snow. Right now, the clouds aren't as heavy as they have been, but I remember Abby saying the storm was going to be bad for days. We're not out of the woods yet, but I'm fine with that.

I don't mind being snowed in with Mark for a bit. We'll finally get to connect. I'll finally get to spend some time with him and make him see how much better our lives will be now that we're together.

Humming to myself, I open the refrigerator and pull out some eggs and cheese. I'll make the two of us omelets and then we can figure out what we're going to do today.

I wouldn't mind playing a board game with him. Maybe we could even start a puzzle. Those aren't my favorite, but he's probably going to be in a lot of pain and we need to keep his arm as still as possible. Anything that will keep the two of us inside and warm is ideal.

I'm scrambling the eggs in a bowl when I hear footsteps behind me.

"Hi, Dad," I say, adding a pinch of salt and pepper before I turn around to look at him. "How are you feeling this morning?"

There's a slight pause before he responds. Emotion flits across his face and I know he's not thrilled with being called dad, but he's going to have to get used to it.

"Chelsea."

His voice is dry, and I immediately put the bowl of eggs down and grab him a glass of water. It was left on the counter last night after dinner so I don't know who it belonged to, but it doesn't matter, does it?

He takes it and drains it before handing it back. I put it in the sink then wipe my hands on my jeans.

"Did you sleep okay in the chair? I'm making eggs." I hold up the bowl to show him then pour the eggs into the pan, enjoying the way they sizzle. In a minute I'll add some cheese, then we can cut it in half and share it.

"Chelsea, we need to call the cops." He puts his hand down on the counter next to me and I whip around.

Surely he's joking.

There's no way he'd call the cops right now, not when things are perfect for the first time in forever. I won't let him. My hands clench into fists at my sides and I force myself to relax them.

"Why do you think we need to do that?" My voice is light. Unconcerned. To show him how much this conversation isn't bothering me, I grab the spatula and turn to poke at the eggs.

"Because... your mother... she's gone. Tim and Abby and Henry are missing. I know what you said last night, but—"

"You mean about turning you in to the cops and telling them you killed Mom?" My back is to him and I'm glad he can't see the way his words hurt me. All I wanted was for him to be my dad. I knew, from the moment I learned the truth about him, that he couldn't be worse than Tim.

That he had to be *better*.

The way Mom talked about him, what she wrote in her diary, I knew he was a good man. A better man. The type of man I deserve for my father, and there's no way in hell I'm going to let him back out of it now, not when everything's finally working out the way I want it to.

"Chelsea."

He puts his hand on my shoulder, and I jerk away from him, causing his hand to fall back to his side.

He sucks in a breath.

Yeah, I bet that did hurt.

"Dad. Listen to me." I turn to talk to him, keeping the spatula between us. "Mom is dead. You killed her."

He flinches.

"I loved her," I say, and my voice breaks without me meaning it to. "But she would want me taken care of. You think Tim was going to do that? You think he would put himself second for me to make sure I was taken care of? No, not a chance. He came here for money, right?"

He nods.

"Besides, he's gone. Abby's gone. How do you know the two of them didn't run off together?"

"She wouldn't." He steps closer to me, his eyebrows knit together. "I know Abby. I know she wouldn't do that. She loves me, she—

"Loves Henry. Loves him enough to flee with him into the storm in the middle of the night without telling you what she's doing. Please, Dad, think it through."

He doesn't say anything. His face twists as he mulls over what I said, but I don't want to give him too long to think about it. This entire time, everything I've done has been to keep the Hardys on their toes. Keep them a little bit off-balance.

Locking Abby in her room. Messing with the baby monitor. Cutting the cables in his truck.

He'll never know I was the one behind all of that of course. I don't want him thinking he can turn against me, thinking that he can't trust me. He wouldn't see the love behind everything I did.

"We'll come up with a story of what happened," he tells me, the words spilling out of him so quickly I wonder if he's given himself time to think about what he's saying. "You and me. We'll come up with something."

I nod, then turn back to the stove. It only takes a minute to finish the omelet, then I cut it in two and plate it, jerking my chin so he'll follow me to the table. He does, slowly sitting down.

I sit in Abby's chair.

"Okay," I say, taking my fork and stabbing my breakfast. "Okay, you're right. We will have to call the cops, but I'll stand by you as long as you stand by me. If you change your story, then I'll tell them you threatened me. That I didn't have a choice in lying because you told me you'd kill me the way you killed my mom."

He's silent. Hasn't picked up his fork.

"Eat." I stab my fork through the air at him and only when he picks his up do I continue. "We'll get through this, Dad, okay?"

He winces but doesn't respond.

"Dad. Look at me." My heart beats out an irregular rhythm in my chest, and I hold my breath until he looks up. I don't want to be angry with him, but I need him to see how this is going to work. He has no idea how far I'm willing to go to have him as my father, how desperate I am to be free from Tim.

And Mom? Knowing that I lost her makes me feel sick, but that's done. I'm not going to lose Mark too, when what happened was an accident. He didn't mean to kill my mom. He *wouldn't*.

But he and I both know the only way to ensure the police believe that is to have me on his side.

"You and me, Dad. It's us against the world." I grin at him and wait for him to respond.

"We'll need money, Chelsea," he says, speaking slowly, like he's starting to wrap his mind around what's going to happen. "You know that, right? I sent your dad so much money and we didn't have much here."

"We can run the B&B," I offer. Then it hits me. "There are some people who'll pay a lot of money to stay where someone died."

He looks sick, and I hurry to speak, to try to smooth things over, to get him back on my side.

"But whatever you think, Dad. And if we need more money, there's always one thing we can do."

"And that is?" He still hasn't taken a bite of the breakfast I made him, but I'm not mad. It's nice to talk to him and to come up with plans about our future together.

I shrug. "Find Abby. That's what you really want, isn't it?"

FIFTY-ONE

ABBY

18 Months Later

Do I feel bad about screwing Tim over at the last minute?

No, I do not. Absolutely, one hundred percent, no. Just like I don't feel bad about screwing over Mark.

One screwed other women. The other was more than happy to resort to blackmail so he didn't have to work a day in his life.

If the drugs in the water hadn't worked to knock Tim out, I would have been more than happy to give him the ten thousand dollars in the Oyster bank to make him go away. But it worked and he didn't wake up in time to stop me, so all the money ended up mine.

Henry and I fled, getting a bed in a hotel two towns over, then hitting the bank right when it opened. All of the money I'd been squirreling away was waiting there for me, in addition to a new cell phone, new IDs and keys to a car I'd had sitting in a library parking lot for a week.

There wasn't any way I was sticking around Oyster for the fallout.

But it all worked perfectly. From sending Tim the social-media post so he could push Lottie to book the B&B, to working with him to ensure that he and I would walk away from our spouses with our money, leaving them behind, it worked. The one thing I didn't expect was for Lottie to die.

But that wasn't a great loss, was it?

I stand up and walk down the front steps of our new house. It's tiny, especially when compared to the Saltside Inn, but there's a fenced-in front yard and a small plot for vegetables, and just enough room for the two of us. It was scary packing up and moving from Maine to Florida, where I'd never been before, but it was the right move for us.

For the longest time after we moved, I checked the news, terrified the police were going to come looking for me. Of course they were interested in talking to me about everything that happened at the B&B, but I was in the wind, and from what I saw on social media, Chelsea stood by Mark.

She told the police Lottie had been trying to kill Henry. That she was going to kill everyone. That Mark was the reason she was still alive. That she needed him to be her guardian now that her mother was dead. That he was her real father.

And in all the interviews I saw on TV, he stood next to her, his jaw tight, his eyes dead.

But hey, he's alive. I never meant for him to die, never wanted him to get hurt. I wanted to leave him in the past, take Henry and run. After I'd looked out for myself, that is. That's what Tim agreed to help me with, only he thought he'd be getting a lot more out of it than just leaving his cheating wife and her illegitimate child behind.

When I see Mark now on the news, I feel nothing. A lot of people would probably want to know why I didn't just divorce him.

Why I would stay with someone for that long if I hated them the way I hated Mark.

And the answer is easy, but I have a pretty good feeling a lot of people wouldn't like it.

I wanted him to suffer. To show some accountability for what he did. To own up to his mistakes. For me to get the happy ever after I so badly craved. Sure, inviting the Rowes into our home turned out to be more dangerous than I thought. I wanted to get them there, let Mark know what I knew, then disappear into the night with Henry, leaving Mark to pick up the pieces of his past indiscretion.

Tim was more than happy to play the game with me since he wanted as much money as possible. Of course, he didn't know I'd have a plan for him too, and that in the end I'd turn on him. All of it, bringing the Rowes into the house, pretending I didn't know them, acting like I thought Chelsea had a crush on Mark, it was all to ensure Mark didn't know what I was really up to.

"Hey, Henry, watch out for ants," I call.

Henry's obsessed with anthills and keeps hunting them down in our yard. It doesn't matter how many times I tell him he'll probably get bitten or stung, he wants to hold them and bring them in the house in his pockets. I watch him, watch how he pries a stick into the dirt to try to dig out some new friends, then turn and walk back up to the porch, my flip-flops slapping against my feet.

It's hot in Florida, but I've embraced sweet tea, ceiling fans, and sundresses.

If I'd left Mark when I'd found out about the affair, then I wouldn't have any of this. We would have divorced, I'm sure of it, and I never would have had Henry. I wouldn't have had the opportunity to skim so much money from the accounts as I did.

Sure, him sending money to Tim every month hurt our bottom line, but I can't put all the blame on Mark. Not if I'm being honest about where the money was really going.

And I'm finally ready to be honest. With myself, at least.

So I waited and tried to get pregnant, hating every moment we were intimate but knowing it would all be worth it for me to have a child. That's all I wanted at that point. Then Henry came and he was perfect, but I was *so tired*. Have you ever been a mother? There's no way to combat the exhaustion. I needed time to sleep, to heal, to make sure all of my ducks were in a row. I needed time to get money. To talk to Tim.

Then I bought the car. With cash of course, so there wasn't a paper trail. It's a junker of a Corolla, but it's served the two of us pretty well. I set up the accounts, the new phone, the fake IDs.

Those were the hardest, I'll tell you what. But I got them and then it was time to show Mark that he couldn't continue to push me around like he had. Eventually I reached out to Tim. I came up with the plan for the anniversary discount. And he agreed to come, but not because he thought he'd be helping me get rid of Mark, but because he wanted more money.

Greedy.

And he wanted to be free from Lottie. From Chelsea.

Understandable.

So I looped him in on my plan. He talked up the B&B to Lottie and she, ever the opportunist, jumped right on the chance to sleep under the same roof as my husband. I had a pretty good feeling she would.

I guess there are some people who might say that I'm greedy too, but they'd be wrong. I'm not greedy. I was willing to do whatever it took to earn the life Mark had promised me and then failed to give me. I knew I'd need money for that, and I also knew having a child was the one final thing I wanted.

So I stuck it out until I got what I wanted. I have no regrets.

The mail truck drives by, pausing for a moment at our mailbox. I lift my glass in a wave, then put it down with a soft thud on the table next to me. Henry hasn't looked up from his dirt pile.

"I'm going to grab the mail, Hen," I call, walking to the front gate. There's a latch on it that Henry hasn't figured out yet, and I don't want him peering over my shoulder in case he picks up how it works. Keeping him safe and happy is my main goal in life.

I can't very well do that if he escapes the yard, can I?

Our mailbox is white, with our new fake name written on the side in navy blue. Before opening the front to grab our mail, I trace my fingers over the letters.

BRADFORD

One quick tug and the lid falls open. I reach in, fully expecting a pile of junk mail with maybe a bill thrown in for good measure.

Instead, I pull out a box.

I turn it over and over in my hands and close the mailbox, slipping back through the gate and hurrying up to the porch. My name is written on front, *Tracy Bradford*, in a script I don't recognize.

A chill runs up my arms, and I glance up to make sure Henry hasn't left the yard.

He hasn't. He's right there, right where I left him. I hurry now, wanting to be with him, feeling vulnerable.

That's silly, isn't it? Our little neighborhood is so nice. I've never felt unsafe here, but I do now.

Trying to look calm, I walk up the porch stairs then perch in a rocking chair.

"Hey, Henry, why don't you come up here, okay?"

Without waiting for a response, I pull a pocketknife out of my pocket and slit the tape holding the box shut. It's not wrapped in paper, so my name and address are written right on top of it. Still, the rest of the box is unmarked, and I have no idea what might be inside.

It's light.

I weigh the box with one hand while I set the knife down on

the table next to my tea. My fingers tremble as I lift the flap, pulling the little side flaps out, then lift the top of the box.

"What in the world?" I sit, almost unaware that I'm sinking down to my rocking chair. "Who is this from?"

Nobody answers me, although it's not like I expect anyone to. Still, my ears prick as if waiting for some voice to respond to me.

There's a piece of paper inside, folded up into a tight little square. I pluck it out and set the box down then slowly smooth the paper out on my lap.

There's nothing written on it but numbers. Two rows of numbers, the first nine digits, the second, eleven.

I don't have any idea what this is.

Worried now, I turn it over, hoping there will be some explanation written on the back, but there's nothing there, no instructions on what to do. I grab the box, tip it upside down, and shake it.

Cold creeps up my spine. Dropping the box to the porch, I stand and shield my eyes from the sun with my free hand.

Where's Henry?

Oh my God, where's my son?

"Henry?" My voice is quiet. Too quiet. He'll never hear me, not if he's wandered around the side of the house.

I stand, dropping the paper to the porch alongside the box. "Henry! Where are you?"

No response.

Oh God, this can't be happening. Not again.

"Henry!" I scream his name now and there's no way he can't hear me calling for him, not unless he's gone or he's trying to avoid me so he can keep playing with his stupid little ants, but Henry's a good boy; he always answers me, even if he knows that will scare away the little critters he loves.

"Henry! Where the hell are you?"

I almost trip running down the stairs. My hand skids down

the handrail, and a sharp splinter lodges deep in the fleshy part of my palm, but I don't slow down.

"Henry!"

Movement catches my eye. I'm halfway around the house, but the front gate swings open, caught by the wind, maybe? Did I not close it properly? Was it moved by someone walking by?

No, he can't be gone. He can't. I love him, I need my son, I—

"Mommy!" Henry's voice, coming from the sidewalk. Not scared though, not upset, not the voice of a little boy who someone tried to take from his own front yard, just the voice of a little boy who's so excited about something he can barely hold it in, and I already have the sinking feeling it's not ants. It's something else, it's something worse—

"Mommy, look what I have!" He's running to me, a grin on his face. His knees are filthy from kneeling in the dirt, but I don't care about that, don't care about anything, I only care about him. "Look!"

It's only when he's right in front of me and I'm about to bend down and scoop him up, scoop up my little four-year-old boy who loves me more than anything, that I realize he's clutching something in his fist.

FIFTY-TWO

ABBY

"What is it?" I shouldn't snatch it from him, but that's exactly what I do. I feel like I'm choking, drowning even, but I take the paper from him and hold it out, my hand shaking too hard for me to tell what it is.

"The nice girl gave it to me!" He's so proud of himself, my sweet boy, proud of someone giving him this.

"Nice girl?" I choke out. Now I've stopped shaking enough to see that what he handed me wasn't just a piece of paper but a photo. "What nice girl?"

"Her." He stabs his finger onto the photo, right onto a face I know all too well. "She was here! With a truck. They had a puppy, and I went out the gate to see it."

"You shouldn't do that," I say automatically, but I don't hear what I'm saying, and I don't think Henry does either.

"She wanted me to give you this. She said hi." He beams at me, happy he passed along the message. "Can I go play now? Can we have a puppy?"

"Not right now."

Later, I'm sure I'll look back and be able to remember

what's happening out here, but right now I feel like I'm stuck in a fever dream, like everything is out of my control.

His face crumples. "But you said—"

"I said not right now!" My tone is too harsh and he sniffles hard, then turns and runs down the stairs, crouching back in the dirt.

I should go after him, but I can't take my eyes off the photo.

Off Chelsea. Off Mark.

My hand trembles when I turn it over and read the back. It's in Mark's handwriting, his chicken scratch something I'd be able to recognize anywhere.

Then why didn't I recognize the numbers on the paper?

"You and Henry look good. We're thrilled to be your new neighbors."

My heart drops as I read. The house down the street, the one that's been for sale for months... surely not; he wouldn't, would he?

I'm back out on the sidewalk, running, the acid in my stomach burning and threatening to make me throw up, but there it is, the *For Sale* sign, still there, still proudly stuck in the dirt like the house could ever be anything other than just a shack on the cul-de-sac, when a truck backs out of the driveway.

My mouth goes dry.

It whips around. Heads towards me. I know the truck, know the elbow sticking out of the driver's window. It slows down in front of me and Mark leans out, his lips curved up into a cocky smirk.

"Hey, neighbor," he says, but I'm already shaking my head.

"No," I say, grabbing the window frame of the truck. "No, Mark. No."

"Oh, it's going to happen, Abby."

There's laughter from the passenger seat and I glance past him. Chelsea. I look away.

"You got the numbers?"

"The numbers?" My tongue feels numb. My legs are weak.

How the hell did he find me here? What do they want from me?

"Account numbers." Mark's tone is light and airy, like the two of us are having a friendly chat. "I saw you get the box."

"You were watching?"

"Routing number and account number, Abby."

He doesn't have to dignify my question with a response. Of course he's been watching. Of course he has. How he found me, I don't know, but it doesn't matter right now.

My tongue is thick. It fills my mouth, making it difficult for me to breathe.

"The numbers." I nod. "I got them."

"I want it all. Everything you took from me. Send it all. You have a week or we're moving in." He looks over and grins at Chelsea.

She grins back. I want to smack it right off her face.

"You can't do this," I say. The words feel useless, pathetic. "You got the B&B, Mark. You get to live your life now. Mark, no, he's your son, he's—"

"And she's my daughter," he says, interrupting me. "Do it, Abby. I want it all. Do it, and we're gone. You almost ruined my life. Don't make me come back. Don't make me buy that house. Don't make me take my son back. I want more than the B&B. I want everything you stole from me."

"No." Tears stream down my cheeks but I barely notice them. "No, you can't do this."

He barks out a laugh. Chelsea imitates it. *I hate her.*

"You'll do what I say, or I swear to you, you'll never get rid of us. You have one week. Pay up and we'll go away. Fight it, and you'll wish you left me a long time ago."

They peel away from the sidewalk, the truck groaning as he

mashes down on the gas. For a moment, all I can do is stand and stare at the taillights.

The bastard. He thinks he can threaten me, threaten my son? Does he not realize how much farther I will go to protect Henry? My hands ball into fists as I stomp back down the sidewalk and through the gate.

This time, Henry looks up at me. "You okay, Mom?"

"Great, Henry," I say, grabbing his hand and pulling him with me into the house. "Why don't you come get some ice cream?"

"Ice cream!" He jumps and pulls away from me, running ahead of me into the house. I'll get him settled with ice cream first, then I have an email to send, with an attachment I'm sure will be more than enough to get Mark and Chelsea out of my hair for the rest of my life.

He thinks he has the upper hand, but I know everything. I know about the battery backup the security cameras at the B&B used. Mark agreed to the one pointed at the front door, the one pointed at the driveway, the one that kept watch over our mailbox. He wasn't as on board with ones in the B&B itself, but I promised him we wouldn't have any in the guest rooms, only in the public spaces. As much of the building and property as possible was under constant watch.

Night vision. Motion sensor. Smartphone alerts. Professional resolution.

Yes, even in the snow.

They made him feel safe.

But he never knew about the other ones, the ones I had installed along the perimeter of our property as well as along the cliffs, just in case of an emergency.

If he'd seen the billing statement for those, I would have had a lot of explaining to do. More important than him not knowing about the extra cameras, he doesn't know about the permanent cloud storage for our recordings.

But I do. I set it up, and since I paid all the bills each month, Mark never questioned anything.

Him killing Lottie wasn't ever part of my plan, but he would have been hard-pressed to murder her somewhere where I wouldn't catch it on tape. I knew how to get those recordings, to save them, to make sure Lottie's murder was on tape, to ensure that nobody would ever be able to watch the tape and not convict him.

My mind races as I scoop Henry some ice cream and then send him to the TV to watch a cartoon. As soon as he's settled, I hurry to my computer and log on.

"Home Security Nation videos," I whisper as I navigate to my cloud. It only takes me a moment to type in my password and access my saved videos.

On my screen, Lottie screams. I have the sound turned off, but I saw the way Mark caught her across the chest, how he knocked her off the cliff.

"God, these cameras were worth the money," I mutter, leaning in to get a better look. At first, I was afraid nothing would be recorded, but it couldn't have been more perfect.

I save the file to my desktop then attach it to an email. In the subject line I write "Lottie Rowe murder". For a moment after entering the detective's email address, I pause, my mouse over the *send* button.

But then I look up and see Henry sitting on the sofa. He has ice cream running down his arm but is so focused on the TV that he doesn't seem to notice he's turning into a sticky mess.

I never meant for Mark to go to jail. Honestly, I didn't. I meant to take his money, take our son, and start a new life. I meant to punish him for what he did to me when he had an affair and broke my trust. It would have been fine with me if he and Lottie had ended up together, if he hadn't accidentally killed her. They deserved each other. And they deserved Chelsea.

But if Mark doesn't go to jail, then I'll lose my son. He'll *take* my son.

I click *send*.

A LETTER FROM EMILY

Dear reader,

Thanks so much for reading *The Hotel*! If you enjoyed it and want to keep up to date with all my latest releases, sign up at the following link. Your email address will never be shared, and you can unsubscribe anytime.

www.bookouture.com/emily-shiner

The Hotel was a blast to write! I hope you enjoyed it, and if you did, I'd be very grateful if you could write a review. Not only do I enjoy hearing what my readers think, but reviews make a huge difference in helping new readers to discover one of my books for the first time.

I truly love hearing from my readers and personally respond to every message I get. Please feel free to reach out to me via emily@authoremilyshiner.com, or you can get in touch on my Facebook page, through Twitter, or my website.

Thanks,

Emily

KEEP IN TOUCH WITH EMILY

www.authoremilyshiner.com

 facebook.com/authoremilyshiner

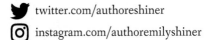 twitter.com/authoreshiner

instagram.com/authoremilyshiner

ACKNOWLEDGMENTS

Working on my second book with Bookouture has been a dream come true! Thank you to everyone there who works tirelessly behind the scenes to bring a book to life, especially my delightful editor, Kelsie Marsden.

Also thank you to my parents, who have supported me through it all, no matter what big career change I made. I'm sure I've caused them more grief than they deserved over the years, but I keep telling them I'm keeping them young. This is where I belong, and had I been honest with myself from the beginning, I would have started writing books a long time ago.

To my sister, who loves to read as much as I love to write and is a wonderful proofreader! I guess there's nothing like having a perfectly good excuse to tell your little sister when she's wrong, but I so appreciate all of her help.

Readers are everything, and hearing from you makes my day! Thank you to everyone who has picked up one of my books, who has reached out, and who has shared it with another reader. Writing can be lonely, but there's an incredible reader community out there, and I so appreciate each and every one of you!

Made in the USA
Middletown, DE
21 September 2024

61245622R00172